HENRY WAS THE FIRST TO SEE IT. . . .

"What's that?" He stepped up next to Quaid and pointed. At first, Quaid thought Henry was pointing out at something on the horizon. Then he realized that what Henry saw was much closer.

"Christ," Carlos said, walking along the edge of the trench, toward the front of the boathouse. He was looking down at the water.

There was a dark pile of something that the waves had washed up against the corner of the trench nearest the pier. It was tangled up, half in yellow nylon rope, half in one of the old tires that hung off of the concrete, facing the lagoon.

Frank came up next to Carlos, carrying a seven-foot-long pole with a hook on the end. He reached down with it and pushed on the debris. It bobbed up and down, floating on the water. After a moment they all saw it come free, and then they spotted what had been hooked into the tire.

"Holy shit!" Carlos' voice was barely a whisper.

Most of it was still an unidentifiable mass of fabric and nylon rope—but what drifted free of the tire was unmistakably a human arm!

Masterful Suspense Fiction by
STEVEN KRANE,
available in DAW editions:

TEEK
THE OMEGA GAME

Steven Krane

THE OMEGA GAME

DAW BOOKS, INC.

DONALD A. WOLLHEIM, FOUNDER

375 Hudson Street, New York, NY 10014

ELIZABETH R. WOLLHEIM
SHEILA E. GILBERT
PUBLISHERS

First Printing, September 2000
1 2 3 4 5 6 7 8 9

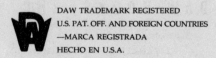

DAW TRADEMARK REGISTERED
U.S. PAT. OFF. AND FOREIGN COUNTRIES
—MARCA REGISTRADA
HECHO EN U.S.A.

PRINTED IN THE U.S.A.

This book is dedicated to all the kindred spirits I left behind at Agora, just to let you all know that the Mousetrap scam was bad, but it could have been a lot worse ;)

I wish to express my gratitude to Peter Suber, the inventor of the game *Nomic*, and to Douglas Hofstadter, who popularized the game, and (most importantly) introduced it to me in his book, *Metamagical Themas*. While the game presented in *The Omega Game* is not *Nomic* in its strictest sense—it doesn't use the initial rule set created by Mr. Suber in the appendix of his book, *The Paradox of Self-Amendment*—it does fall into the realm of *Nomic*-like games. I apologize in advance for the sinister cast I have given an innocuous game. The necessities of drama and my chosen genre required it. This fiction aside, I have played *Nomic* myself for a number of years, and I assure all interested readers that the pathology I illustrate within these pages is not inherent in the game. To mutilate a Shakespearean quote, "The fault is not in our rules, but in ourselves."

BOOK ONE:

OPENING

First Move

Quaid Loman woke up—or at least became fully aware of his surroundings—sitting on the edge of an unfamiliar bed. His hands shook, sweat dripped down the back of his neck, and he needed a drink more than at any time in the past six months.

He tried to remember the previous night, and he couldn't.

Quaid rubbed the palms of his hands deep into the orbits of his eyes, and fairy ghosts of color shot across the insides of his eyelids. It was a reflex, born from other long nights he couldn't remember and the longer mornings that followed.

It took him a few moments before he was awake enough to realize that the hangover blood-throb—the price of admission for such an evening—was absent.

Even so, Quaid's breathing was measured, careful. His body still expected the pain. When he finally moved, it was with a slow deliberation, restrained by a fear that was almost an

ache itself—the anticipation sharp as it had
ever been.

Not just the first drink, Quaid's barely rational
thoughts stepped on themselves, *the first*
thought *of drink.*

As if to mock him, the pain refused to come.

If anything, that made the craving worse. *One*
drink. It'll take the edge off, better than aspirin for
the pain. . . .

Six months of sobriety, and he'd blown it.

Quaid pulled his hands away from his face,
still expecting the hangover fist to begin squeezing his brain. He blinked a few times at a
blurred, horribly bright hotel room. Each time
his eyelids rose, he tensed against the searing
light.

He almost wished for the blinding headache,
the nausea, the burn of acid in his throat and
deep in his chest, the throb of his own pulse in
his ears. That would almost be better than waiting for it to hit, his whole body a muscle tensed
against the cramp that any moment would knot
it into a ball and tear it from the bone.

He blinked. His vision blurred, adjusting to
a too-bright day. After a few long moments of
squinting, Quaid began to believe the hangover
wouldn't come.

He was fully awake and the visceral fears of
the reptilian hindbrain gave way to the fears of
a more rational mind. He bore none of the physical stigmata of a drinking binge—

But last night was a hole cut out of his mind.

It had been removed so completely that not even a silhouette remained to give him an idea of the shape and size of the missing memory. This place, and how he had come here was knowledge so thoroughly gone that he couldn't be certain if he had forgotten, or had never known in the first place.

It wasn't his first blackout—

It *was* the first where his body didn't pay for it afterward.

"What happened? Where the hell am I?" Quaid whispered to himself. His words carried the pasty taste of sleep. He was trembling slightly when it sank in that he didn't even remember sitting up. It was as if he had just been teleported here, sitting naked on the edge of a stranger's bed.

There was a nightstand within reach. He leaned over, another reflex, and fumbled for a moment, but his hand found his glasses. He put them on, and the room shot into focus.

Now he could see where he was.

"Shit . . ." Quaid shook his head.

A hotel room. Even though it had been a while since he had a job that required travel—or much of anything else—he recognized the character of the room almost instantly. That wasn't a great surprise. What surprised him was that the look of the place was several orders of magnitude out of his league right now. There was real wood paneling, stained and waxed; Victorian wallpaper bearing a fruit-bowl motif

large enough to be a mural, and a plaster scallop-
shell molding circling a ceiling centered on an
antique brass ceiling fan that looked like it came
straight out of the nineteen-twenties.

The vague European feeling to the room was
brought home when he looked down near the
baseboard and saw an outlet with two small
round holes. . . .

God knew *where* he was, but that wasn't an
American wall outlet.

Before his marriage and everything else had
fallen to the booze, he had been on enough business trips for all hotel rooms to seem the same
to him. The Radissons blending into the Hiltons
into the Residences into the Hyatts. He had even
gone overseas a few times.

No expense account had ever sprung for a
place like this, even before he'd become a lush.

Quaid looked at the paneled walls and tried
to come up with some explanation of how he
had come to be here. His memory was empty
of any answers. No way he could have af-
forded this.

He tried to force himself to remember the
prior day, but all he could recall was a series of
nonspecific moments that could be yesterday, or
last month.

His mind locked onto one memory as the
most recent—at least as the freshest.

He remembered entering the elevator on the
way to his current job. He had a vivid image of
a teenager on the elevator with him, wearing a

violent red and blue tie-dyed T-shirt, lycra shorts, and a black bicycle helmet. His mind was fixated on the kid's appearance, so incongruous in the gray office building where he spent his gray workdays.

Quaid tried to force a memory of what he was doing, what he was thinking.

A crumpled sheet of paper in his hand. Anger. Apprehension. Fear?

Red and blue tie-dye.

What was I thinking?

Glorified temp work. Maybe he muttered it out loud. . . .

Had he actually gone up that elevator to quit the first steady job he'd had in over half a year?

What the hell had he been doing?

He couldn't remember the rest. Like a half-forgotten word, the more he tried to force the memory, the more it retreated.

Quaid felt sick, and it wasn't from a hangover.

He got to his feet and walked over to the window. It was burning daylight outside, and the sun should have been driving daggers into his forebrain. However, the only pain he felt was a hollow self-pity for his own stupidity. It was a feeling that he had managed to nurture quite often in his long lurch toward sobriety.

"So I quit," he muttered. The words were still thick and pasty, as if he'd been asleep for years. He shook his head as if he couldn't quite believe himself. He kept shaking his head as he looked out the hotel room window.

"Where the hell am I?" he repeated to himself. The view out the window didn't help him come up with an answer.

The window had wooden louvers and shutters, not your typical Radisson touch. Looking out it, to one side, he saw a bluff that rose about sixty feet above an unmarked, snow-white beach. Beyond was a lagoon of water a brilliant shade of blue, a color that he'd only seen in *National Geographic* specials. Tropical woodland crowded around on the other side, except where a road of white gravel snaked past the side of the hotel.

He looked at the palms rustling in the breeze. He had to be in the Caribbean, the Virgin Islands, the Pacific maybe. . . .

Until now, at the hotels he frequented, a good view had been one that didn't face the airport.

Maybe I finally landed a decent job. . . .

Christ, if that was the case, where had his memory gone? Quaid couldn't believe, even with his history, that he would do something stupid like celebrate a new position with enough one-arm curls to wipe out his still-drying synapses.

That wasn't quite truthful.

He didn't *want* to believe it. When he was honest, he wouldn't put it past himself.

But he *had* awoken in worse predicaments than this one. When it came down to mornings after, waking up naked in a luxury hotel in Fiji,

Tahiti, or wherever didn't even rank in the top twenty—with or without his memory.

"Things could be worse," he said, allowing himself a chuckle.

That phrase had been a personal motto of his before he'd hit bottom and joined AA. The day she left him, Judy had said that they were going to etch those words on his tombstone.

He didn't know if repeating the phrase now was a conscious effort at being ironic with himself, or if he was slipping into old patterns of denial.

He really could use a beer right now.

Quaid shrugged off the craving and got up to look for his clothes.

He opened drawers and cabinets. Bureau, wardrobe, and even the end table—all were empty. They didn't even contain the obligatory Bible or tourist pamphlets. Not even hotel stationery. That seemed odd enough, but Quaid didn't stop to ponder it—he was feeling more and more exposed without any clothes on. It seemed ludicrous that he'd come here with his glasses and nothing else.

To his relief, he found his clothes in an open suitcase, sitting on a stand in a closet. He stepped into the closet and had the disturbing realization that it was one of *three* suitcases.

He had never packed that much for a business trip. Those usually only rated an overnight bag. Even when he and Judy had gone on vacation together—the last time two years ago—they'd

only taken two suitcases and an overnight bag
between them.

Three suitcases could have contained every
scrap of clothing he owned. One suitcase he
didn't recognize as his, and it looked brand new.
He bent over it and saw it still had a Wal-Mart
inventory tag on it.

*Wish I knew why I came here. It's got to be an
interesting story.*

Quaid pulled on some jeans and a polo shirt
that seemed light enough for the climate, and
began noticing more oddities about this hotel he
found himself in. First off, there was no television. That, combined with the absence of any
tourist literature, struck him as odd enough that
he started *looking* for other things out of place.

He found them—or, more correctly, he didn't
find them.

There was no phone. Not only was there no
phone in the room itself, but when he tried to
hunt down his cell phone in his luggage, including the mystery case, which just held more of
his clothes, he came up blank.

Whoever had packed him for this trip hadn't
included the phone. That shouldn't have bothered him, since he was probably miles outside
the roaming area, but its absence made him uneasy. He was also somewhat disturbed that his
luggage didn't include any other electronic devices. Not his ThinkPad, not his Walkman, not
even his calculator.

The hotel didn't even have its own radio.

Quaid looked out the window at the empty beaches. The only thing moving out there was a lone gull catching an updraft, and the occasional breaker rolling across the too-blue water. He was overwhelmed by a feeling of isolation, as if this room was cut off from everything else in the world. As if he was the only human being for thousands of miles.

The thought lasted for about five minutes, until he heard a woman screaming.

"Thomas?"

The word left Beatrice Greenhart's lips before she had fully awakened. Her dead husband's name spoken in the tones of a prayer, a talisman against the unknowns hiding in the darkness.

Hearing her own plea to the absent Mr. Greenhart awoke her fully with a sense of sourceless dread. It was a feeling stronger than any she had felt since the morning of her husband's stroke. She realized, with a combination of disgust and disorientation, that the bed she lay on was not her own.

She sat bolt upright and threw the covers off of herself as if they had been trying to strangle her.

"No . . ." Her voice was a whisper. This wasn't her house.

The air she breathed carried the copper taste of panic. She gripped her head as if she could pull the evil thoughts out of her body.

It claimed Thomas, it's come for you . . .

"No." Her voice sounded old and frail in her ears.

It takes your mind first, your memory . . .

"No! Stop it!" Beatrice yelled in her loudest, most bitchy voice. It didn't matter who it was she was shouting at—she managed to compose herself by force of will. Mr. Greenhart had not condoned pointless blubbering. She shouldn't start now.

There was nothing wrong with her or her memory. Her brain was fine, intact and working perfectly. She pushed herself out of the alien bed and hugged herself.

She wore her own nightgown, and slowly convinced herself that, yes, she did remember going to sleep last night. She had gone to sleep in her own bed and had woken up—

Where?

She walked to a shuttered window, the wood floor cold against her naked feet. She pushed the shutters open on a wooded vista filled with alien trees.

There was little question. She had been kidnapped. Drugged or assaulted while she slept and abandoned here. Wherever *here* was. God only knew how long her captors had kept her unconscious, but Beatrice was thankful that it wasn't any failing within her own skull that had done this to her.

Her pulse started racing as she looked out at the palms from her window and thought of the kidnappers, and where they might be now. She pressed her palms against her forehead and tried to force herself to exhibit some of Mr. Greenhart's practicality.

That had been Thomas' strong suit, no nonsense, no worry, no daydreaming, no "wishy-washy bull crap" as he was fond of saying. He had been a nuts-and-bolts, here-and-now kind of man. If Beatrice had told him about her fears of kidnappers—as she had with her fears about muggers and rapists years ago—his response would have been something like, "Are there any here now? Get down to business, woman."

Beatrice got down to business.

She wasn't going to accomplish anything standing around in her nightgown, so she looked around the room hoping that her abductors had left her something she could wear.

They had.

In a well-worn suitcase that Beatrice had last seen in her attic's crawl space, she found most of the contents of her bedroom closet. The contents gave her a chill. They must have been watching her for a long time, they had only packed her recent clothes. She had been getting stouter in the past few years, and only about half the clothes she owned still fit her.

At least they were *her* clothes. She doubted she would have been able to put on unfamiliar clothes when she didn't know their origin. Her skin still crawled when she thought about someone else's sheets and blankets touching her. Thank God they had left her nightgown.

That brought another shudder.

They could have stripped off her nightclothes while she had slept. They could have done *other* things. . . .

Down to business, woman!

She didn't know *what* they'd done while she slept. Like the absent kidnappers, it didn't bear thinking about.

She grabbed the clothes that were on top and pulled them on. She dressed quickly, trying to rush ahead of the random speculations that were trying to frighten her. In the back of her mind, Thomas' ghost was telling her that her business was to get dressed, then find a phone and get herself back home.

What have they done to me? What are they going to do to me?

However much she tried, she would never reach his level of businesslike detachment. Though, at least, she could manage a business-like demeanor. She forced herself to slow down, not to let her panic control her movements. She pulled on a pleated charcoal-gray skirt in a deliberate, unhurried manner, even after she realized that this room had no phone.

That only makes sense. What kidnappers allow their prisoner a phone? The door is probably locked. . . .

Her pulse raced again as she thought about having to leave by the window. There was a flagstone patio a story or two below. A fall that would easily break a hip, or a spine—

Thomas' ever-practical voice was with her, saying to put on her shoes and try the door first, before she started worrying about the window.

She put on a pair of flats with cushioned soles and walked up to the elaborate Victorian door. The knob danced with scrollwork, and at eye level was a circular trapdoor that served as a peephole. Cautiously, Beatrice opened the peephole and looked out.

She received a small circular view of another elaborate Victorian door across the hall. An engraved brass plaque identified it as the door to room 215.

Beatrice held her breath and tried the elaborate knob. It turned easily, and the door pulled inward. The surprise of an unlocked door, if anything, frightened her more. She caught her breath and tried to stand up a little straighter. Her kidnappers must have just abandoned her here, in this hotel, after they were done with her. . . .

"Find someone to call the police," she told herself as she stepped out into the hallway. She left the door open behind her as she took a few tentative steps into the hallway. It was a long hallway, with a T-intersection on either end. She stood near one end. About midway, on the wall opposite Beatrice's door, she saw the top of a stairway. She started walking toward it.

It was definitely a hotel; the brass plaques numbering the rooms told her that. The carpet was dark, with blood-red patterns in it that complemented the dark wood paneling on the walls. The ceiling was high, with a scalloped plaster molding. The fabric wallpaper, on the walls above the wood paneling, featured pineapples and flowers in a twisting vine motif. Between every pair of doors, a thin table supported a pair of clawed lamps with Tiffany shades. She didn't see anyone else in the hall. There was an eerie feeling of emptiness that preyed on her fear. She clenched her fists, refusing to run, or start screaming for help.

She had almost reached the stairs, when she heard a voice behind her. "Madam? Pardon me. Do you speak English?"

She spun around, as if she had been struck. Her first thought was that her kidnappers had returned. They wouldn't let her go home. Now that she was awake they would do what they wanted, because they wanted her to *know* what was . . .

She was shrinking from the stranger, ready to run from him, when Beatrice's brain finally caught up with what he had said. "What?" She shook her head as if to clear it.

The man seemed to take Beatrice's answer as affirmative. "I didn't mean to startle you." He was bald and had a snow-white mustache, and wore a blue work shirt and jeans. He had to be several years past retirement, but he was built as if he still did heavy manual labor every day. His face was lined and hard, but right now there was a lost expression on his face.

"This is crazy," he said, "but can you tell me where we are?"

"Are you playing games with me?" She had a sudden conviction that this man was part of it. Why else would he be asking her such a question? Here? Now?

"No—"

"*Stop it,*" Beatrice said, her fear pushing her voice an octave higher and several decibels louder. "Stop trying to frighten me! *Tell me why I was taken here!*"

"I didn't—" The man took a step back, frowning. "Let me start over. My name is Frank. I woke up in a hotel room down the hall, and I don't remember how I got here."

"*You?*"

Frank's words muddled Beatrice's fear up with an uncertainty and a disorientation as severe as that she had awakened with. She hugged herself, trying to force herself not to feel the impact of what he was saying.

"Are you all right?" Frank asked.

"*No!*" Beatrice felt her upper body shake under arms that clutched her sides hard enough to make her ribs ache.

Too much. Too fast.

"Why am I here?" she asked, the edge gone from her voice. "Why would anyone want to take me here?" She looked up at Frank's blurry face, mortified at her tears but unable to stop them. "Where is *here*?"

There was a long pause as Frank looked at her. The hardness in his face broke for a moment.

"You, too?" he asked, reaching out for her shoulder.

Down the hall, a door burst open to the sound of screaming.

Quaid ran out into the hall outside his room and into a Victorian hallway with textured fabric wallpaper, wood paneling, and blood-red patterned carpeting. He could hear commotion down the hall from him, around a corner where another hallway entered his from the right. He heard smashing glass and a female voice screaming, *"Who are you? What have you done to me?"*

Then he heard more glass smash against something.

Quaid rounded the corner just in time to nearly collide with a black man at the convergence of the two hallways. The new guy was backing away from the scene. He didn't even bother to look at Quaid; he kept looking down the hall, holding up his hands and saying, "Calm down, girl."

The woman he was talking to could have benefited from his advice.

She was standing in the middle of the hallway holding the remains of a table lamp. The glass shade was scattered in multicolored fragments across the carpet. She held the brass lamp up-

side-down with both hands, as if she was ready
to hit a world-series home run with the thing
and the black guy was a wild pitch.

She stared at the black guy, then at Quaid,
apparently trying to determine who was the bigger threat. Quaid had no clue what was going
on. From the screams he'd thought a rape or a
mugging, looking at her he wasn't so sure now.
She was barely covered in a sheer black nightgown that—with everything else—showed that
she was unhurt. In body, at least.

"Who are you?" she yelled at the two of them,
and the other guy looked at Quaid with an expression that said he didn't want to be here.

They weren't the only three in the hallway.
There was an elderly couple standing on the
other side of the woman. Quaid had missed the
pair at first. The hysterical woman and her
weapon grabbed most of his attention.

She whipped around to see the couple, as if
Quaid's notice had given their presence away.
The old man stepped protectively between the
two women and backed his companion away
from the scene.

"Don't you come near me!" She shook the lamp
at the couple, and the man kept backing away.

"The bitch is nuts," said the man next to
Quaid. His voice was quiet enough that Quaid
knew the guy didn't intend him to hear, much
less the woman. But the woman whipped
around and yelled, "I am not *crazy*!" She swung
the lamp in the black guy's direction, and even

though she was over six feet away and couldn't connect, the move made the guy stumble backward and fall on his ass.

Someone had to try and defuse the situation before anyone got hurt.

Fortunately, Quaid had long and repeated experience in dealing with explosive rages. Unfortunately, most of those times he'd been the one holding the lamp.

Quaid took a few tentative steps forward, trying to picture himself as Judy before she had given up on him. He winced when he walked on the remains of the glass shade in his bare feet.

He tried to duplicate Judy's disarming look of concern as he asked her, "What's the matter? Maybe I can help you." *Christ, was Judy as scared then as I am now?*

He stopped approaching before he got within what might be perceived as a threatening distance—and about as close as he could get without being in easy clubbing range.

"What's the matter?" She repeated his words with a dripping sarcasm that said that she thought Quaid knew perfectly well what the matter was. For all he knew, he should've. "Who do you think you are? You can't do this to people. There're laws . . ." He saw the muscles twitching in her face. The end of the lamp was shaking.

Quaid focused on the woman. If he could monopolize her attention, maybe one of these people with a more complete memory could slip away and get the local cops, or paramedics, or whatever. He risked a step forward and sucked in a breath as a shard of lampshade sliced open a chunk of his heel. "Do *what* to people? What's happened to you?" That was one of Judy's tricks, keep asking questions. Keep plugging away.

The lamp lowered a bit, which Quaid found encouraging.

She was looking at him, as if until now she hadn't quite seen him. She couldn't have been more than twenty-five or so, though up close he could see signs of premature aging around the eyes and mouth. She was attractive; at one point she might have been shaped like a model, though right now she was too bony, her posture too beaten. Her hair was a flaming red that seemed to have come out of a bottle. Looking into her eyes, this close, made him wonder again if she *had* been raped.

"Who are you?" she asked. Her tone was normal now. She wasn't shouting the question as if it was an accusation.

"Quaid Loman," he replied, and resisted the temptation to hold out his hand. "What's your name?"

"C–Connie."

"Why don't you put down the lamp and tell me what's going on?"

She didn't put the lamp down, but she did lower it all the way. Quaid could hear the the guy behind him exhale. She seemed to melt a little and asked him a question that made him stop breathing for a moment.

"How did I get here?" she asked him. "Where am I?"

Very slowly, he asked, "Don't you remember how you came here?"

She shook her head. "It's the white slavers, isn't it? They want me to be a prostitute in some sick third-world country—"

"Connie, do we look like white slavers to you?" Quaid didn't know what else to say to her. He was still trying to understand the implications of finding someone else with an incomplete memory. He looked over his shoulder at the black guy, who had managed to get to his feet by now. He was older than Quaid had first taken him for. From the back he could have been in his twenties, but his face was lined and his mustache was dusted with gray. "You aren't a white slaver, are you?"

"No, man. I fix cars for a living."

"What's your name?" Quaid asked, splitting his attention between him and Connie. He had some thought that if he introduced all these strangers, it might calm Connie down.

"DeVay, Carlos DeVay—" He looked past Quaid and at Connie. "I didn't have nothing to do with you being here, madam."

Quaid looked back at Connie, and past her to the older couple. When he looked at them, he realized that he had mislabeled them as a cou-

ple. From the body language, and the way the woman was watching the man with as much suspicion as she was everyone else—with the possible exception of Connie—Quaid could tell that the two didn't know each other.

The man was large, bald, with a bull neck and a white mustache. The woman was pear-shaped, with a tight helmet of brown curls. She peered at everyone through a narrow, suspicious squint.

"What about you two?" he asked. "What about your names? Connie can trust you, right?"

"I am Mrs. Thomas Greenhart, young man. If anyone has some explaining to do, it's the young lady—not to mention—"

"I think we can understand her dilemma," the man said. "Can't we, Mrs. Greenhart?"

Mrs. Thomas Greenhart gave the man a look that accused him of betraying a confidence. Quaid was beginning to have an uneasy feeling exactly what that confidence was.

The man stepped forward, still keeping his body between Connie and Mrs. Greenhart, "Frank Pisarski," he said. He looked at Connie and said. "I don't think you need to worry about us. I believe all of us are in the same boat."

Connie looked at him, "What?"

Quaid asked, "How did you get here, Frank?"

Frank Pisarski spread a pair of strong hands and said, "Haven't a clue."

Carlos let out a long whistle. "Oh, man! You, too?"

"Mrs. Greenhart and I just ran into each other, just realized our mutual amnesia, when Miss—" He paused, looked at Connie and, when a surname wasn't forthcoming, continued, "—when Connie here ran into the hall."

Connie looked at Quaid and he saw the question in her eyes even before she asked it.

"Yes," Quaid said, "Me, too."

Second Move

Quaid thought it was a bizarre tableau. Five amnesiacs standing in the middle of a plush Victorian hallway. It was a scene from a bad foreign art film. He was half ready for one of the others to start laughing and explain the joke.

What wasn't funny—was disturbing, in fact— was the absence of hotel security when a distraught woman was busting up their furniture.

Frank looked at him, Connie, and Carlos. "We all need to talk."

Quaid saw Connie tense and he risked putting a hand on her shoulder. "I think we need to take Connie back to her room and give her a chance to clean up."

"It's not *my* room," Connie whispered. Most of the panic seemed to have left her.

"Where is it?" Quaid asked her. "I think your clothes will be around somewhere."

She nodded and gestured with the hand that wasn't carrying a lamp. On the right wall a few feet away, a door hung half open. What Quaid

could see of the room beyond was a twin of
his own.

"Why don't I take that?" Quaid took the opportunity to relieve her of the lamp. She let go
of it and retreated toward the room, backing up
to keep an eye on the others. When the door
closed, he took a limping step toward the table
the lamp had come from. The lamp had been
one of a pair. There was an oddly decapitated
look to the one without a shade.

"You handled that well," Frank told him.

"Uh-huh." He didn't want to go into his experience handling irrational rages. He changed the
subject. "So what's your story, Frank?"

Quaid could see Frank's expression cloud up;
it was like he was admitting a weakness he
didn't want to reveal. "I don't know. This morning I was shaving and I realized, looking at the
mirror, that I didn't recognize the bathroom."
He rubbed his chin and frowned. "I don't know
where I am, or how I got here. But I seemed to
have packed for a long trip. I was afraid I'd
suffered a mini-stroke."

Quaid noticed Mrs. Greenhart tense.

"Try waking up in the shower," Carlos took
a few steps toward them, minding the glass on
the carpet. "I nearly broke my neck. If that happened to her, I don't blame her for freaking."

"You, too, Mrs. Greenhart?" Quaid asked.

"I don't want to talk about it." She shook her
head and placed a hand to her temple. "Awful
thing. Awful that someone would do this."

Quaid looked at all of them. "You're right, Frank. We have to talk. Then find the concierge or whoever runs this place." Quaid looked down at the bloody footprints he was leaving. "But I need to go back to my own room for a moment, get something on this foot."

"We'll wait here for you."

"Keep her calm," Quaid said, nodding toward the door Connie had disappeared behind.

Frank nodded and Quaid hoped he could play the kindly grandfather type, though he looked a little too tough for that.

Quaid carefully limped around the corner, avoiding the glass. As he did, Carlos followed him. "Can I join you?"

"Yeah, sure." Quaid tried hard to absorb the significance of five strangers in the same hotel suffering from the same kind of amnesia.

Carlos paced him all the way back. "What you think happened?"

Quaid was having a problem coming up with an explanation for his own amnesia. "I don't know. Carbon monoxide?" It still didn't explain why he was *here*.

Quaid pushed open the door to his room and walked into the bathroom. Carlos waited by the door, looking around. After a moment he heard Carlos say, "No phone in here either?"

"No phone, no radio, no TV." Quaid sat down on the john and started washing off his wounded foot. He had to pull a sliver of glass out of it, but otherwise the cuts didn't seem too deep.

"That's what I was doing in the hall," Carlos said from outside. "I didn't know what was happening. I needed to find a phone and call my wife."

"That's understandable."

"Yeah, right." There was an ironic tone to his voice. "We've been separated five years. She left *me*. This happens, and the first thing I think to do is call the bitch up."

Quaid shook his head as he dried off his foot, and walked out into the room. He hunted down some socks and a pair of shoes while Carlos stood in the doorway, waiting for him.

"I know how that is," Quaid said. "My wife left me about a year ago." In his head he was still amazed at the fact that it had still taken him another six months and a restraining order before he had admitted that he had a drinking problem.

"That's rough, man. Like I said, me and Lucy are just *separated*—like after five years it's going to work out somehow."

Quaid shrugged. "I don't know. Your first impulse was to call her. Me, I haven't seen or talked to my wife—ex—since . . ." Quaid let it trail off. Court orders against him wasn't the best subject to bring up right now.

Carlos leaned on the doorframe. "So you think it's carbon monoxide that's fucked with our memory?"

"I don't know. It can give you brain damage—"

"Yeah, but I'd like to know what I'm doing here in the first place. I mean, I pull thirty, thirty-five a year. After child support I don't have money to be wintering in the Virgin Islands."

Quaid pulled on his shoe, winced, and looked up at Carlos. "Winter? I thought it was April."

From his expression Quaid could tell, from Carlos' point of view, it was definitely *not* April.

"What's the last month you remember it being?"

"January."

Connie knew this was wrong. All her life, people had told her that she overreacted to everything, worried about things that people shouldn't worry about. Peter would tell her that it was all in her head, when he'd tell her anything. More often, he'd give her that infuriating look of pity.

But she *was* here, this *was* happening, and it *was* wrong. They had finally taken her away.

She pushed her way into "her" hotel room. Once inside, she leaned against the door and shook. She had told Peter about them, about the people watching her. He had never believed her—or, more likely, he was one of them. "Who's the crazy bitch now, Pete?" she asked the walls as her fingernails bit into her palms.

It was worse than Ferndale, the feelings she

had here. There weren't any chicken-wire windows, they didn't strap her to the bed, but the
trapped feeling—if anything—was worse. At
Ferndale she'd known where she was, who was
in charge, what would happen if you broke their
rules. Here, she was adrift, and worse, missing
part of her mind.

Knocking from behind her made her gasp.

"Are you all right in there?" It was the voice
of the older man, the bald one.

They were inmates, too, weren't they? Victims
of the same people who had drilled away part
of her brain. But how could she know? How
could she be sure?

"No," she choked out. She turned and put a
security chain up on the door.

She looked down at what she was wearing.

How long had it been since she had worn a
nightgown? How long had she been running
from them, hiding? The price tags were still on
the thing. "Where are *my* clothes?"

She found a new-looking nylon gym bag
tossed in the corner. She picked it up and placed
it on the bed. They had laundered her clothing.
She had forgotten what it was like to wear
things that didn't smell of beer or a storm sewer.

She almost didn't put them on. It was a trick
of theirs, to give you things that you think you
need or want, make you dependent on them.
That was how they had gotten her, wasn't it?
That last night at the shelter, the last night she
remembered. It had been so cold that she had

given in to the volunteer who wanted to drag her inside. She had known stepping inside would bring her closer to the social workers and the doctors who wanted to take her mind, drug her, make her into something less threatening to them.

She never should have gone to the shelter. She should have toughed it out on the street. It wasn't exactly safe, but at least she would have seen them coming.

A pair of denim shorts and a sleeveless gray sweater. At least it wasn't snowing here. Just thinking about the cold made her joints ache. Lord, maybe that was the point. They dragged her off to someplace pleasant, so she would *want* them to control her, so she would *ask* them to pull the shade across her mind, to think the way they wanted her to think.

She walked up to the window and looked outside. A wind caressed her face, and she backpedaled, surprised the window was open. Beyond the window was a vast expanse of lawn descending a hillside down to a snow-white beach. She was looking out the second floor of some large Victorian structure. She could see scroll-cut woodwork above her, and a cylindrical tower at the end of a wing to her right.

The window was open.

She ran her hands across the sill. They hadn't confined her here, hadn't locked her in. Somehow that terrified her. Her abductors had broken down a fundamental boundary between

freedom and captivity. By forcing her into this
position, giving the illusion of freedom, they destroyed whatever sense of freedom Connie
might have had.

"Connie?"

Friend or foe?

Were they part of the dark forces that had
brought her here, or were they fellow abductees?

Did it matter?

Connie sighed.

*I am not crazy. I know the dark men brought me
here. I know this is wrong.*

She walked over and removed the chain from
the door.

Quaid continued to compare notes with Carlos on the way back to Connie's room. Carlos
had lost three months' worth of memory more
than he had. That led to the disturbing realization that he had no idea how much time of his
own he had lost. Days? Months? Years? The
only thing he knew for certain was that Carlos
had lost three months more than he had.

The door to Connie's room was open, and he
could hear Mrs. Greenhart's voice. "You aren't
making any sense, Mr. Pisarski."

For Connie's benefit, Quaid knocked on the
door and waited for someone—Frank—to call to
them, "Come in."

The room was a twin of his own, the only
difference was the floral mural on the wallpaper,
and a different view of the water.

Connie sat on a wooden claw-legged chair, facing halfway from everyone, toward the widow. A small pile of clothes was scattered on the bed, next to a navy-blue gym bag that looked brand new. The striking thing was that that was the only sign of disorder in the room. The rest of the room—*like mine*, Quaid realized—was as spotless and ordered as if she had just moved in.

Mrs. Greenhart stood by the doorway, peering at everyone suspiciously. Frank was staring out the window, past Connie. His broad frame blocked out most of the view.

Quaid looked at Mrs. Thomas Greenhart and asked her, "What's not making any sense?"

"It is March seventeenth, he knows it is." She directed her attention at Frank. "You're just wrong." There was a sharp edge in her voice that, in any other situation, Quaid would have interpreted as anger. But, looking at her, Quaid thought it was more likely fear.

"Didn't we just have this conversation?" Carlos turned to Quaid.

What impressed Quaid was the fact that Mrs. Greenhart had an exact date. "How do you know it is the seventeenth?"

"Because I always visit Mr. Greenhart on the sixteenth." She said it with such conviction that it was almost convincing. "They had to have taken me while I was asleep."

Connie looked up in her direction. She didn't

say anything, but her lips were pressed in a hard white line.

Frank turned toward Quaid and Carlos. "She's adamant that she hasn't suffered any memory loss."

"My mind is as sharp as it ever was. I'd know if anything was wrong." Mrs. Greenhart folded her arms as if to dare anyone to tell her different.

"What about you?" Carlos asked Frank.

Frank chuckled, somewhat ironically. "I remember mailing out a filing extension to the IRS, last minute."

Connie was hugging herself, and Quaid realized that she was silently crying. He walked over and stood by her.

"You can't tell me I couldn't tell if I had forgotten a whole month . . ." Mrs. Greenhart was still talking, but her voice was trailing away.

Carlos said, "Quaid thinks it might have been carbon monoxide."

Quaid put his hand on Connie's shoulder. "Are you all right?" It was a stupid question. Objectively, none of them were "all right."

Connie shook her head and said, "They stole Christmas." She looked up at him. "They don't want me with my children. Might get some bad ideas from Mommy. Can't let her corrupt their minds, can they?"

"You didn't lose it," Quaid said, trying to sound confident.

"Once a year Pete lets me see them. Once a year . . ."

"You just can't remember right now," Quaid continued. "This probably isn't permanent."

Frank turned around and looked at him. "You sound like an expert." The way he said it made it sound like an accusation. Quaid got the impression that Frank didn't have much use for "experts." He looked at Quaid with narrowed eyes. "Are you a psychologist?"

Connie's shoulder tensed under Quaid's hand. He stood up. "No, a database programmer."

Frank shook his head. "So you don't have any better explanations than I do."

Quaid shrugged. "The same thing hit all of us." He looked at Connie, who was shaking now. "And we could all probably do with some medical attention."

"You can't tell me I've lost a month," Beatrice said, again.

Frank looked at her and shook his head. "Let's find the concierge."

Third Move

Frank didn't much care for the place. It was old, Victorian, the kind of place Vincent Price, Bela Lugosi, or Boris Karloff would feel at home. *Especially now that they're all dead.*

He'd looked out the window in Connie's room and had seen a couple of turrets and at least two major wings. But, despite the size of the place, it felt dark and claustrophobic. The floral wallpaper in the halls was so garish and busy that it gave him a headache.

Despite Mr. Loman's theories, Frank didn't see himself picking this spot for a vacation. A cabin on a lake in upstate New York, and motel in Atlantic City. Those were the kind of vacations he went on. What was he doing with a room in this place?

The memory loss was easier to explain, at least to Frank's mind. Carbon monoxide, or another gas, some form of mass poisoning. That would explain five people with the same problem. Frank wondered if it had affected the other inhabitants. . . .

If it was some poison gas, the five of them had gotten off relatively lightly. Others wouldn't have, and they would be in for some grisly discoveries later on.

They reached the staircase where a brass plaque pointed them down toward the lobby. The stairs below spilled out into a lobby filled with more stained glass, dark wood, and blood-red carpeting. Four old ceiling fans spun lazily above the two-story-tall space.

"No central air," someone muttered from behind him. Frank thought it was the black guy. Frank shrugged and started down the stairs. The sooner they found someone in charge here, the better.

"It's an old building," Loman said.

"I know, but there's no vents. Get what I'm saying?"

Frank kept descending the stairway. Speculations had lost their productive value, they just needed to find the hotel manager, or a phone.

At the foot of the stairs he faced the windows that looked out the front of the building. The hotel was up on a bluff that gave an unobstructed view of the lagoon.

"We're rooming all over the place upstairs," DeVay kept saying. "How'd gas affect all of us?"

"A lot of it?" Loman didn't sound too sure.

The main entrance stood open, facing several acres of lawn that descended toward the beach.

Frank felt a breeze that carried the smell of salt and drying seaweed.

Why would he come here? All he had ever wanted was to spend his retirement in solitary peace. Worse, the gap in his memory made him unsure of his other faculties. He understood Mrs. Greenhart's firm denial too well, he just wasn't that good at deceiving himself.

The others caught up with him, and the five of them stood in the center of the lobby. Frank turned around, hoping to see someone manning the registration desk. He wasn't quite certain exactly what he was expecting, but he *wasn't* expecting a grimy teenager sitting on top of the desk.

The kid wore a black leather jacket that hung loosely over a shirtless chest. His pants were ragged denim that was torn open at the knees. If his attire wasn't enough, his expression marked him immediately as a smart-ass.

The kid's response to seeing them was to vault backward over the desk, landing facing Frank and the others. "Don't tell me you work here," Frank muttered, stepping forward. The kid looked more like the type to rob the place.

That thought made Frank stop in his tracks and raise his arm to keep Loman and DeVay back. *What if this is a robbery, and he's going for a gun?* He felt himself tensing to dive at the bastard.

To Frank's relief, the kid leaned on the desk,

both hands in view. "More plebes, huh?" the kid said. "What's your room numbers?"

From behind him, Frank heard Mrs. Greenhart snort. "I never—"

Frank stepped forward, making a point of keeping himself between the kid and everyone else. "What's your name, son?"

"Call me Duce. You guys bring it up to fifteen."

"Fifteen what?" Frank asked.

"Tenants, tourists, prisoners. Take your pick." The kid shrugged.

Smart-ass and a half. "Do you work here?" Frank asked. He tried to keep the annoyance out of his voice.

"Fuck if I know." Duce flashed a toothy grin that was an open invitation to a fist.

"Watch your mouth, son."

The kid didn't even seem to hear him. "Any of *you* remember how you got here?"

The question shouldn't have surprised him. Even so, he was struck speechless for a few moments. Frank stared at this Duce character as if the punk had just revealed some nasty secret they shared between them.

Frank stepped up to the desk. He placed his hands on the counter and felt his muscles tense. He spoke quietly, but the words were taut, like piano wire ready to snap. "No. We don't. *Do you?*"

Duce shrugged. "Seems to be going around. None of the others know what's going on—and if you haven't noticed," he spread his arms, "there ain't no staff to ask about it."

Frank felt his hand ball into a fist. Suddenly, Loman's hand was on his arm and he was asking, "You mean there are others here? How many?"

Frank turned to face Loman, irritated at the interruption.

Duce turned to Loman and nodded back to the wall behind him. Against the wall was an antique cabinet that consisted of square pigeonholes, each with a small brass plaque giving a room number. About a dozen of them contained a manila envelope.

"Count the letters. I come up with twenty." He looked at Frank again and said, "So what room number you in?"

"What business is it of yours, young man?" Mrs. Greenhart said, the contempt in the words was palpable. Frank was already looking over Duce's shoulder at the pigeonholes. There was a package for his room, and Connie's. . . .

Duce, however, took Mrs. Greenhart in stride. "No staff here, someone's got to pass out the mail."

Frank looked back at her and Connie. "Maybe this will explain things."

Duce grinned and shook his head. Real attitude problem there.

Frank tapped on the table and said, "202." He gestured back at Mrs. Greenhart who gave him a withering state. Eventually she said, "211."

Duce reached behind him and pulled out a pair of manila envelopes that were exactly the same except for the address labels, which had a name and room number, nothing else.

"Frank Pisarski and Beatrice Greenhart?"

Duce tossed Frank's on the counter in front of him. Mrs. Greenhart stepped up and pulled hers out of Duce's hand.

Loman said, "233, I think. I wasn't paying attention."

" 'Kay," Duce said, turning around. "Give me a name?"

While Duce hunted down Loman's envelope, Frank picked up his. It wasn't heavy, it felt as if it contained only one sheet of paper. He glanced up to see Mrs. Greenhart had already opened her envelope. She stared at the document inside, muttering to herself.

"Madness," she whispered, staring at the legal-sized sheet of paper.

"Here we go," Duce pulled out an envelope and shoved it across the counter, in Loman's direction. Loman's room number on the envelope was actually 223. He stepped up to the desk, next to Frank, and picked it up.

Connie followed him, but stayed a step behind, looking over his shoulder.

"And you?" Duce asked.

"C–Connie. I don't know my room number."

Duce nodded and turned around to rummage in the mailboxes.

Frank shook his head and opened his own

envelope. Behind him he could hear Mrs.
Greenhart insisting, "This is not funny. Not
funny at all."

Inside was a single legal-sized sheet of paper.
It was laid out like a contract, albeit a short one,
and the first thing that caught his attention was
the signature.

It was his own.

Frank had never seen this paper before now,
but it unquestionably bore his signature, and the
signature was dated May first, again in his own
handwriting. Behind him, Beatrice was muttering something about forgeries and lawsuits.

Frank started reading it. Despite his hopes, it
didn't explain a damn thing. It was a preprinted
form that only had five paragraphs on it:

AGREEMENT BETWEEN **FRANK PISARSKI**
AND THE PLAYERS OF THE GAME:

1: **FRANK PISARSKI** is a Player in the Game.
2: The Players must participate in the Game.
3: The Players may agree to change the rules.
4: The Players must obey the rules or forfeit.
5: The winner of the Game is the last Player
   who has not forfeited.

Frank Pisarski 5/1/00

"And what the hell is this crap?" Frank asked.

"No," Beatrice said. "I didn't sign this. I never
signed anything like this. And the date's
wrong." She tramped up to the desk and tossed

the paper and the envelope on the counter. "I do not play games."

Duce was still rummaging and came out with another envelope—exactly the same as the others. "We got only the one Connie." He held it out, and when Connie didn't look as if she was about to take it, Quaid took it and handed it to her.

She stared at it for a few moments, as if handling shards of glass that might slice right into her. She opened it very slowly.

"Did you get the same thing?" Frank picked up Mrs. Greenhart's letter. The same five paragraphs, a different name and signature. He turned to Loman, "You?"

"Yeah," Loman shook his head at his own paper. He turned toward the lobby, saying, "Carlos, I guess you've got one, too. . . ."

When Loman trailed off, Frank looked back toward the lobby. Empty. No sign of Carlos DeVay. "Where did he disappear to?" Loman whispered.

The scenery was even more spectacular than it had been from the window. The hotel had been constructed to command the best view of the water, and exiting through the front doors he could see all the way down to the lagoon, which had to be a mile or two at least.

"Lord have mercy," Carlos whispered to himself.

It was finally sinking in. Up until now he had

been focused on the loss of his recent memories. Fear over the loss of part of his mind, the fear intensified by the feeling that he couldn't sense what was missing. Three months at least, by talking to that guy, Quaid. Inside his own head, Carlos knew that if there hadn't been someone to tell him, he wouldn't know if his absent memories covered days, or years.

Once he'd walked out the door of the hotel, it clicked inside him that he was seriously *elsewhere.*

The most recent memory that he had was lowering a 442 engine block into the pristine body of a 1972 Oldsmobile. The garage had been cold as a morgue, the windows frosted, and his breath coming out in white fog. The chain was so cold it burned his fingers even through his work gloves. January in Detroit.

It wasn't January, and he was a million miles from Detroit.

Carlos headed away from the hotel, toward the water. He walked on an immaculately manicured lawn that was so green it was almost blue. Above him the sky was a cloudless azure flecked with the white dots of distant gulls. The water was deeper blue than the sky, severed from the land by a strip of beach that was platinum white. The white-yellow sun burned everything with a near-shadowless brightness, hot even from its low point over the palms to Carlos' left.

After the grays of an urban winter, and the

dark colors of the hotel's interior, the color out here was almost painful. Carlos' eyes watered.

Color might rule here, but sound was a reluctant weak sister. It was so quiet that Carlos had to concentrate to realize that there were any sounds at all. The breakers in the distance, beyond the protective arms enclosing the lagoon. The distant call of a seagull. The rush of the wind through the palms to the right and left.

And a gentle clinking.

Clinking?

Something metallic was being struck repeatedly. Not behind him, but ahead. Carlos had to squint to make out what was ahead of him. Almost lost in the reflective glare from the water was a small concrete patio. A tall flagpole sprouted from it, the clinking he heard came from the ropes striking it in the wind.

Carlos walked up toward it. It seemed the best position outside from which to get his bearings.

"No one raised the flag today," Carlos said to himself. It was irritating, and somewhat ominous, to discover that such a basic clue to his location was absent. He didn't even know what country he was in.

The flagpole's base was raised above the surrounding ground, so Carlos didn't see the cannon until he had almost reached the flagpole.

He was standing at the cusp of the bluff, the point at which the land stopped its gentle slope and began its dive toward the beach in earnest.

The ground dropped away from the base of the flagpole at about a thirty- or forty-degree angle. Just in front of the concrete base, a niche had been cut out of the hillside. A semicircular dug-out around a flat surface paved with flagstones. Dead center sat a black nineteenth century cannon. Carlos walked past the flagpole, and a few more feet, until he was at the edge of the dugout.

The flagstone surface on which the cannon sat was about fifteen feet below, so Carlos circled around the perimeter, walking down the slope until he reached the front of the dugout.

It was a commanding view of the lagoon. Carlos could see the entire beach from here. Unlike most display pieces, Carlos bet that this cannon was still sitting where it had been originally stationed. It probably could have hit anything that entered the protection of the lagoon.

He placed a hand on its black surface, expecting the cold feel of cast iron. He pulled it away, cursing. The sun had been up long enough to make the surface burning hot. Sucking on the heel of his hand, Carlos saw a glint of brass at the base of the black-painted weapon.

"Finally." A historical plaque commemorating some battle or other would at least give some clue to his location.

Carlos moved around the end of the cannon and looked down.

"Well, what the . . ."

The plaque, shining near gold in the sunlight,

was blank. Carlos stared and rubbed his eyes as if it was some illusion that would go away. It wasn't.

He knelt down. His first thought was wrong. It wasn't a brand new plaque that had yet to be engraved—and what idiot engraves a plaque *after* it's mounted—it was at least as old as the rest of the hotel. Carlos' fingers traced the edges where the finish was still a pebbled, weathered green.

The plaque shone because the inscription that had been embossed upon it had been deliberately and thoroughly erased. Carlos could just see where lines of text had once been. The surface that had held the inscription was smoother, more polished.

There was no hope of reconstructing what the plaque had said.

From somewhere down the hillside, Carlos heard a voice call to him, "Hail the cannon!"

Quaid couldn't see any sign of Carlos in the lobby. As he looked he heard Beatrice Greenhart fuming. "This is all some elaborate hoax. As soon as I find a phone, someone is going to pay for this outrage."

Frank Pisarski sounded just as pissed. "Pretty elaborate for someone's idea of a prank."

Quaid turned around and called over to Duce. "Everyone here got one of these?"

Duce nodded and waved a loose strand of hair away from his face. "Everyone so far. I stayed back here to hand them out." He pulled a crumpled sheet out of his pocket and held it up. It was the familiar contract. He looked at Beatrice. "And if you have as good a memory of yesterday as everyone else does, I wouldn't be so quick to assume that isn't your signature."

Beatrice harumphed and repeated, "I don't play games."

"Whatever this is, signature or not, it isn't legally binding." Frank looked down at the paper in his hand. "It wasn't witnessed, notarized, or anything."

Quaid looked at his own sheet. "U.S. law, you're probably right."

Connie and Beatrice both looked at him. Beatrice's expression was a sour squint. Connie just looked frightened.

"What do you mean by *U.S.* law?" Frank looked as if he already knew the answer to his question, and didn't like it.

Duce volunteered the answer. "He means you ain't in Kansas anymore."

Quaid looked out toward the entrance to the lobby. It still hung open on a tropical island landscape. "If we're in Hawaii or the Virgin Islands, U.S. law applies—but this place isn't wired for American current." Quaid looked around the lobby until he found a wall outlet to point at.

Frank shook his head and rubbed his forehead. He looked like a man who had to restrain himself from punching something—probably Duce. "This just gets better and better."

Connie was staring at the baseboard as if the European wall outlet was some alien creature. Beatrice was muttering something about the American embassy.

Duce appeared to be thoroughly amused.

"Others?" Quaid addressed Duce, whose smile didn't waver.

"Yeah," Duce said.

"Where are they?"

"Oh, they went outside," Duce shrugged. "Looking for a boat, radio, phone maybe—"

Quaid nodded. "Frank, look after Connie and Beatrice—"

"Mrs. Greenhart, young man."

"—Connie, and *Mrs. Greenhart*, would you? I'm going to check outside—Carlos might have gone out while we were talking to Duce here."

"Yeah," Frank said. He turned and gave Duce a stony look that did nothing to the kid's shit-eating grin. "I want to ask 'Duce' here a few questions."

Connie was still staring at the wall outlet. Quaid asked her, "Are you going to be all right?"

She nodded, not moving her gaze. "I don't remember . . ." Her voice trailed off. She finally looked away. "This isn't all right."

"Frank's going to be here with you."

"They're here, too," she whispered. Then she looked up at Quaid and said, "I'm fine."

It sounded insincere, but there wasn't much he could do. He left somewhat reluctantly, heading out the front doors.

Quaid found Carlos standing next to a flagpole about two hundred yards in front of the hotel. He was talking with about four other people.

He walked up and called, "You missed the mail." When Quaid got up next to him, he handed Carlos his own copy of the "Contract." "Apparently, we all got one."

"So I've been informed." Carlos waved at the group of new people.

Quaid turned and faced the new group. "I suppose introductions are in order. Quaid Loman."

The first person was an Asian man, Japanese, Quaid suspected. He wore a white shirt and tie, sleeves rolled up and jacket slung over his shoulder. "Henry Sukomi," he said as he reached forward to take Quaid's hand. His palm was sweaty. "Are you any closer to the heart of this mystery?"

"Sorry."

"Damn," Henry said. Quaid could hear southern California in his voice. "All I got is a piece of paper with my signature, one I've never seen before, and the deep personal conviction that we should be celebrating New Year's right now." He grimaced and shook his foot. "And now, sand in my shoes."

"Wow, another piece of the mystery game." She was a brunette in a T-shirt and blue jeans who couldn't be older than Duce. Her T-shirt said, "If you're not part of the solution, you're part of the precipitate." She held out her hand and said, "I'm Bobbie, and this is Eve, and Louis."

Eve was a statuesque black woman dressed in a green suit, looking as if she'd just left the same corporate meeting as Henry. She was shaking her head and saying, mostly to Bobbie, "I don't like the idea of taking this 'game' seriously."

"Eve's right, hon," Louis added. He was the most striking member of the quartet. He must have weighed nearly four hundred pounds. He was the only one who was dressed for the locale—a pair of shorts, a loud Hawaiian shirt, and a straw hat. Despite that, he was obviously the least comfortable. As he spoke, he removed the hat to wipe the sweat off his face and the bald top of his head.

Bobbie looked at Louis with obvious distaste.

"It's all some twisted joke," Louis kept saying, his jowls vibrating. "Give us something to do to keep us from looking for a way off this island."

"Keep us here?" Quaid asked. "Why?"

"Eve has this theory," Bobbie said.

"We've been kidnapped," Eve said. "Taken here against our will—"

"Uh-huh?" Carlos said. "How do you know that if no one here remembers how we arrived—"

"We *all* can't remember." Eve said. "That can't just be chance, or an accident. It was *done* to us. And there is no reason to do that to us if we came here voluntarily."

"We got two folks back at the hotel who won't argue with you." Carlos rubbed his chin. "I'd like to hear from the kidnappers, myself."

Quaid nodded. "What about the signatures on these contracts?" He still held his own copy, the edge of it fluttered in the breeze.

"You don't remember signing that," Eve said, grabbing the fluttering edge of the paper with one hand, pointing at it with the other. Without waiting for his answer, she continued. "So you don't remember the conditions under which you signed it. You could have had a gun to your head."

"Maybe the amnesia is part of the game," Bobbie said.

Henry looked from Carlos to Quaid and asked, "I don't suppose you two have come up with any better theories?"

"Other than possible carbon monoxide poisoning, no." Quaid looked down at his "contract." "And that doesn't explain this."

Quaid looked up at Eve. "Do you have any theories on *why* someone might do this?"

"After what they've done? They've stolen months from my life, taken me away from my job, trapped me in this godforsaken place a thousand miles from anywhere— I don't *care* what their motivations are."

Eve never raised her voice, but she had no trouble communicating anger. Listening to her, he had the impression that "they," whoever "they" were, would be sorry if Eve caught up with them. He looked over at Louis, who was mopping his bald spot. "What about you?"

"Me?" he asked. "This elaborate setup? I have one or two ideas who—"

"Hello out there!"

Quaid recognized Duce's voice coming from back by the hotel. Everyone turned in that direction. Duce was standing in the lobby doors and calling to them.

"We're all meeting in the ballroom."

"Well, maybe this is it," Henry said. "The explanation we've been waiting for."

Quaid doubted it, but he kept his mouth shut as they all walked back to the hotel.

Fourth Move

The ballroom was set behind the lobby, filling a large portion of the area that separated the two wings of the hotel. Quaid, Carlos, and the other four entered through a pair of wide double doors that led in from the lobby. The room had fifteen-foot-high ceilings. Light came from two equally elaborate crystal chandeliers. A stage faced them across a parquet dance floor.

They seemed to be the last to arrive.

The room was filled with the echoes of folding chairs opening and scraping across the floor. People were standing, milling about, others were setting up chairs, while others—Quaid noticed Beatrice Greenhart among them—had taken seats facing the stage. He stood by the door and counted nineteen people, including himself.

Duce followed them in and closed the doors, making it an even twenty.

"That's everybody," Duce said into the room. Quaid couldn't tell if he was addressing anyone specific.

Quaid walked over to the right side of the room, where Mrs. Greenhart was. Frank and Connie were over there, the people he had begun to think of as "his group." Carlos sat with him. The others who had come in with them took seats together at the rear.

The ballroom was large enough that twenty people didn't seem like a hell of a lot. Looking around, Quaid realized that he'd already met half these people. It was interesting to see how the crowd seemed to group itself in clusters of about five people or so—

"What are we doing here?" Connie asked him. He looked and saw she still had her contract clutched in her hands.

Quaid rested a hand on her shoulder and hoped it was more comforting than threatening. "Someone had the presence of mind to get us all together." *Us all.*

He had used the pronoun before he'd realized the deeper implications. Was this everyone? The entire population of this hotel? Were they *all* victims of unexplained displacement and amnesia?

All players in the "game?"

He looked around at the crowd. The room was abuzz with people talking to each other, but there was a subdued air about them, an expectancy.

Everyone is waiting for an explanation, Quaid thought. He realized he held the same expectation. Rather, the same *hope*—that someone would deign to play Rod Serling and narrate this episode of *The Twilight Zone*.

But expectation— What Quaid really *expected* was that the architect of this meeting would be yet another memoryless fellow traveler.

Duce took a seat up front, and when he did, one of the ten people Quaid hadn't met stood up and took a few steps toward the stage. He was in his mid-forties, with jet-black hair cut short and an immaculate goatee that sharpened an already angular face. He wore a pair of glasses with gold frames and rectangular lenses. He had on a black button-down shirt with sleeves that he'd rolled up to the elbows.

The man cleared his throat, and the room silenced.

The newcomer looked at everyone in turn. Very deliberately, Quaid thought.

"In case you're wondering, I *am* the one who called everyone together—at least I hope it's everyone. But in answer to the obvious question, no, I don't know what's happening here."

Frank stood up and said, "So would you mind telling us what your point is, or are you just wasting our time?"

Someone in the crowd said, "Amen."

"I hope not. But I think everyone here has the same goal. If we don't compare notes, we're going to be working at cross-purposes. Duplicating effort at the very least."

Eve's voice called out from the back. "And you just decided that?"

The man shrugged. "If not me, somebody else. It doesn't matter. Now that we're here we can try and make some sense—as a group—of what's going on."

Another man, whom Quaid hadn't met, stood up and addressed the speaker with a low Southern drawl, "Two questions. Who all are you? And who died and left you in charge?"

The question was received by a few laughs and a few agreeable mutterings, but the man who'd called the meeting seemed unfazed by the question. "My name, sir, is Tage Garnell. And I assure you that I am not in charge of anything."

"Good man," the new man went on. He hooked his thumbs in the front of his belt and leaned forward. "I know who the hell you are now. How about who the hell is *us*?" He wore a checked shirt, the sleeves rolled up on rather substantial biceps, with a pair of mirrored sunglasses hanging from the shirt pocket. Blond hair was cropped close to his skull, and he wore a rusty-colored mustache. "I want to know who all you people are, and what the hell we're doing here."

There were murmurs of assent from the audience, including—he noted—Mrs. Greenhart. Quaid took the opportunity to stand up and face everyone himself. "I think that's a question that we'd all like answered." His mouth went a little dry as he looked at all the people. But he'd talked to crowds as big or bigger recently. "My name is Quaid—"

And I'm an alcoholic. . . .

"Quaid Loman. I woke up on the edge of the bed in my room this morning—I'm assuming it's my room—and I had no memory of coming here, planning a trip here, or signing anything—" Quaid gave an abbreviated rundown of his morning.

"Fair enough," said the guy in the checked shirt. "I'm Jarl Theodore. I was on the road in Louisiana, last I can tell. Went to sleep in my rig, woke up here."

Suddenly it became very much like an AA meeting. People stood up and gave their names, and in most cases a story of how they came to be there. Or to be more exact, the last memory they had before becoming aware they were here. No one admitted to having any clue why they had come—or had been taken—to this place. No one seemed to have any firm idea of exactly where this place was.

Frank spoke a piece, saying he was a steel-worker from Pittsburgh who was currently unemployed. He didn't say if he had retired or had been laid off. He summarized his meetings with Mrs. Greenhart, Connie, Quaid, and Carlos. He left out the portion about the lamp. He introduced Connie and Mrs. Greenhart, neither of whom stood to speak.

Carlos followed Frank, and was much briefer. Of the others that followed, the ones he had met already were just as diverse a bunch. There was Henry Sukomi, the Asian gentleman in the suit. He was a Japanese civil engineer from Los Angeles. Bobbie Grant, the young woman with the T-shirt, was an organic chemistry major at MIT. Eve Robinson, the black woman who was certain that they had all been kidnapped—and told that to the rest of the room—worked as a marketing rep for a pharmaceutical company based in Atlanta. Louis LeMonde—whose surname matched his girth—was a used car salesman from Buffalo.

The new people—which is how he thought of them even though they all seemed to have awoken into this predicament at about the same time—all contributed their own bit to the introductions—in all, it took nearly two hours to hear from them.

The remaining ten were—

Susan Polk, an elementary school teacher from Grand Rapids; Abraham Yanowitz, a doctor from Tampa; Erica Urquort, a septuagenarian from Lexington, Kentucky, who was a romance novelist of all things; Gordon Hernandez, who managed a Wal-Mart in Phoenix; Iris Traxler, a well-endowed blonde who said she was from Las Vegas, and said "entertainment industry" in a way that made it an obvious euphemism; Madison Oyler, a short, stocky native of New Orleans whose nose had been broken several times said "investments" as euphemistically as Iris said "entertainment"; Olivia Grossmann from Washington, D.C., a member of a lobbying group called the Christian Faith Foundation; and lastly, A. J. Kaplan, a United Airlines pilot from St. Louis.

Quaid probably wasn't the only one here who was trying to think of some common thread between them. Something that might explain why they, and not some other random collection of people, had ended up in this hotel.

Tage Garnell, the man who'd decided to bring them all together, went last. "I come from Green Rock, New Mexico—a place none of you have probably heard of. I spent a little time in the military—I'm a reservist now—and right now I do security consulting."

Jarl Theodore stood up, looked around the room, and said, "I guess that answers my first question. Now here's the kicker: What do we do about it?"

If there was a question specifically designed to introduce chaos into the dialogue, that was it.

Frank watched as the people around him degenerated into babbling idiots, each trying to shout over the others. He hadn't had the greatest respect for the motley crew that shared this "game" with him, the fact that half of them tried to talk at once cemented the impression.

"This is bullshit," he muttered.

Frank stood up and looked over the unruly mass. No one seemed to take much notice of him except Loman, who appeared to be watching the guy by the stage, Tage Garnell. Loman and Garnell got high marks from Frank because neither one was making a fool of himself by trying to shout over everyone else.

Good as his word, Frank thought, looking at Garnell, *he isn't trying to lead anything. Not even a damn conversation.*

Frank, for one, had had enough. He picked up his folding chair. It was heavy wood with a hinged seat. Frank grabbed the seat with one hand, the back with the other, and slammed it shut three times in a rapid succession.

The sound of the seat slamming closed resonated like a gunshot.

"People! *People!*"

He slammed the chair again for emphasis.

"Shut up!"

He had shouted so hard that his face was flushed and he had to suck in a few deep breaths to fill his lungs back up with air. He did, however, achieve the desired effect. The room was silent, with nineteen pairs of eyes looking at him, some with unveiled hostility.

Frank set down his chair and cleared his throat. "We have time to hear everyone. *But not all at once.* One person at a time."

The trucker made the same comment about people taking charge that he had made earlier. *You don't like it? Why don't you do something?*

"We got to get us a boat and get off this rock." The voice came from the back. The guy with a lump of a nose. Oyler, Frank remembered, Madison Oyler. A thuggish-looking gentleman who'd been evasive about his profession. *Looks like a loan shark.*

"Unfortunately, there seem to be no boats," said Henry Sukomi. He loosened his tie and continued. "We searched the docks and there's not even a life raft available."

Oyler shook his head and closed a small notebook he had in his lap.

"Boat or not, it's foolhardy to attempt the ocean out there until we have some idea where we are." A new speaker. The pilot. Frank had forgotten his name. *Probably should be taking notes myself.*

Frank sat down, satisfied that the conversation was civil for the moment. As he sat, the pilot continued, "Do we even know for sure that this is an island?"

Carlos felt the same uneasy sense of being *elsewhere.*

The question the pilot posed silenced the room for a moment.

The sense of solitude here, it would make sense that it *was* an island. But couldn't it easily be some isolated coastline of Mexico, or Thailand, or even Florida? Carlos hadn't even been aware that he had been making an assumption.

How much more was he taking for granted?

Abraham, the doctor, stood up. He was balding and had a very full, graying beard. He was a few shades shy of Santa Claus. "If we are going to be here for more than two days—which seems likely to be the case, island or not—we need to assess our available supplies. Food, fresh water, emergency medical equipment."

Bobbie, the chemistry student, asked, "You think that's necessary?"

"There's rather rugged terrain out there. If one of you should fall— Without proper treatment a compound fracture could be fatal. There are venomous snakes and insects. Allergic reactions. Heat stroke. This many people, cut off from medical care for any extended period, concerns me."

Carlos stood up. "Don't you all think that we need to get out there and see what else is on this island—or whatever?"

"Yes," Frank said from next to him. "If the pilot is right, five miles away could be an Interstate."

"What about the game?" The speaker was Erica Urquort, the novelist. She looked old and frail, and didn't stand to speak, but her question knifed through the room better than Frank's shouting had.

"There's no game." Madison Oyler stood up, took a folded sheet of paper from the notebook in his lap, and proceeded to tear it into pieces.

There was almost an air of ritual about it, the way he tore up his own copy of the "contract."

"Just a piece of paper," he said.

Carlos overheard Mrs. Greenhart in front of him saying, "Amen."

"Son," Erica said. "Someone has gone to a lot of effort here—"

"Obviously . . ." Madison tossed his torn paper to the ground. The pieces scattered around his feet. "But they aren't here, *we* are."

"If someone went to all this trouble to start this 'game,' I don't think they'd just let us walk away from it." Erica was shaking her head. "I doubt things will be as easy or simple as you imagine."

"Don't talk as if you know what's going on here." Madison waved at the floor. "Thinking you do will be your worst mistake."

"I think we're supposed to come up with our own rules." Bobbie, the student, was looking at her own paper.

"We have to leave." Madison said. "Forget the game, if there ever was one."

Quaid stood up. "This so-called 'game' is the only clue we have to why we're here in the first place."

"You shouldn't give a rat's ass about why you're here. We have to find a way out before—"

Jarl Theodore hooked a thumb in Madison's direction, interrupting him. "I'm with him. How are we all getting home?"

"We need to send some people inland, see where we are—" said A. J.

"Not before we get some first aid gear together—" Abraham.

"Who all you planning to send—" Jarl.

"Has anyone done a thorough search of this

hotel?" Eve asked. "There has to be a phone, a radio, somewhere."

The babble had returned, with people talking over each other again.

"May I make a suggestion?" Tage Garnell spoke up and waited for the room to quiet. Tage seemed infinitely patient, and for some reason Carlos felt his words were ominous—as if the suggestion was somehow going to be threatening.

"Thanks," Tage said once the noise had subsided again. "We shouldn't divide or duplicate effort here. Our actions should be coordinated. Without a leader, we need some sort of decision making process."

"So are you nominating yourself for leader?" Quaid asked, his voice sounded more than a little accusatory. Jarl, the trucker, nodded in approval.

Tage shook his head. "No. Quaid, wasn't it? I simply think we might be best off making group decisions by majority vote. At least until we elect a leader, if we ever need one."

Quaid looked around a little sheepishly and said, "Sounds reasonable to me."

There was a chorus of agreement from around the room.

"That's acceptable to everyone?" Tage asked.

There was scattered affirmation from the audience. It lasted a few moments until Carlos heard a voice in back exclaiming, "Bullshit!"

Carlos turned and saw Madison Oyler standing up and facing the rest of them with a dis-

gusted expression. "I don't believe you poor
bastards. You know what he's doing!"

"Mr. Oyler—" started Dr. Abraham Yanowitz.
Madison didn't let him finish his sentence.

"What am I doing?" Tage asked him.

Madison Oyler looked at the rest of them,
then at Tage, and shook his head. "You all stay
here and play debating society. Play your game.
I didn't sign up for this, and I'm going and
finding a way off this rock." He turned around
and stormed out the ballroom doors.

During the three hours after Madison Oyler
stormed out, they made a number of decisions.

After several false starts, it came to a show of
hands and a long argument about whose job it
was to count votes. In the end they voted Frank
Pisarski into the job.

They voted on several teams to take on the
major tasks ahead of them; mapping out the
area they found themselves in, and itemizing the
available resources in the hotel and the immediate are around it.

Five teams: two "inside" teams—A and B—to
go over the interior of the hotel, and the immediate vicinity; three "outside" teams—C, D, and
E—to go over the outlying beaches and buildings, and—in the case of Team D—eventually to
go out into the surrounding wilderness and give
them some sort of map of their location.

Ten people, Quaid included, volunteered to
be on Team D, which would eventually go out

and find out where they actually were. The most risky job they had—as Abraham, the doctor, kept pointing out. Team D had to be in good shape. And couldn't include people with skills they might need back here in the meantime. A. J. made the team because he was the one with the best mapping and navigational skills. His three teammates ended up being Eve Robinson, the woman who, aside from Connie, might have been the most upset about their apparent kidnapping; the chemistry student, Bobbie Grant, who was probably in the best shape of all of them; and Gordon Hernandez, the Wal-Mart manager, who beat out Quaid's bid to be on the team by a single vote.

The "home" teams were easier to determine. Neither Erica, the seventy-year-old novelist nor Louis, the four-hundred-pound used car salesman were up to running around the grounds. As the only doctor, Abraham needed to remain in a central location in case anyone was injured. And Quaid didn't know how many others had seen it, but Connie was too unstable to go anywhere. There were two volunteers to stay in the hotel. Iris Traxler and Susan Polk. Mrs. Greenhart ended up inside by refusing to express a preference.

That left the remainder of them to be on Teams C and E, to search the vicinity of the hotel.

By this point the debate had taken so long

that there was no problem getting a consensus on their first priority. Before any of their "teams" did anything, they had to find out what kind of food supplies this place had.

Fifth Move

Connie didn't know what to do. It was all beyond her ability to absorb. All these people— It was as if they were all back at Ferndale, but without the locks, or the nurses, or the orderlies. But it wasn't Ferndale, and Connie didn't think any of these people would belong there. The people caught up in Ferndale didn't think like "normal" people, like *these* people.

Connie had to get away from all of them, to think.

So, once the meeting was over, Connie slipped away from her side of the ballroom, while the people who "knew" her here were talking among themselves. Frank and Quaid, who Connie thought of as Baldy and the Nerd, were talking about where they might look for potable water and first aid kits. The black guy had moved off to another group of people near the doors, a group that included the fattest man she had ever seen. Sourpuss, Mrs. Beatrice Greenhart, stayed seated, apparently itemizing things to fume about.

It was easy for Connie to slip away without anyone noticing.

Once outside the ballroom, the door shut behind her, everything was quiet. It was the first time she had been alone since she had woken up, panicked, in her room.

She caught her breath and tried to make sense of herself and this place.

Is this what they actually do with the oddballs, the square pegs?

It was easy to believe that the powers that be, the ones who make the master list of proper thoughts and behavior, might steal away the people who didn't fit into their plan. They went to such lengths to classify, to number, to categorize, to process. . . .

But here?

And why would they take these others?

Of course they would take her. She knew about them. She did everything she could to keep them from paying attention to her, keeping track of her, numbering her. She had burned her social security card when she left Ferndale. They tried to give her checks, but she burned those as well. If she had cashed them, they would have known where she was. She had no address, no number, not even her original name. No one should have been able to trace her.

Except for them.

They would have means to detect abnormal thoughts, wouldn't they? That was why she kept seeing them, having to hide from them, even after all her efforts.

She followed a hallway that led outside, behind the hotel. The windowless door wasn't marked as an exit, so she stepped back a bit when it swung open on an exterior courtyard. She stood there a moment, unable to walk through.

They had taken her—and when they took you, you weren't supposed to leave. She had been in Ferndale. She had even been in prison for a while when Mayor Grinch decided that living without an address was a seditious act against the City of New York.

When they took you somewhere against your will, the first rule was you did not try to leave. When you did, they put you somewhere else, somewhere worse.

The door wasn't locked, and there's no one else here.

But she knew they were watching *her*. She had yet to step outside this building. What if that was just what they were waiting for? What if she took a step and one of their doctors, or social workers, or police, came up and said, "We're so sorry, you were making such progress, but now . . ."

She could picture the sad shake of the head, the expression of pity. The man, she knew, would be wearing Pete's face. So sad, when inside he'd be so pleased with himself. *See*, he'd think to himself, *I knew she was nuts. . . .*

She could turn around, pretend she didn't want to go outside. That would really fuck with them, wouldn't it? The last thing they would expect.

"Oh, hell," she muttered and stepped across the threshold, tensing for the sirens, expecting a herd of burly men in hospital scrubs to grab her.

When she heard the door shut behind her, she jumped.

They locked me out! was her first panicked thought as the door slammed. She whipped around and grabbed the handle, trying to yank it back open. It swung back out easily.

"You bastards are enjoying this," she said to whatever listening devices they were using on her. It was all some sort of test, and she didn't know if she had passed or failed.

God, it smelled good out here.

Connie sucked in a few deep breaths and walked out into the flagstone courtyard. There was an English garden here, nicely kept out to a stone wall about two hundred yards away from the back of the hotel. Beyond the wall, the grass went wild, as tall as her head, until it met the jungle that surrounded this place on three sides.

So much green. She took another deep breath; the perfume of the flowers was sweet and alien.

What if it wasn't the watchers who had taken her here? What if she had been *saved* from them? What if she was finally free of their controlling grasp?

For the first time since waking, Connie relaxed.

The feeling lasted until she realized that that was obviously what they *wanted* her to think.

Beatrice Greenhart was the first to notice Connie was missing. The woman had been sitting next to her, but by the time the meeting was breaking up, the seat next to her was empty. Beatrice looked back at the two men nearest her, Mr. Loman and Mr. Pisarski, but they were engaged in their own conversation.

Beatrice turned around just in time to see Connie slip out the ballroom door.

It wasn't her business, but that young woman was upset. Not that she didn't have a right to be, but Beatrice didn't like the idea that she might hurt herself.

She excused herself to the gentlemen, who didn't seem to notice her, and followed Connie out of the ballroom. By the time she reached the door, a few of the others were leaving. That nasty teenager, Duce, almost bumped into her, and she had to suck back her breath in disgust. The child wasn't even wearing a shirt, and his naked chest was shiny with a layer of sweat.

"Aren't your parents appalled by the way you dress, young man?"

"Whoa, lady, do I make remarks about how your folks dress you?" He glanced back at her and shook his head, and kept going toward the lobby.

"Brat," Beatrice muttered. *If it hadn't been for young men like that—*

Don't dwell on the past, down to business, woman.

Now where would Connie go? Well, if she was trying to escape everyone, the lobby wouldn't be a great choice. Beatrice walked directly away from where Duce was headed.

She followed a hallway that paralleled one of the side walls of the ballroom. It ended in a door that was just swinging shut. Beatrice followed the hallway and went out the door.

Outside was a flagstone courtyard nestled in the arms of the hotel's two wings. There were a few stone benches, a fountain, and a garden that seemed to spread out halfway to the wilderness. Beatrice smelled unfamiliar flowers and had to suppress a sneeze.

Connie was out here, hugging herself and walking away from the hotel. Beatrice watched as she looked up at the sky and surveyed the garden. There was a growing dirty feeling inside herself.

Old, meddling voyeur, she isn't Melissa. Thomas would be very upset if he knew you were thinking this way—

Beatrice backed up and reached for the door. Connie was fine without her. . . .

But then, Beatrice saw Connie's head lower and her shoulders begin to shake. Connie started stamping one foot and shaking her head from side to side.

Beatrice's reluctance evaporated. "Child, are

you all right?" She spoke in a voice so soft that Quaid or Frank probably wouldn't have recognized it.

Connie spun around at her words, almost falling backward into the reflecting pool at the base of the fountain. "What?"

Beatrice stepped forward and said, "Please, are you all right?"

"All right? What makes you think I'd be all right?"

She's so much like Melissa, Beatrice was thinking with one part of her brain. The other part of her brain—the one with Thomas' voice—was telling her, *She isn't our daughter.*

Somehow it didn't seem to matter that Connie was at least a decade older than Melissa, a foot taller, thinner, with the wrong-shaped face and different hair color. Physically, Connie couldn't be more different from Melissa.

But that fear in her eyes.

"I want to help," Beatrice said. Her own voice seemed to crack a little.

Connie shook her head and stamped her foot again. *"Then tell me what they want!"*

"I don't know," Beatrice said. She stepped up and held out a hand for Connie. Connie looked at it, turned around, and started marching off toward the garden.

Beatrice felt a sick empty pit in her stomach.

"Leave me alone," Connie said.

How many times did Melissa say that?

Connie wasn't her daughter, this wasn't her

responsibility, and Connie's behavior wasn't out of line with what had happened to any of them. The thought of being brought here by some unknown men still made Beatrice's skin crawl. Inside her, no-nonsense Thomas was telling her to let it go, there were bigger things to worry about.

Tage Garnell, the doctor, and the pilot had all made good businesslike suggestions to resolve their mass abduction. She should be getting herself together to join her team and look for something useful.

Talking to this woman wouldn't bring Melissa back.

Beatrice didn't move. "Why do you want to be alone?"

Connie turned around. "Why should I tell you, Sourpuss?"

"Tell me and I'll go away."

Connie nodded. "Honey, you've got to do better than that. Do you know how many people have tried to get me to tell them my 'feelings?' " She raised her hand and put the quotes around the word with her fingers. "The best. Paid more a year than your house is probably worth. You own a house, right? You have that settled-in look to you. 'I've found my nest, and I ain't moving.' "

The verbal onslaught was sudden, and Beatrice suddenly didn't know what to say. "I'm just . . ."

Connie snapped her fingers. "You've got to

be quick on the uptake here. They're watching. Of course, they're always watching, aren't they? But I mean here, as the old lady said, they have an investment here. Their game, you know. Now I know why I'm here, they've been eyeing me a long time, but you?" She waved back at the hotel. "Them? Nine-to-five drones, home-owners, bank accounts, cars, little model citizens of the fascist welfare state. Where do you fit into this? Why don't you tell me how you feel?"

Beatrice just shook her head. She felt the same disorientation she had when she had woken this morning. Ever since Thomas had left her, she had tried so hard. This was all too much for her. She walked over to one of the stone benches and sat down.

"Down to business, woman," she whispered to herself. The words felt hollow.

"What," Connie said.

"I'm afraid," Beatrice whispered.

Connie walked up to her and knelt on the flagstones at Beatrice's feet so she could look up into her face. "You're afraid of them?"

"I don't even know who they are."

"That's the point. If you *knew*, they wouldn't be them."

Beatrice snorted and raised her hand up to her mouth to hide an embarrassing smile. Connie was looking up at her, smiling, too. Beatrice composed herself. "I apologize for following you. It was truly none of my business." She began to stand up, but Connie put a hand on her arm and pushed her back down. At any other time, Beatrice might have flinched away from the contact, but this time she was almost grateful for it.

"Why did you follow me?"

Beatrice shook her head. "I was stupid and silly—"

"You tell me yours, and I'll tell you mine."

"I don't—"

Connie lowered her hand and said, "Me first. You might not have noticed, but I'm not normal. My sin is not to fit the tight little Barbie mold that everyone seems determined to give me. I see the elves in Central Park—high on crack and dying of AIDS. I make their heads hurt, so they have to lock me up or make me invisible. I try to hide. But here I am, so they must have found me." She shook her head. "Great joke on me, put me in with all these straights. Watch the goofball freak the normals. Gets their rocks off, maybe. I really had to get away from that funky middle class suburban vibe in there. I bet every last one of them has cable TV or a cell phone. So I came out here to feel sorry about the fact that no one understands me. I do that a lot even when I'm not kidnapped and shipped to the tropics. Your turn."

Beatrice blinked a few times, unsure if Connie had really finished her statement. After a while she answered. "You reminded me of my daughter."

Connie looked at her and frowned. "Come on,

that is so weak. I give you a dissertation and you give me a set of Cliff Notes. You spawned a redhead—"

"No," Beatrice shook her head. "You don't look anything like her. It's just . . . You *seem* like her. The way you look at everything, distant from it. The lost look in your eyes. She didn't think anyone understood her either."

"Oh, she's a nut, too?" Connie said.

"She killed herself," Beatrice said quietly.

Connie stared at her.

"I kept thinking that she must have been so sad. But how can you live in the same house and not see it? Thomas and I were actually in the house when she did it; took a knife to her wrists. She left a note about some boy and the police . . ." Beatrice shook her head. "You don't kill yourself over some boy you've known less than a year. My God, I lost Thomas, and he was all I had for over thirty and did I . . ." Beatrice couldn't talk anymore. She was shaking and sucking in deep breaths, but she didn't allow herself to sob.

Connie stood up and wrapped her arms around her.

"I'm sorry . . ." Beatrice choked out.

Connie said, "Shh."

The two of them rocked in the garden for the better part of an hour.

Sixth Move

It was early evening before Quaid saw Madison Oyler again.

Two hours after the meeting in the ballroom had broken up, Quaid was heading toward the outbuildings by the lagoon with Frank, Carlos, and Henry. Team E was going to check out the coast while Team C was going to check inland for more outbuildings. Their priorities at the moment were food and fresh water, But they had in mind to catalog anything that might be useful.

Henry Sukomi was leading the way, since he was the only one of them who'd been in this area before. It had gotten hotter, and Henry had ditched his jacket and had rolled up the sleeves of his shirt.

"Twenty people," Carlos said as they started down the hill toward the beach. "What the hell are we doing here?"

"What any sane people would do," Frank answered. "Trying to get word to civilization."

"Come on, you *know* that's not what I mean. Who brought us here? Why?"

"You're making an assumption," Quaid said. "We're not in a position to do that."

"What do you mean, *assumption*?"

"The same one that Eve Robinson—Connie and Beatrice, too, for that matter—is making. That we were 'brought' here."

"Quaid," Frank reminded him. "We *are* here."

"But we don't remember our arrival, do we? My point is, we can't say *how* we came to be here. We could have been kidnapped—"

"*Could* have?" Frank shook his head. "Son, how else could we get here?"

"We may have come here ourselves."

"Quaid, I think you were doing better with the carbon monoxide story." Carlos turned around and started going back down the hill. The others followed, and after a moment Quaid sighed and joined them.

Their feet crunched on the white gravel path, and a slightly abrasive salt wind carried the ocean smell to them. "All I'm saying is we don't know. Any more than we know where we are."

Henry shook his head. "I'm all for not taking anything at face value. But it's a stretch to believe that I might have put myself in this situation voluntarily."

"That's just it," Quaid said. "What situation *are* we in?"

Henry started to say something. But he caught himself and Quaid could see that Henry had gotten his point. Frank sounded somewhat less convinced. "What are you getting at?"

"We don't have *any* solid information about what's going on here," he said. "From what we know it's possible that Eve's right and some diabolical organization has kidnapped us and stolen our memories. From what we *know*, it's equally likely that our cruise ship is going to arrive at dusk to take us to the next island on our tour and the memory loss is some unrelated accident."

The path cut into a stand of tropical trees. The dappled sunlight made Quaid's companions into abstractions—light picking out an eye here, a nose there, an isolated hand. . . .

Quaid rubbed his eyes as Carlos said, "I told you before. I don't make enough to afford a vacation like this—whatever the fuck it's done to my memory."

Quaid nodded. He wasn't convinced they came here voluntarily. What he was convinced of was the fact that they didn't *know*. He was having the same problems with the kidnapping idea, which had as many, if not more, logical flaws in it. First among them was the absence of their alleged keepers. If they were captives, shouldn't there be some sign of the fact?

Quaid's hand was shaking as he rubbed his eyes. An unwanted thought found him wondering if there would be any rum stashed in one of these outbuildings. They were in the tropics, rum would make sense, wouldn't it? His own drink was scotch, but beggars can't be choosers.

When they came out of the woods, down the

beach from the outbuildings, the sea air carried more of a chill. They now faced the ocean, near the entrance of the lagoon. Here, the white sand beach had given way to rocks that the breakers struck with a rhythmic pounding, sending spray to mist the air around them.

The buildings they approached were newer than the hotel that overlooked them. Two were little more than shacks flanking a third, more substantial structure. The large building was made of whitewashed cinder block that was blinding in the sunlight. It faced out toward the ocean. That wall was an open, gaping door facing the waves.

"Boathouse of some sort," Henry said. "When I was down here, I just looked around enough to see that there wasn't any boat." He stopped next to the wall facing them. "The door was padlocked, so we left it alone. We just looked in the window."

Quaid stepped up and looked in the window himself. There wasn't a lot to see. It was like an oversized garage with a trench going down the center of it. He saw signs of a winch above, but the bright sunlight cast very deep shadows and he couldn't make out much.

"I can't really see anything," he told Henry.

"Sun was better this morning," Henry said.

"Someone wasn't as dainty with the door as you were," Frank said.

Quaid looked up and saw him coming around

the far corner of the boathouse. He was holding up the remains of a padlock, bent and dangling.

"What? Someone pound that with a rock?" Carlos walked up to Frank and took the lock. It came apart when he took it.

"That's what it looks like." Frank waved them around to the door. It did, indeed, look as if someone had pounded the door with a rock. The wood was dented around the padlock, the paint was gouged, and the hasp that'd held the lock was bent, twisted, and pulled half off of the doorframe.

"Mr. Oyler," Quaid suggested.

Henry shrugged. "Well, he did leave looking for a boat."

"Guy's more of a bastard than he let on if he found one and didn't come back." Carlos shook his head and tossed the fragments of the lock to the ground.

"Well, come on." Frank pulled the door open. "Let's see if Mr. Oyler's home."

They walked into the boathouse. The shadows were impenetrable for the few long moments it took Quaid's eyes to adjust. However, it was fairly obvious that nothing as large as a boat was hiding in the shadows. The walls were lined with cabinets, and hooks held tools and rope. Mounted on the wall near the door were what looked to be controls for a winch that dangled chains above them. The concrete trench in the center of the floor was maybe twelve feet wide. The floor of it sloped away from them, until near the open eastern end of the boathouse it descended into the water. To the right, on the door side of the boathouse, a pier jutted out into the water, paralleling the path of the trench.

Quaid looked straight out from the head of the trench and could see ocean all the way to the horizon. The only interruption was a bit of coastline from the eastern end of the lagoon, a bare, rocky spit of land that jutted in from the left. The sounds of the waves breaking against the pier and the boathouse were shallow within this natural breakwater. The only other sound was a gentle creaking as the wind gently moved the chains above their heads.

Their isolation was tangible here.

Henry was the first one to see Oyler.

"What's that?" Henry stepped up next to Quaid and pointed. At first, Quaid thought he was pointing out at something on the horizon, raising the faint hope that he might have been right about the cruise ship returning. That thought only lasted a moment before he realized that what Henry saw was much closer.

"Christ," Carlos said, walking along the edge of the trench, toward the front of the boathouse. He was looking down at the water.

There was a dark pile of something that the waves had washed up against the corner of the trench nearest the pier. It was tangled up, half in yellow nylon rope, half in one of the old tires that hung off of the concrete, facing the lagoon.

Floating debris, Quaid thought. *Some old garbage*

that'd been thrown overboard, to wash up here eventually. Like his thoughts about the cruise ship, this idea was overly optimistic.

Frank came up next to Carlos, carrying a seven-foot-long pole with a hook on the end. He reached down with it and pushed on the debris. It bobbed up and down, floating in the water. After a moment they all saw it come free, and spotted what had been hooked into the tire.

"Holy shit!" Carlos' voice was barely a whisper.

Most of it was still just an unidentifiable mass of fabric and nylon rope—but what drifted free of the tire was unmistakably a human arm.

Seventh Move

Quaid tossed his glasses aside, and half-ran, half-dove down the concrete ramp. Henry vaulted off of the edge from behind Frank and Carlos.

"Holy shit, get him out of there—" Carlos' shout was drowned out by the sound of Quaid and Henry hitting the water at the same time.

When the water hit Quaid, it felt ice cold, the shock of it leaving his skin a rasp of gooseflesh. Henry was already tugging at the nylon-wrapped bundle of flesh and rags as Quaid came up beside him.

"Help me turn him over!" In Henry's voice Quaid heard a cold terror that they were too late.

Both of them grabbed the body, hoping there was still a chance to save him. Henry took hold of the shoulders; Quaid grabbed onto the tangled, soaking, mass and pulled the free arm toward him. The arm moved sluggishly, tangled in clothing that felt as cold and heavy as lead. As Quaid levered it toward him, the hand reached toward the sky, the skin bone white, the fingers gnarled as if frozen in an attempt to reach for safety.

Quaid had no real footing. The water was shoulder-deep at the front edge of the ramp, and he could feel his left foot drifting into even deeper waters. As the arm arced over, rotating the body between him and Henry, his right foot lost its purchase.

Quaid's head plunged under the water as the arm splashed on top of him. He took in a choking lungful of water through his nose. For a few desperate moments he couldn't make sense of up or down, left or right. He knew that he was frozen in place, but it felt as if he were tumbling down through empty space, the pressure of the water in his sinuses trying to grind his brain into the back of his skull.

Something tore into his shirt and yanked him forward. Quaid's head exploded out of the frigid water, and he slammed into the same algae-slick tire that the body had washed up against. He grabbed madly for it, his fingers slipping over the slick rubber as he coughed water through his mouth and nose.

Someone—maybe Frank—asked him if he was all right. He couldn't speak for coughing, so he simply nodded as he spit up more water.

Quaid was getting his first complete gasps of air when he heard Henry say, "It's Oyler, all right, and he's dead."

Keeping a good grip on the wall, Quaid

pulled himself around to where he had solid ground beneath his feet. Henry had pulled Oyler back a little, away from the entrance. Quaid made his way toward both of them, pushing through the water with his legs and holding his arms out for balance.

Quaid's ears still rang from his brief immersion. Over the ringing he heard Carlos shout down, "What happen? He try to swim for it?"

Quaid didn't need Henry's shaking head to tell him that that wasn't it. Now that Oyler's body was turned over, it was obvious that the nylon rope binding him wasn't some accidental tangle, or something the tide had flung around the body. The rope was wrapped around by design, binding his legs together. He could see that originally both arms had been tied fast to his chest, the loose arm that had been hanging on the tire must have been the result of Oyler's last frantic efforts to free himself.

"*Good lord,*" he gasped as he pulled up alongside of Henry.

Henry was staring into Oyler's face. Oyler's eyes, still open, stared back.

Oyler had freed his arm and had grabbed hold of the tire. That would have been enough to prevent his death by drowning. Quaid could see now, even with his blurred vision, that wasn't how he'd died.

Beneath Oyler's beefy face and broken nose, beneath the mouth caught in a final crooked grimace, across the pallid skin of his neck, was an open slash cutting across six inches of tendon and artery. A wound a man could only survive for minutes, if that. Even in the water, his clothes had been darkened by the tint of blood that had long since emptied from his body.

Quaid found himself amazed at the strength of a man who could nearly fight himself free of his bonds, in the water, with his throat slit from ear to ear.

"Someone killed him," Henry said. He started backing up the ramp, dragging Oyler's body. "Someone killed him." He kept looking into Oyler's face. Henry's head was shaking, but his eyes remained locked in a gaze with Oyler's own.

"Someone *killed* him!" There was a nasty edge to Henry's voice.

Quaid plunged through the water, following Henry, his legs too unsteady to keep up, his soaked clothes pulling against him. Henry, on the other hand, seemed to practically race back to the head of the ramp once the water had retreated to waist deep.

Carlos and Frank ran to him. Being on dry ground, they beat Quaid there. Henry was still shaking his head, repeating, "Killed him. Slit his throat. I . . . I . . ."

Henry stood ankle deep in water, about three feet from the head of the ramp. He still held Oyler's shoulders, out of the water now. Oyler's head hung backward, pulling the neck wound open obscenely, almost as if the neck might sep-

arate and drop the head at Henry's feet. "No—
Not— I can't—"

Frank reached for Henry's shoulder. Henry
flinched violently, and Oyler's body fell from his
grasp. It seemed to Quaid that it took three or
four minutes to fall. He could see Oyler's head
bob, as if nodding in agreement with the statement Henry was unable to voice. Past the lacer-
ated skin, Quaid thought he saw the tendons
underneath Oyler's jaw flex in reaction to the
movement of the head.

Then the corpse splashed into the water.

Henry stared at the corpse at his feet as if he
had been the one to slash Oyler's throat.

"I'm sorry," Henry turned away, finally
breaking eye contact with Oyler.

Quaid walked up next to Henry, slogging
through the shallower water. Carlos handed
Quaid his glasses and knelt next to the body.
"Something *bad's* going on here."

There wasn't any real answer for that. If anything, it was an understatement. Quaid put his
glasses back on and the corpse snapped into too-
sharp relief, more grotesque than ever.

"Are you all right?" Quaid asked Henry.

Quaid saw Henry nod without turning
around. "Y–Yeah. I never saw a dead body before. N–never touched . . ." Both his hands
balled into fists. "I need some air." He pushed
past Quaid and headed for the door. When he
reached it, he was practically running.

Before it swung shut, Quaid heard the sounds of retching.

Frank stared at the door. "Guy would make a lousy paramedic."

Quaid looked down at Oyler and could feel some of what Henry was going through. "Cut him some slack," Quaid said. "I don't think we were prepared for this."

"Yeah," Frank knelt down next to Carlos. "But between your swimming ability and Henry losing it, we're damn lucky we aren't pulling three bodies out of the water."

Quaid felt his face flush with embarrassment and anger. He'd been trying to save the poor bastard, after all. His hand balled into a fist. He hadn't struck anyone ever since he became sober, but—

"Question is—" Carlos reminded them, "who killed this guy? Why?"

That sucked the anger out of Quaid. Compared to someone's death, a little bruise on his ego didn't merit much of anything—even silent embarrassment. "Let's get him out of the water."

They all pulled him up onto the concrete. Once Oyler was out of the water, moving him required all three of them. Some macabre portion of Quaid's mind wondered at the process that turned living flesh into so much wet cement.

They laid Oyler out next to the door.

"Wearing the same clothes," Frank said. He

bent down and checked Oyler's head, around his arms and legs, then he pulled open his shirt down to where the nylon rope still bound him.

"What are you doing?" Quaid asked him.

Frank shook his head. "Trying to get some idea how this happened. There don't seem to be any injuries, aside from the lethal one, and some rope burns—"

"That ain't enough for you," Carlos said.

"Did he strike you as a guy that'd get into this without a struggle?" Frank pulled at one of the ropes. "This guy's bound tight. You think he just let someone walk up and do this to him?"

Quaid put a hand on Frank's. "Are you trained in forensics or pathology?"

"What do you think?"

"Don't disturb the body. You'll screw up evidence you don't even know's there."

Frank took his hand away and stared at Quaid. "Son, you're welcome to call 911. If you can find a phone."

Carlos nodded. "He has a point, Quaid. I don't see any police labs around here."

"I know."

"If there's a killer, I think it's kind of important that we find him as soon as possible. Waiting to find a cop is going to give him that much more chance to get away—"

"—or do it again." Carlos finished Frank's statement.

"Look, we *do* have a doctor," Quaid said. "At

least save the investigation of this for someone who might have a little training in the area."

Frank looked down at Oyler and slowly nodded. "Okay, you have a point." He wiped his hands on his pants and stood up. "Two of us should stay with him." Frank waved at the body. "One of us needs to take Henry back and break the good news to the others."

Carlos looked at the body and asked it, *"Why?"*

Good question. Did someone here have a personal grudge against Madison Oyler? They only had each other's words that they were all strangers. Or, more ominously, was this the first move by their keepers in this game they were playing?

Carlos walked back to the hotel with Henry. He didn't like leaving Quaid and Frank alone back there with the body, but he had volunteered when it became obvious that the two didn't trust each other. And this way, if they went at each other, Carlos wasn't going to be in the middle of it.

"You going to be all right?" he kept asking Henry.

Henry's response was, for the most part, little more than a grunt. *Never know how you'll react to something till it happens.* Carlos didn't think of himself as insensitive. He wasn't all touchy-feely, but he wasn't soulless either. He had seen a stray dog hit by a car, brought it as far as the curb, and had wept over it when it died.

Oyler's body hadn't had any effect on him whatsoever.

Cold-hearted mother, he silently berated himself.

It wasn't that he was unconcerned. The idea of some throat-slashing freak out there really frightened him. The murder disturbed him. The *body* had no effect at all.

The two of them walked through the lobby doors, Henry dripping all over the carpet. "Hey!" Carlos called out. "Someone here?"

There wasn't an immediate answer. Henry looked over at him and said. "Can you do this yourself?" Henry looked down at his drenched clothing.

"Yeah," Carlos said. "Go back to your room. If there's another meeting, someone'll get you."

Henry nodded and headed for the stairs. Carlos walked around the stairs to the reception desk. On the desk was one of those old-fashioned bells, a silver hemisphere with a button on top. Carlos hit it a few times. *"Hello?"*

The bell's sharp ring echoed through the lobby.

Soon, he heard a few people coming from the eastern wing. He backed up so he could face the hallway and saw half of "Team A" coming down the hallway to meet him. Fortunately, it was the half that had the doctor.

"Doc," Carlos said as Dr. Yanowitz came into the lobby, "Am I glad to see you."

Iris Traxler, the stacked blonde from Las Vegas stepped up next to the doctor. "Is there something wrong?" asked Dr. Yanowitz. "Is someone hurt?"

"You could say that," Carlos said. "But I think he can wait until we get everyone together."

"What's happened?" Iris asked. "You're soaked."

Carlos looked down and saw that he had managed to get fairly drenched himself, even though he didn't take a swim with the corpse. "You should see the other guy," Carlos said.

"Who's hurt?" Dr. Yanowitz asked, "How badly?"

"As bad as it gets," Carlos said. "Mr. Oyler's dead."

It took time to get all seventeen of them together. Carlos wondered how Frank and Quaid were doing with the corpse. That thought was punctuated by the evil worry that there might be three corpses when they got around to returning to the boathouse.

No, Carlos thought, *Frank and Quaid—at least Frank—can take care of themselves.* Then, again, Oyler looked as if he could have taken care of himself pretty well.

Team C—Tage Garnell, Olivia, Duce, and the trucker—were the last to arrive at the impromptu meeting. Carlos did a quick head count and saw that everyone was here except the trio down by the boathouse. Henry had changed clothes, but he still looked like he had been through hell. He was pale and flushed, and his hands were shaking.

Carlos stepped up to the stage, followed by Dr. Yanowitz. He wished to God that he wasn't the guy who had to break the news. He hated talking to large crowds. As he stepped up in front of the stage, he started feeling the way Henry looked.

Great, I look at Oyler's corpse and feel nothing. I try and tell people about it and now I toss my cookies.

"Yeah, uh, we're all here now, so—"

"No," someone piped up, "we're missing three."

Carlos stumbled over the interruption. "No. I mean, yes, we are, but—" Carlos wiped his palms on his pants. He noticed that he had algae stains below the knees. For some bizarre reason, he started wondering if there was a laundry in this place. "Frank and Quaid aren't here. They're at the boathouse. With Oyler."

"So the bastard found his boat?" the trucker asked.

Carlos shook his head, and for a moment was struck by how stupid the question was. Didn't he realize that Oyler was dead?

Christ, of course he doesn't, I haven't told them yet.

"N–no." Carlos said. "He's dead."

"What—"

"How—"

"Who—"

"What do you mean dead—"

"P–please. *Please!*" Carlos tried to shout over the crowd. His voice didn't carry like Frank's, but the babble subsided to something just short of pandemonium.

"What happened?" A. J., the pilot, asked.

Carlos nodded. Good question. He wished he had an answer. "The four of us, Team E, were looking over the boathouse. Someone had broken in before us. We found him floating in the water." Carlos closed his eyes. Now, of all times, it was sinking in to him that someone had been murdered. Someone he'd seen walking and talking earlier today. . . .

His voice caught. "Sorry. We found him in the water. Someone killed him."

"Oh, God," Carlos saw Connie stand up. Her chair clattered to the ground. "They're *killing* us now."

"Who killed him?" That question came from the back, from Louis LeMonde. His doughy face was filled with concern, his massive body was almost vibrating with panic. "Why would someone kill him?"

"I don't know." Carlos said quietly.

The room around him lost control. People were shouting over each other, shouting half-heard questions at him and the doctor. The only one who didn't join the babble was Henry, who sat and stared at a spot on the ground about a foot in front of his shoes.

Surprisingly, the one voice that cut through the crowd belonged to an old woman. "Isn't it obvious what happened?"

As the room quieted, Erica Urquort stood up. The septuagenarian looked up at the stage with a light in her eyes that belonged to a teenager— to Carlos' thoughts, a very disturbed teenager. She looked less frail than she had during the first meeting. "I *warned* him," she said. "He chose not to listen to me."

"Madam," Dr. Yanowitz asked, "are you saying you were expecting this?"

She took off a pair of reading glasses and let them dangle by a chain from her neck. "Our keepers here invested a lot of time and effort to organize this 'game' we're supposed to be playing. I think it was naïve to think they'd allow one of us to decide not to participate."

Carlos shook his head. "You think he was killed because of the damn *game*?"

"His last words? He told us we could play our game without him." In her hands she held a familiar piece of paper. She held it in one hand as her other replaced her glasses. "We've all read this: 'The players must participate in the Game,' and 'The players must obey the rules or forfeit.' "

Erica sat down, apparently having had her say.

From the back Carlos heard the voice of Tage

Garnell, the first time he had spoken since the meeting had started. "You're saying you think he was killed because he 'forfeited'?"

"Maybe that's what they *mean* by forfeit," Erica said.

Eighth Move

It was an hour or two after dark when Carlos led Dr. Abraham Yanowitz and Erica Urquort down to the boathouse. The doctor was here to do an autopsy—such as he could with the equipment available. Miss Urquort was there to take notes for the doctor. She had been a secretary in her youth and still could take shorthand dictation, an archaic skill that was useful now that there didn't seem to be a single tape recorder in the area.

Fortunately for them, the white gravel path that led to the boathouse was lit by small lamps set in the ground. Carlos had been worried about Miss Urquort slipping and breaking a hip or something, though she looked like a pretty tough old lady.

Once they were starting down the hill away from the hotel, Dr. Yanowitz said, "I realize now why the Warren Commission was fatally flawed."

Carlos turned to look at him. He couldn't read the doc's expression. His face was genial, but there was a turn to his lips that, while it wasn't quite a frown, seemed to be uncharacteristically dour.

"Okay," Carlos asked, "why?"

"You can't do a murder investigation by committee."

"How are we supposed to do it?" Carlos asked.

"Not by going around the room and asking everyone's alibi," Dr. Yanowitz sighed. "If the killer was in that room, he or she could have easily tailored a story to mesh with everyone else's."

"Our keepers killed Mr. Oyler," Miss Urquort said. "That is the only logical explanation. No one else would be motivated to."

"We only have each other's words that we're strangers," Yanowitz said. "And how do we know that someone in that ballroom wasn't one of our 'keepers'?"

"You have a point, Dr. Yanowitz."

Carlos agreed with Miss Urquort. Dr. Yanowitz had a point, if not several points. The meeting after the announcement of Oyler's death had been predictably chaotic. Most of the time was filled with people stating where they were and with whom between Oyler's leaving the ballroom, and Oyler's being found.

According to what people said, no one seemed to have been alone long enough to do the deed. A deed that included subduing Oyler, tying him up, and slitting his throat. Everyone seemed to be with at least one other person for the hour after the meeting; afterward everyone was with their respective "teams."

Teams A and B were in the hotel, Team C had been outside checking the inland side of the hotel and a greenhouse there. Team D had been checking things along the other side of the lagoon.

But how far could anyone trust that testimony? Carlos knew that it would be natural even for innocent people to amend their own testimony to agree with people they had already heard.

A few concrete things had come out of the meeting. They all voted that, from this point on, no one should go anywhere alone. Rooms would be shared, and if people left their rooms, they would do so in parties of two or more. Dr. Yanowitz and Miss Urquort were voted the autopsy team. Lastly, Tage Garnell, Quaid, and A. J. Kaplan were voted to search Oyler's room for any clues. It seemed slightly more than a coincidence that the "official" investigation included a member from each team, as if the teams were some sort of representative blocs now, rather than arbitrary divisions.

They approached the boathouse; floodlights washed the pier outside, and sodium bulbs burned yellow through the windows. "Here we are," Carlos said, walking around to the door.

Frank yanked the door open in front of them. "And what took you so long? It's after ten."

"The wheels of democracy," Dr. Yanowitz replied, "grind slow and exceedingly fine." He stepped into the boathouse and glanced at Oyler's corpse, covered now by a blue tarp. He set down a gym bag he carried. "We had to vote on what to do, after all."

Quaid yawned. "Well, at least we can have a professional look at the body."

"Internal medicine," Dr. Yanowitz shook his head. "How long ago was the body found? Anyone have a watch?"

"Four hours," Frank said.

"Note that, Erica," Dr. Yanowitz said.

Miss Urquort nodded, took out a small legal pad and pen. She walked around the concrete trench and sat down on a small crate.

"I wish there was a table in here." Dr. Yanowitz pulled aside the tarp and started examining the body.

"I need to take you two back," Carlos said. He looked at Quaid. "You were voted on to the other investigation team."

"What other investigation team?" Frank asked.

"What are we looking for?" A. J. asked as the trio pushed themselves into Oyler's room.

"I don't know," Quaid said. "But we can't afford to overlook any potential clue to what's happening here."

"Do you have a theory?" Tage asked him.

Quaid looked at him, Tage's goatee was still perfect, but his cheeks had darkened a shade or two over the course of the day.

"All I know," Quaid said, "is that we have nowhere near enough information to make an informed judgment."

Oyler's room itself was no surprise. It was laid out just like Quaid's, and Connie's, and probably every other room in this place. Shuttered windows—only darkness behind them at this hour. Bed, wardrobe, bathroom, no telephone, no radio, no television.

"I admire the restraint of your speculation," Tage said as he started going through the bureaus. "It would seem most likely, though, that the death of Mr. Oyler, as Miss Urquort has said, is related to the 'Game.'"

"Uh-huh," Quaid said. He pulled a large suitcase out of the closet and lugged it over to the bed. "Our 'keepers' killed him."

"It does seem that there is another party present here." Tage said. "Our 'keepers' as she says."

"Seems to be the easiest conclusion to draw," Quaid said as he cracked open the suitcase. There was nothing terribly surprising in here at first glance. Oyler had expensive taste in shirts. He was pretty sure he was looking at five to six hundred dollars' worth of fabric lying on top.

"You don't sound certain," Tage said.

"I'm not certain of anything." Quaid started taking the folded shirts and laying them down on the bed. "For instance, how do we know that our memory loss coincides with our arrival here?"

Tage looked across at him and actually gave him a thin smile. "Well, that's a novel concept."

"We might all be strangers here—but what if we were here a day or two before this morning? Long enough . . ."

Tage nodded. "Long enough for someone to develop a motive to kill Mr. Oyler?"

"It feels better if the killer isn't one of 'us,' doesn't it?" A. J. said. He looked up from the wardrobe and the suit jackets he'd been rummaging through. "But we did question everyone, all accounted for. Who had a chance to slit the poor bastard's throat?"

Quaid shrugged. "If the killer is one of us, it goes without saying that he—or she—is lying about where they were at the time."

"And at least one other person," Tage said. "A conspiracy. Everyone has someone corroborating their whereabouts."

Quaid nodded and pulled out several pairs of pants. "Does that seem *less* likely than a conspiracy by persons unknown to kidnap twenty completely unrelated people, erase their memories, and deposit them in some isolated resort?"

Tage stood up from an apparently fruitless search of the bureau. He took off his glasses and seemed to stare into the middle distance. "You have a point." He waved his glasses at him without looking in his direction. "Take Occam's Razor to this situation— You're the one who had the theory about carbon monoxide?"

"Yes."

"Maybe not CO, but something pervasive. A gas, a virus, some sort of infection . . . Gas perhaps. The effects would be most likely to dissipate at the same time. The staff here, they would be underpaid, maybe native and superstitious, or maybe just occasional workers here for the season—whatever season this is. They see, or assume they see, a life-threatening situation and escape in the single boat they have." He nodded. "Or, perhaps, more kindly, they escape to get us aid and are either swamped—or are traveling such a distance that they are just now reaching help. . . ."

"No keepers," A. J. said.

"No keepers," Tage agreed, "and someone amid those left behind only needs to know Mr. Oyler and be less affected by the 'gas.' They only need to remember a motive where Mr. Oyler does not. We know that whatever affected our memories had different effects on different people—amounting to months' worth of difference."

"I'm impressed," A. J. said. "That has got to be the most coherent explanation of what has happened here that I've heard yet."

Tage replaced his glasses. He looked over at A. J. "It does cover *almost* everything."

"Except the Game," Quaid said.

"Except the Game. Though, given this theory, Mr. Oyler's reaction to the Game gives his assassin a perfect opportunity to cover his—or her—own motivations. Erica's suggestion that Oyler's death was a so-called forfeit becomes the obvious first conclusion." Tage rubbed his chin. "You're certainly right to not accept any assumptions, Mr. Loman. We're in the position of a solder dropped into a jungle. We don't know if we're behind enemy lines, or even if there is an enemy. We don't know if there's a war, and if we're anywhere near it."

"Apt analogy," A. J. said.

Quaid nodded his own agreement and returned to the suitcase. He wanted to keep an open mind about what was happening here, and he was starting to wonder if there was such a thing as a too-open mind.

Quaid found something he didn't expect buried in the bottom of Oyler's suitcase. "Shit," he blurted out.

"What is it?" Tage asked him.

Quaid picked up a holster, complete with automatic weapon, and handed it to him. Tage looked at it, frowning, and undid the snap that held the gun in the leather. He pulled out the gun, pointed it toward the ceiling, pulled the slide back, and made a series of arcane motions that resulted in the weapon coming apart in several pieces which he placed on the bureau.

"Colt 9mm," Tage said. "It was loaded." He placed a single bullet down on the bureau next to the handle of the gun. "There was one in the chamber."

A. J. walked over to the bureau. "Some 'keepers.' What kind of kidnappers let their prisoners run around armed?"

"He must not've remembered that he'd packed it," Quaid said. "He didn't even realize, or check, the suitcase he came here with. If he'd been carrying that, he might still be alive."

"Maybe," Tage said. "Maybe not." He sighed. "Our main issue right now is what to do with this. It's a real danger to anyone who doesn't know how to handle it."

"Put it to a vote, like everything else." Quaid said. There was an ironic tone he couldn't quite keep out of his voice.

Tage didn't acknowledge the sarcasm. "We can do that when we gather tomorrow. Until then is what worries me. Mr. Loman is correct. We cannot assume that Oyler's murderer is not one of us, and we don't want to give that person the opportunity to obtain a loaded weapon—"

Not before we vote on it, Quaid thought.

"Here's a suggestion," A. J. said. "You took that thing apart. Just give each of us a piece of it and we won't have to deal with a working gun until we put it together tomorrow."

Tage smiled. "You, my friend, are quite the Solomon." He picked up the clip and the single bullet, which he replaced in the top. He handed the piece to A. J. "You keep the bullets."

He handed Quaid the segment with the barrel, and pocketed the remainder himself. A. J. went back to the wardrobe and resumed his rummaging. After a while, he said, "You know what's missing?"

"What?" Quaid asked.

"The notebook. He had a notebook with him in the first meeting." A. J. looked at the two of them. "Didn't you notice?"

Quaid tried to remember and finally nodded. "Yeah, I do. We didn't find one with his body."

"And there doesn't seem to be one here," Tage said.

"Maybe that's it," Quaid said. "What if he had notes about what was happening, from *before* the gap in our memories?"

"That could answer everything," A. J. said. "That might even be a motive for one of us . . ."

"Weren't we talking about not making too many assumptions?" Tage asked.

Quaid nodded and went back to the suitcase.

After a moment, A. J. said, "I think I found something."

In his hand he held a small case. It was open, and he was staring at the contents.

"What do you have there?" Tage asked.

"Case of business cards," A. J. shook his head and handed it to Tage. Tage looked at it then passed it to Quaid. The case was small, brass, and had "Steven Coombs" engraved on the cover. *Steven Coombs? Who in hell is Steven Coombs?*

It wasn't a set of his own cards that Oyler had kept in it—or Steven Coombs' cards for that matter.

Apparently it was where he filed cards he came across in the course of his business, whatever that was. A few cards had already been flipped through, so the one that Quaid saw first was about halfway through the stack.

ALPHOMEG entertainment
"The First and Last Word"

The logo was embossed and a glossy blue that reflected the light. There was no representative listed on the card, no contact number, just the name, logo, and the vague motto. Seeing the card gave him a uneasy feeling, almost a sense of dejá vù. The feeling was ambiguous, as if he were looking at something very dangerous, but also very valuable.

Quaid flipped through the other cards. None of the others were as cryptic, or carried the same impact. The other cards were mostly from Los Angeles or New York City—names like Fox, Disney, Neilsen, Paramount, Rolling Stone . . .

Who the hell was this guy?

"This is something," Tage said. "A window on Oyler's past." He looked at Quaid across the tops of his glasses.

"If it belongs to Oyler, and not a Mr.

Coombs." A. J. shook his head. "Do we have the wrong room?"

Quaid looked up at A. J. From the expression on the pilot's face, he had felt the same disturbing familiarity that Quaid had when he'd seen the Alphomeg card.

Quaid couldn't distill the feeling into words, or come up with a single coherent memory to associate with it. He picked out the Alphomeg card and asked, "Do either of you recognize this?"

Both Tage and A. J. shook their heads "no."

Ninth Move

Dr. Abraham Yanowitz kept thinking of one of his colleagues from medical school. They had started out together, but Ezra's course of study diverged from Abe's. Ezra became a pathologist, dissecting corpses for the coroner's office of Durham County, North Carolina. For the longest time, Abe couldn't understand the concept. You went to medical school to learn how to heal. That was the point. Ezra had seemed to have the same attitude Abe did when they had both started.

Years later, Abe had met Ezra at a convention and asked him. Ezra had seemed surprised that Abe would question him. "Of course I want to heal," he said. "Too much." Why work on corpses, then? "They never get *worse*."

Ezra didn't have it in him to accept a patient dying on him—an inevitability with just about every serious medical discipline but one.

Abe wished Ezra was here. Pathology—he'd only had the few required courses—and in forensics he had not a whit. Besides, Abe didn't like corpses. He never had. In that way he was Ezra's opposite. A dead body marked the ultimate point where Abe stopped being useful. That, and a corpse was the one thing he was squeamish about.

However, Abe could not fault the logic that— if this was going to be done—he was the only one here remotely qualified to do it. If he was going to argue with a point, it would be the necessity of doing it at all. He had argued for taking the body to the freezer in the hotel's kitchen and saving it for the authorities. . . .

It wasn't a popular suggestion. The consensus attitude was that they had to do something about it—*now*.

That meant him.

Quaid, Frank, and Carlos had moved Oyler's body for him, placing it on a workbench that they'd covered with a blue tarpaulin. The table was longer than an autopsy table, but narrower. Oyler's right arm was against the boathouse wall and his left was about half an inch from falling off the other side.

Abe had hung a work light, a bulb in a small metal cage, on a beam directly above the body. It washed Oyler in a harsh white light that was only broken by the shadows of some mothlike insects as they attacked the bulb.

A garden hose emerged from one wall of the boathouse, and after checking the water pressure he had uncoiled it so the nozzle on the end was in his reach.

He unzipped the bag he carried, and started emptying all the equipment he had liberated from various parts of the hotel. A few large kitchen knives, a hacksaw, a pair of dull-gray carpet knives, a box of large binder clips, gallon-sized freezer bags, an old-fashioned kitchen scale with a huge round dial, several square baking pans, a bottle of isopropyl alcohol, two sets of pliers, a tape measure, a pair of green rubber gloves, and a white apron.

The last thing he pulled out was an old thermometer that he had taken off the wall in the kitchen. He carefully snapped the small metal staples that held the glass tube to the plaque. Once he did, he turned to look at Miss Erica Urquort. "Are you going to be all right?"

She was standing there, pad and pen in hand, nodding. "I'll be fine, Doctor."

I'm glad you are. He was going to be cutting a dead body open after midnight. He wasn't sure if *he* was fine.

He put on the apron and snapped on the gloves. He picked up Frank's watch, which Frank had reluctantly parted with. "Start taking notes. It is 11:15 P.M. Four and a half hours after the body was discovered."

First things first.

Abe rolled Oyler on his side and slid his pants down. Holding Oyler steady with one hand, with the other Abe removed the glass tube of the thermometer, shook the liquid down toward the bulb, and inserted it.

Abe was very careful, the glass was really too fragile for this sort of work, but his only other option had been a meat thermometer that didn't register under 100 degrees.

Abe waited five minutes, then carefully withdrew the glass tube and replaced it on the plaque so he could read the temperature. "At 11:20 the body's core temperature is approximately 89 degrees. Combined with evidence of rigor in neck and jaw, and fixed lividity in the dorsal aspect, that suggests a time of death five to seven hours ago."

Abe rolled Oyler back and stepped up to the head of the body. "We have a white male, approximately forty years old, 180 pounds. The body is—" he paused while he picked up the tape measure, "71 inches long."

Abe put down the tape measure. "The body is fully clothed. Black sport coat, severely wrinkled and showing probable immersion. White button-down shirt, with pink stains that deepen toward the collar area. Probably diluted bloodstains. Black trousers. The left shoe is missing." Abe went on with the details of the clothing for another ten minutes. If this ever went to a court, he wanted all the evidence noted, however trivial.

"The body is bound by yellow nylon rope." Abe described the location of the rope, where it was tied, and where Oyler had managed to pull his right arm free.

Abe then enumerated the contents of Oyler's

pockets. Keys, pen, loose change, wallet. The wallet was water damaged, but held a New Orleans driver's license, a social security card, and the rest of Madison Oyler's identification. Inside was about two hundred in cash, and a boarding pass for a Delta flight from New York City to New Orleans, one way, coach. The passenger's name was Steven Coombs.

"Have you got all that?" Abe asked as he dropped the wallet and its contents into one of the freezer bags.

"Yes," Erica said, and started to read back his narration verbatim.

"Okay—" Abe said. "Just checking."

Talking through every step, he cut away the ropes and Oyler's clothing. It all went into a large garbage bag.

With Oyler naked on the table, Abe started with the catalog of trauma, beginning at the head. "Examining the head, there is matted blood in the hair." He prodded the scalp and felt his finger slide deeper than it should have at a spot to the rear of Oyler's skull. "There is a depressed skull fracture, roughly circular and about one inch in diameter along the posterior of the skull. There are abrasions to the face and scalp." Abe leaned in and looked at some of the cuts. "Some of the deeper abrasions on the right cheek have a dark material embedded in the flesh." Abe picked up a carpet knife and used it to pick out one of the small black specks embedded in the flesh of Oyler's cheek. The foreign object came free with some difficulty—it had to have been really embedded to avoid being washed away. Once free, he held it up to the light, resting on the blade of the knife. "It appears to be dirt, soil. Possibly from a fall, striking his face on the ground."

Abe moved down. Placing his fingers on the skin of the neck and spreading the lips of the wound there. "Massive trauma to the anterior neck an inch below the lower mandible. The wound is from a sharp blade, most probably a knife. It is six inches in length, beginning one inch below the left ear, cutting across the larynx, terminating a half inch above the right collarbone. The wound ranges from a quarter inch on the left side to an inch in depth on the right, slicing open the trachea, severing the right carotid artery."

Abe lifted his hands from the wound and the skin; dull white areas showed where his fingers had pressed. He looked at the dead tissue and shuddered. He wondered if Erica noticed his discomfort.

"Okay," he said, breaking the forced professional monotone. "I'm not a forensic pathologist, but it appears that the wound was delivered by a fairly strong man standing behind the victim. Right-handed. I don't see much in the way of hesitation marks. A large sharp knife across the throat, quickly." He looked at the head again, where a knot of hair surrounded the skull fracture. "The blow to the skull came earlier. The blood from the neck wound didn't have time to dry on his clothes before he was pushed, or fell, into the water. The blood from the skull fracture had time to clot the hair."

"He was hit on the head, tied up, then his throat was slit?"

"Uh-huh." Abe continued down the body. He described the ligature marks on the wrists and arms, more soil under the fingernails, incidental bruising on the torso, more ligature marks on the legs. He looked for the defensive wounds to the right hand, but didn't find any.

Frank's watch read 1:30 when he was done with the external examination. Abe sighed. "So much for the easy part."

He picked up a knife.

Connie lay on the floor of Beatrice Greenhart's hotel room and stared at the ceiling. She couldn't sleep. The moon shone through the slats of the shutters, cutting silver strips out of the darkness.

"Beatrice," Connie asked, "are you awake?"

"I am now," came the grumbled reply.

"Are you scared?"

"What's the use of being scared," Beatrice responded. "It's stupid and silly." There was a hint of strain in her voice when she said it.

"Why would they take us here, just to kill us off?"

"Pointless to worry about things like that," Beatrice said. "We don't *know*."

"We know," Connie said. "We just forgot." She looked back up at the darkness above her. "They made us forget. That's what they want, our minds."

"My mind is perfectly fine, young lady. I'm not senile. I remember everything. I was taken here in my sleep."

"That's what they want, what they've always wanted. For you to think their way. Follow their rules."

"Please go to sleep."

Connie nodded and silently stared upward. They wanted her to play this game. They had killed someone to make that point clear.

Connie closed her eyes and felt them watching her.

Quaid dreamed of Madison Oyler.

In his dream it was a moonless night when he followed Oyler down to the coastline. Oyler waded into the water, and Quaid followed, the inky water wrapping itself around him.

Quaid knew that he had to catch him, because Oyler *knew* something—

Oyler kept ahead of him, and Quaid couldn't quite catch up. Quaid could have stopped at any time, but the need to know—know *what*, he wasn't quite sure— That need kept him after Oyler, swimming in the frigid water.

Eventually he managed to catch up, but it was too late. Oyler's skin was white, colder than the water around him. The body bobbed facedown. Quaid had caught up with a corpse.

Quaid turned around, but he couldn't see the shore. Nothing but water in every direction.

Quaid floated there, exhausted, Oyler's corpse bobbing next to him. He had little strength left, and panic gripped him with that odd paralysis that only seemed to happen in dreams.

While Quaid tried to think of which way he needed to go to get to shore, Oyler's corpse moved.

"Don't make deals with the Devil!" it said as its arms reached out and pulled him under.

Frank had just turned the corner with Jarl Theodore and Gordon Hernandez, when Gordon looked up at the sky and announced, "This is bullshit."

Frank stopped next to the guy. It was the first time he'd spent any time with these two, and he didn't really know what to make of either one. "What's bullshit?" Frank asked.

Gordon's face showed an expression of disgust, which looked grotesquely twisted from being underlit by the lights along the path. "You tell me, what are we guarding against?"

"Okay," Jarl said. "Maybe you slept through it, but you see, this guy got killed—"

Frank put a hand on Jarl's shoulder and said, "Give it a rest."

"This is pointless." Gordon shook his head and turned away from them, facing the dark lagoon and the trail of lights that followed the path to the boathouse.

"What's your problem, man?" Jarl questioned, his voice carrying equal parts anger and bewilderment.

"Do you have a problem with how we decided these patrols?" Frank asked. "I noticed you didn't vote for them."

Gordon nodded without turning around. "Forget that three people can't guard an area this size. I have to manage security for a place at least this size, one floor, and we have security cameras and guards that don't have to go everywhere in pairs— Even so, I could have gone with this crap, *if* it wasn't such an exercise in self-deception."

"Meaning?" Frank asked.

"The killer's in *there!*" Gordon turned around and pointed at the hotel. "Anyone who doesn't see that is begging to be next."

"Yeah," Jarl said. "And we all happened to take Greyhound here. Someone set all this crap up. Took us all here. Not to mention the fucking game."

"Yes," Gordon said. "Someone set up this game." He walked up to Jarl and placed a finger on his chest. "And how do I know that someone wasn't *you*?"

Guarded, the hotel slept. One by one, lights in the rooms went out, until, at last, the grand Victorian was blind and silent. The only sounds over the lagoon; the footsteps of the guards, the steady break of the waves, the sound of nocturnal insects, and—in a small outbuilding—the quiet wet sound of Dr. Yanowitz cutting Madison Oyler's flesh.

Tenth Move

Quaid woke up sitting in the easy-chair in his hotel room. He experienced a few minutes of familiar disorientation. This time, however, he could remember last night, and the feeling of panic toned down into a sense of quiet unease.

Apparently, their cruise ship hadn't returned during the night.

God, if there was ever a time that called for a drink . . .

Quaid shook his head and put his fist up to his temple. Christ, he shouldn't think like that—especially after he had managed to decline a gathering of good ol' boys around the recently discovered wet bar adjoining the dining room.

Louis LeMonde, Tage Garnell, A. J.—Quaid didn't remember all the folks that were spinning theories round the bar, but he had been a good boy and hadn't succumbed to temptation. He remembered being waved over and shaking his head.

He gave some lame excuse. He didn't even remember what, now. But he could see the lie recognized in several sets of eyes. For some reason he couldn't tell them the truth.

No, let's not pretend. It's shame pure and simple. You can't admit it to anyone who hasn't fallen into the same pit you have.

So, instead, he had managed to make a half-dozen people suspicious of him. That, when he was one of the people to have discovered an unexplained corpse lying around. *Good work, Quaid.*

He stood up and pushed open the shutters. Another perfect day in paradise. Six in the morning, or earlier—the sky was barely brushed with daylight.

Quaid turned around and saw Carlos asleep on his bed.

Buddy system. Quaid rubbed his temples. *No one sleeps alone.*

He wondered what time Dr. Yanowitz finally got back to the hotel.

His back ached and he regretted being hospitable last night, giving Carlos the bed, taking the chair. He rubbed his lower back and made his way to the shower.

By the time he toweled off and left the bathroom, full daylight had gathered outside, and Carlos was sitting on the edge of the bed rubbing his face.

"Morning," Quaid said, towel wrapped around him as he went over to his closet to gather a fresh change of clothes.

"Yeah," Carlos muttered. "Need to go to my room . . ."

Quaid nodded. Carlos needed his own change of clothes. He wonder how many other people were discovering that they'd overlooked that detail last night.

Someone knocked on the door just as Quaid pulled on his shirt. He looked at Carlos, who shrugged. Carlos had slept in his clothes—or he had tried to; it looked as if he hadn't gotten any sleep.

Quaid opened the door with one hand while he buttoned his shirt with the other.

Standing outside the door was Duce. He was still shirtless, and still wore the same leather jacket he had on yesterday. It made Quaid wonder if he had any other clothes with him.

"Yes?" Quaid stepped into the doorway and saw Henry standing in the hall off to the side. He had a new suit on, but it looked as if he was still recovering from yesterday.

"Messages from on high," Duce said. "Who'd you shack up with last night?"

Carlos called from the bedroom, "What the fuck do you want?"

Duce handed Quaid a pair of familiar-looking envelopes. He looked down at them and asked, "Where'd these come from?"

"The mailboxes in the lobby," Henry said. "Six people patrolling outside, and no one thought to watch the lobby."

Duce shrugged. "Seven down, twelve to go . . ."

Duce and his chaperone continued down the hall. Carlos came over to Quaid and took his own envelope. "I need to get back to my own room, clean up, get some new clothes—"

Quaid nodded. "I'll go down with you . . ." He tore open the envelope, unsure of what he would find. Though, what he did find he already half expected.

It was another legal-sized sheet, just like yesterday—but the text was a lot longer now. The title now read:

CURRENT RULES OF THE GAME:

Rule one had been modified. It now took up about half the sheet.

1a: Carlos DeVay is a Player in the Game as part of Team E.
1b: Connie is a Player in the Game as part of Team B.
1c: Duce is a Player in the Game as part of Team C.
1d: Tage Garnell is a player in the Game as part of Team C.

It continued like that, through 1s. Nineteen people. Everyone *except* Oyler. Then there were the original rules, with number three changed radically;

3: The Players may agree to change the rules. This shall be done by majority vote of all the Players, until such time as a leader is designated. Actions that affect all the Players shall be determined in the same manner. It shall be the duty of Frank Pisarski to count these votes.

Then there were the additions . . .

6: There will be five teams, Team A, Team B, Team C, Team D and Team E. Team D shall investigate Inland. Teams C and E will investigate the immediate vicinity of the Hotel. Teams A and B shall investigate the Hotel itself.
7: All Players shall be part of a team.
8: All Players must stay in groups of two or more people at all times.
9: There shall be patrols of the grounds by groups of three people during the night. They shall take three four-hour shifts.

It was hard to suppress the shudder that went through his body as he read the new document. Whoever had drafted it had been privy to all their meetings, and the details of what they had decided. He couldn't help but think that these had to have been written by one of them. . . .

"I guess we're playing their game whether we want to or not," Carlos said.

*   *   *

After Carlos had a chance to shower and dress in his own room, the two of them went downstairs to get something to eat before the nineteen of them formed another "official" gathering.

The dining room was on the ground floor of the eastern wing of the hotel, opposite the wing that held his room. The place was long and narrow, with high ceilings. A half-dozen people had already gathered here, and the breakfast of choice seemed to be cold cereal.

By one end of the room a pair of swinging doors were propped open on the kitchen. A stainless-steel cart stood by those doors, piled with five boxes of cereal and a pitcher. A nearby counter held bowls and a plastic tray of silverware.

Carlos grabbed himself a box of Raisin Bran. He stood by the cart and looked at the box for a few long moments before he walked into the kitchen. He *hated* cold cereal for breakfast. It was hangover food, and it reminded him of the worst six months of his life. There had to be something a little more substantial in the kitchen.

The kitchen was modern, with large stainless-steel stoves and a walk-in refrigerator. Above a giant island in the center of the kitchen a forest of copper pots hung from a rack that was chained to the ceiling. He freed an omelet pan and managed to hunt down some eggs and a slab of English-style bacon in the cavernous refrigerator.

Quaid had just gotten his breakfast going on one of the commercial cooktops when he heard someone near the entrance say, "Aren't you breaking the rules, Mr. Loman?"

Quaid looked up from his breakfast and saw a woman standing by the door. She was dressed smartly in an understated tan blouse and matching skirt. Olivia Grossmann. He had seen her, of course, but never talked to her. All that really stuck in his mind about her was that she worked in Washington D.C.

"No," he told her, wondering why he felt a sudden urge to explain himself. He didn't realize until then exactly how seriously he took Erica Urquort's assertion that Oyler had died because of a "forfeit," because he'd broken the rules of this Game. "We made implicit allowances for privacy, didn't we? As long as we're only one room removed from someone. How many of us showered together this morning?" He pointed a spatula back toward the open doors of the kitchen, where the dining room had filled even more. "I don't think this counts as striking out on my own."

She nodded. "Perhaps you're right." She walked into the kitchen. She had deep brown eyes that seemed to measure him from behind thick, black-framed glasses. "I wanted to ask you a question, Mr. Loman—"

"Quaid, please." He turned the eggs. Breakfast was almost done.

"Quaid. I have a serious question for you."

"Yes?" he looked up at her.

"Do you believe in God?"

Quaid didn't answer immediately. Instead he turned off the burner under his breakfast. After a moment he gave in to the answer that came first to his mind.

"I believe in a Power greater than myself . . ."

Step two: Come to believe that a Power greater than myself could restore me to sanity.

For no particular reason he felt ashamed that he'd never yet been able to get past the eighth step.

Quaid had gotten sober, and had managed to stick to AA. Of the twelve steps of Alcoholic's Anonymous, one through seven were all about admitting to God, yourself, and the rest of the world that you had screwed up your life. It was about giving your life over to God, or at least something more powerful than the drinking— and for most true drunks, like him, God would *have* to be it, there wasn't anything earthly or mundane more powerful than that particular need.

Quaid had blown through the first seven of the twelve steps in what he had figured to be record time. The way his life had gone in the crapper, it was the last thing he could be egotistical about. But that eighth step . . .

Step eight: Make a list of all persons he had harmed, and become willing to make amends to them all.

It was going to be a long list.

He wondered about last night, about not being able to admit to anyone he had a problem. Did that mean he was backsliding? "Yeah," he told her, thinking about how he couldn't admit it last night. "God's the only thing that's kept me sober." A strange relief filled him when he admitted that, as if he had stepped back from the abyss.

Quaid took his omelet pan and hunted for a plate he could empty his breakfast on. "Why are you asking? You don't even know me."

"Should that matter?" Olivia asked. "It's a tenent of my faith to witness for the Lord . . . I'm starting to believe that this might be the last chance any one of us has to accept Christ."

Quaid remembered now what she did. She was part of a fundamentalist lobbying group. Christian something-or-other in Washington D.C. He concentrated on removing his omelet onto the plate intact. He stared into the eggs as he said, "Last chance?" The conversation was making him uncomfortable.

"We're being tested."

Quaid nodded. He didn't think he agreed with what she meant by that—but someone, somewhere, *was* testing them. "I'm going to go eat breakfast," he told her. He picked up his plate and walked back toward the dining room. As he passed her, she touched his arm. "What?" He half-turned in her direction.

"Please, weigh what's at stake before you dismiss what I'm saying. No one knows, exactly, what form the end times will take—or the rapture . . ."

"Why are you concerned about *my* soul?" he asked her. "There're seventeen other people here, most of whom have a better chance at salvation."

She shook her head. "Not better, or worse. That door only closes once, and it's at the same time for everybody." She patted his arm. "I know. It's an awful thing that this isn't a comfortable subject for most people these days—as if we're ashamed of God." She shrugged. "I'm used to it."

Quaid looked into her eyes. He wanted—*really wanted*—to dismiss her as a religious fanatic. He couldn't do it in good conscience. She had something he didn't. Faith in something.

She let him go and he wandered back into the dining room. Could this all be some sort of divine test? A special crossroads in Purgatory to separate the sheep from the goats. . . .

Quaid supposed that if you took the right attitude, everything could be that kind of spiritual test. Calling it that really didn't come close to providing any practical answers.

In a corner of the dining room he saw Connie, sitting alone at a table, drawing something on a pad of paper. She still looked lost, and somewhat dazed, but she appeared less frightened than she had last night in the audience. He felt a pang of guilt for not checking up on her.

Drinking made him an oblivious, insensitive

bastard, and sobriety had not quite erased all
the flaws that drinking had carved into his character. Not that he had any special obligation to
Connie—just that, of all the people here, she
seemed the most fragile.

Quaid walked over to her table and sat across
from her. "How're you holding up?"

She looked up, a little startled, and pulled the
top sheet of her pad back over what she'd been
drawing. "Fine," she said, looking down at the
table.

"Did you get enough sleep last night?"

She nodded, still avoiding eye contact. He
kept at it, trying to draw her out a little. "I heard
that you and the others here at the hotel found
quite a food supply."

She nodded again. Her red hair was limp, as
if affected by the malaise that floated around her
like a cloud. She wore a green T-shirt that was
new enough to still show lines where it had
been folded.

Feeling a failure at his attempts at conversation, he started on his breakfast. After a few moments of silence, she said, "It must have been
awful."

Quaid looked up from his eggs and found
that Connie was actually looking at him now.

"Finding him like that."

It was his turn to nod wordlessly.

"They killed him because they want us here,"
she said. "They were warning us, you know.
Telling us that they were watching every move.

I mean, they could have taken the body, but they left it for us. It was *for* us. I've been wondering why, you know."

"They . . . Why?"

Her voice had become a whisper. "You *know* who they are. Know but don't know. Don't remember. But they have to have been watching all of us, been watching us since before we came here. They chose us, we're *all* different, don't fit their pattern. I thought that I was different, the special one. But I see now we *all*—" She leaned forward. "*I saw lights last night . . .*" she whispered.

Quaid didn't know if she was about to tell him more, but that was the moment Beatrice Greenhart chose to come by the table.

"You're not upsetting this poor girl, are you?" She looked at him accusingly. "A lot of people have been unkind about her. She doesn't need to be upset, called names."

"No," Connie shook her head. "He's been fine, really."

Beatrice squinted at her, "I'm worried about you."

Beatrice and Connie must have been paired last night. Quaid couldn't help thinking that it had been a bad idea. They were stone and glass, and he couldn't help but think of Connie breaking against Beatrice. "I'm fine . . ." Connie insisted.

Beatrice harumphed and continued off in the direction of the ballroom. Connie got up and followed her before Quaid could ask her any questions.

Quaid wondered if Beatrice and the late Thomas Greenhart had had any children. If so, he suspected that they'd be around Connie's age. As he finished his breakfast, he realized that Connie had left her pad of paper behind. Curiosity got the better of him and he reached over and turned it around. He flipped up the page so that he could see what she'd been doodling before he had interrupted her.

The eyes were the first thing he noticed.

She'd drawn dozens of them, lidded eyes, eyeballs, eyes with wings, eyes with feet, eyes twisted and distorted until they looked like flying saucers—all staring out of the page at him. The eyes were surrounded by an abstract line pattern that took him a few moments to recognize. . . .

An "A" and an "Ω" intertwined, repeated over the entire surface of the page.

Eleventh Move

Abe Yanowitz faced a ballroom of eighteen people, feeling the dull burning ache of exhaustion behind his eyes. He hadn't felt this disconnected from his body since back during his residency when he'd regularly pull eighteen- and twenty-hour shifts. His hands shook as he looked down at his notes. These were his own, scribbled after the autopsy. Erica promised to transcribe his dictation later today.

The woman was amazing. She had grabbed three hours of sleep, maybe, after they had come back. Looking at her, she didn't seem to suffer any signs of fatigue.

Then again, Abe had had less sleep than she had, since he had, after the autopsy, awakened Frank and his roommate A. J. to haul the mortal remains of Madison Oyler to the deep freeze in the hotel kitchen.

Abe rubbed his forehead, remembering the body, naked, Y-incision held shut by two-dozen heavy-duty binder clips, his shroud a trio of black trash bags sealed with silver duct tape. In a separate trash bag, his clothes. In a final one, a series of Ziplock freezer bags, holding various organs.

"Madison Oyler bled to death from a massive insult to the neck area," he read from his water-stained legal pad. He felt distant from everything, as if someone else was speaking. "It was done with a sharp, wide-bladed implement, possibly a carving knife. Death would have followed within minutes from traumatic shock. Examination of the area did not reveal the murder weapon." After the autopsy, and storing the body, Abe had used the daylight to try and play detective. He had done his best to track down and identify the relevant evidence around the boathouse. He'd only been partially successful.

"Before Oyler received the mortal injury, he also suffered a massive trauma to the back of the skull. From the state of that wound and the resulting concussion, I suspect it was delivered at least twenty-five or thirty minutes before the neck wound, or as long as an hour. The blow to his skull alone was enough to incapacitate him."

Abe had a good picture in his head of what had happened to Oyler. He had been hit from behind, hard enough for him to lose consciousness. That had given his attacker enough time to tie him up.

For most people, that would have been over-kill. The head wound, in fact, was extensive enough that it was pretty amazing that Oyler had managed to wake up at all, much less partially free his right arm. There had been a nasty hematoma squeezing the brain under the depressed fracture, and if Oyler's throat hadn't been slashed, he might have eventually died from the bleeding into his skull.

When Oyler had regained consciousness, at the very least, he would have been disoriented, probably with some serious deficits in perception and motor control.

"The blow," Abe said, after reviewing the injury, "was delivered by a blunt, irregular object. Traces of debris embedded in the scalp lead me to suspect a large rock. A visual exam matched these traces with slivers of rock embedded in the doorframe which suggests that the same weapon was used on the door and on Mr. Oyler. We matched the rope he was bound with to a large supply available in the boathouse."

He turned the page. "I am *not* a forensic pathologist, so you all should understand that this bears only slightly more weight than a layman's opinion." With that disclaimer out of the way, he sucked in a breath and dove in with both feet.

"From my examination of the body and the crime scene, this is what I suspect happened. Mr. Oyler approached the boathouse, found it locked, and used a large rock to gain entry. Once he had broken the lock, he dropped this rock and entered. At this point, or very shortly afterward, his unknown assailant reached the door and retrieved the rock. The assailant stepped inside and struck before Mr. Oyler realized his presence."

Abe lowered the legal pad. "Mr. Oyler was rendered unconscious long enough for the assailant to cut the rope and bind him. Then our assailant waited for Mr. Oyler to regain consciousness—"

A number of voices rang out. All they said could be summed up by the single word *"What?"*

Abe waited for the audience to quiet before continuing. "I realize that makes no logical sense. But that is what the evidence shows. Mr. Oyler had several abrasions from struggling with his bonds. He was conscious and alive long enough to free one arm. There are no defense wounds on that hand, so I suspect the arm was freed too late to interfere with the assailant's knife—but from the abrasions, I'd say that Mr. Oyler was allowed at least ten minutes, maybe as long as half an hour, of struggle before his throat was slit and he was shoved into the water. After that, he wasn't alive long enough for any water to enter his lungs."

Abe looked at the room as everyone started talking at once. *Yes, the theory is shit. What do you expect? I diagnose old ladies' gallstones, not murder victims.*

Abe shook his head, sat down, and closed his eyes. It was very hard not to fall asleep.

It took a while before Frank finally stood up and was able to call some order to the room.

He slammed a chair shut and yelled over the voices.

"People!"

The one word silenced the room. Frank wondered if they heard the edge in his voice. If they could sense what was going through his mind. Oyler's corpse. Not just the sight of it being pulled from the waves by that dynamic duo of Henry and Quaid. But almost a time lapse of it getting paler and stiffer, until the final sight he had this morning, the guy gutted from neck to groin—held together by glorified paper clips. *Henry, you weak bastard, that's a sight that should make you puke.*

"We need some focus here. We have some decisions to make." He waved over at Tage Garnell. One of the few people here that Frank hadn't seen act like a fool. "I think you wanted to say something?"

Tage stood up. Unlike the doctor, or most of the people here, he didn't seem stressed out from lack of sleep. "When we examined Mr. Oyler's effects, we found a gun. We need to determine who should get custody of it."

The ruckus in response was bad, but Frank didn't have to shout over it this time.

"We need to hunt down the bastards who killed Oyler." That from Jarl Theodore. "We should form a posse to find them."

"Who here knows how to handle a gun?" asked Eve Robinson. "You? Tage has some military training, anyone else?"

"We need to contact the local authorities—not go on some vigilante mission," A. J. called over to Jarl and Eve. "We should follow the plan. Give the gun to those who're going for help."

"We need to protect ourselves first," Duce said, smirking at A. J. "Or should we just pretend we're safe while you prance off into the woods?"

Quaid stood up. "Should we give the gun to anybody?" Everyone turned toward him. Frank looked at the guy, a thin nerdy type with glasses. *Make it good*, Frank thought, *you haven't done much to impress me.*

Quaid cleared his throat and continued. "We don't know who killed Oyler. It's tempting to blame our 'keepers,' whoever they are, but it seems just as likely that his killer is one of us—"

"Good lord, didn't we go through that nightmare yesterday?" That came from one of the women Frank hadn't talked to yet, the schoolteacher.

"Yeah," said Jarl, looking over his mirrored sunglasses at Quaid. "Everyone's accounted for by at least two others."

"Our keepers are here, somewhere." Henry Sukomi was quiet, subdued, and looked as bad as he had when he'd almost thrown up on Oyler's body. "Someone's delivering these." He waved one of the new "contracts."

Frank cleared his throat. Time to get these sandy gears of democracy moving. "Shall we decide?"

*   *   *

When the voting was finally tallied, it was A. J.'s expedition that received the benefit of the gun.

Quaid thought to himself that, perhaps, it was for the best. The decision got the weapon away from the majority of them—at least it would when Team D made for the hills.

Despite argument to the contrary, Quaid couldn't help thinking that Oyler's killer was one of them. It didn't make sense to blame it on their keepers—the people who had invested in this grand conspiracy to bring them to this place, something that must have taken considerable time, planning, and resources—

Quaid had trouble seeing them, whoever they were, dispatching anyone with a stray rock.

The good news—depending on your frame of mind—was the fact that there were enough provisions in the hotel to last years. They were not going to suffer for lack of food or fresh water for a long time yet. Another sign of planning on their captors' part. Various people itemized what they had found, which took a while. . . .

The meeting was about to break up, sending them off to find items to contribute to Team D's mission to get help, when Eve stood up and announced something that must have been in the back of everyone's mind.

"We can't adjourn yet." She waved the new contract in front of her like a flag. "We need to come to a decision on *this*."

"Decide what?" someone asked, Jarl or Duce, he couldn't quite tell.

Eve looked more statuesque than usual. For some reason he was reminded of Martin Luther nailing his letter to the door . . . Not that Eve resembled Martin Luther, but the attitude was similar. The air of defiance.

"This 'game' we're being coerced into," Eve continued. "It may have killed one of us—*they* may have killed one of us—are we going to continue with this? Let this thing control us?"

Erica Urquort spoke up. Her age didn't reach her voice, which sounded as firm as Eve's. "You want us to abandon it, like Mr. Oyler did?"

"Are you saying you want to be a mouse running through someone else's maze?" Eve asked.

Tage stood up. He adjusted his glasses and looked at the two women across the length of the ballroom. "I understand your concern, Mrs. Robinson. But, it does seem that whatever this game is, it is *our* game. We decided on all these changes yesterday—"

"That wasn't a *game*," Eve said. "We weren't voting on *rules*."

"Here, here," Quaid heard from Beatrice Greenhart. She was nodding to herself. "I'm glad someone here is finally talking sense."

"And how do we stop playing?" Frank asked. "Take a vote and declare we've all stopped?"

"Now there's a paradoxical question," Dr. Yanowitz said. He held his head in his hands, almost appearing to sleep.

"What's a paradox?" Frank asked.

Dr. Yanowitz looked up and shook his head. "Our votes have become the procedure to modify the rules of this game. Can we use that process to stop 'playing'?"

"Why not?" Eve asked. "And what are you talking about?"

"Doing that is implicitly acknowledging that these 'rules' are supreme," Dr. Yanowitz said. "That only the rules themselves define their jurisdiction. Which means that if we *vote* ourselves out of the 'game,' we will still be acknowledging the authority of the rule we create that says we're not playing. In a sense we would still be playing this game—or the meta-game . . ." The doctor looked back and must have realized how many blank stares were aimed in his direction. "Sorry, I'm tired, and this probably isn't the place for those kinds of abstract thoughts."

Quaid stood up, struck with a thought of stunning simplicity. It was so basic, he was surprised that no one had suggested it before. Perhaps it only occurred to him now because this was the first time the game, in and of itself, was a serious consideration. "I think there's a simple solution to this game."

"I hope it's better than voting ourselves out of it," Henry was shaking his head. "After what happened to Oyler—"

"No," Quaid said. "The game ends when we have a winner. Let's just take a vote that everyone here has won the game."

Twelfth Move

Carlos' initial reaction was: *How can something that straightforward lose?*

From his point of view it was a genius solution to a debate that, to him at least, was beside the point, to put it kindly. To Carlos' mind, the point was to get back to civilization, wherever that was. He was generally too nice a guy to tell folks what he thought about all this debate about keepers, and why they were here—that it was all a load of bull.

When your house is burning down, you don't start the arson investigation till you're out of the damn fire.

Somehow, though, it seemed like folks refused to look at it that simply.

The doctor, of all people, spoke up and said, "That won't do any better than voting the 'game' out of existence. With these rules we have, winning isn't some intrinsic constant that will stop the game."

"Come on, old man," said the trucker, Jarl. "Games stop when you have a winner. *Duh.*"

He raised his hands and gave the rest of the room an "isn't this obvious" expression.

Tage was pulling his goatee and giving the doctor a thoughtful expression. "That isn't necessarily so. Many card games have several rounds where someone 'wins' but the game itself proceeds while points or chips are accumulated. Many sports contests operate the same way."

"Christ, then just vote the game over at the same time," Jarl said. "I don't believe this shit."

"It's acknowledging the game is the supreme authority," Dr. Yanowitz said. "I thought that was what we wanted to avoid."

Quaid stood up. "People, I honestly think this is the only way we're going to have to resolve this. If Oyler was killed because of the game—"

A deep sardonic, *"If?"* came from Louis LeMonde.

"—then let's use the game to resolve itself."

"No," said Erica Urquort. "I don't think those who have engineered this will be denied that easily."

Quaid looked frustrated. "So they hit people with *rocks?*"

"What if they're only letting us live to play this game," Connie said in a low, rushed voice. "Have any of you thought about that. They want the game, and while we play it we're useful to them. Once the game is over . . ."

"It's taking too much of a risk," Louis said, wiping his forehead with a towel. "And, like the doctor said, we might be playing into their hands by doing it."

"You can't have it both ways," Quaid said. His voice was noticeably strained. Apparently, the debate had surprised him as much as it did Carlos. "Whoever *they* are, is this going to piss them off, or is it part of their master plan?"

"There's no need to be rude," Mrs. Greenhart said. "Why do we have to vote on a piece of paper anyway. There are more important things. We need to get down to brass tacks—"

"Haven't you been listening—" Quaid snapped, shook his head, and sat down. "Oh, Christ, never mind."

Carlos leaned over toward him and whispered. "You okay?"

"*No!* Apparently I made a fool of myself, yet again."

"No, man, you have a good idea. Ditch the game and one less thing to worry about."

Duce spoke from the rear of the room, a sarcastic lilt to his voice. "I know Jack about any of you, but whoever set this up had *something* in mind. I want to know why I should *share* a win with anyone. If I'm stuck in this Game, I'm getting something out of it." He was staring at Tage as he said it.

Quaid shook his head. "Some great idea, how much will you bet that we're the only ones to vote for it?"

They weren't the only ones to vote for it . . .

But there were more who didn't.

Frank took the tally. Dr. Yanowitz voted against. Erica, Connie, and Beatrice voted against, little surprise there. Henry voted against it without saying a word—Carlos thought it was in reaction to Oyler's death, before that point the guy had seemed rational. Bobbie said it sounded, "too much like cheating." Eve wasn't going to vote on anything that acknowledged the game as such. Duce, true to his word, said, "If this Game's serious enough to vote on this crap, the prize is serious enough, too. Count me out of this vote." Louis cast his vote, saying that he wasn't going to end up like Oyler.

Tage Garnell cast the deciding vote. "As Duce said, we *don't* know what a win means. Not for us, or for our 'keepers.' We don't know enough to say that it would end the Game, or even if such a win is desirable. My deference to Mr. Loman who proposed this ingenious solution, but he himself told me not to make assumptions. I don't have enough facts to support the idea."

"I don't fucking believe it!" Quaid shouted at the garden behind the hotel, squinting in the noontime sun. He had come out here with a serious need for fresh air. *"What are these people thinking?"*

"Take it easy, man," Carlos said.

Quaid would have preferred to be alone. But they were still operating under the damn rules. "Easy? Easy?" He strode past the fountain, turned around, and spread his arms. "Am I the crazy one here, Carlos? Did I make no sense up there?"

"Told you, it was a good idea . . ." Carlos looked back at the hotel. "It's Oyler. That freaked them."

"*So what!* It freaked *me*," he shook his head. "The only argument against it that made any sense was Tage's. I mean, can you believe Duce?"

"Boy does have a point. What does the winner get? Bragging rights?"

"And do you think whatever elaborate conspiracy brought us here would take out the loser with a *rock*?"

"Hmm?"

"Oyler wasn't killed by some mass conspiracy. Not our 'keepers.' Someone walking around this hotel did him in."

"But who?" Carlos asked. "Doesn't everyone here have an alibi?"

"It looks that way." Quaid nodded. "But did you listen to what Dr. Yanowitz said? He was clobbered, tied up, and was finished off later. Someone could have made two trips . . ."

Carlos nodded. "You might have something there. I thought it was goofy having the killer watch the guy for half an hour."

"Maybe more," Quaid said. "And his notebook hasn't turned up yet. Want to bet he was killed for something in that notebook?"

"I'll take a pass on guessing about anything that's going on here." Carlos shook his head.

"Besides, does it matter if we were kidnapped by the CIA or little green men?"

A new voice joined them from back by the hotel. "I think the consensus among UFO nuts is they're little *gray* men."

Quaid turned to see A. J. and Frank coming out of the hotel. Carlos looked at A. J. and narrowed his eyes. "I didn't picture you as a UFO nut."

A. J. chuckled, "I'd say our nemesis is Earthbound." He looked in Quaid's direction. "Didn't Mr. Garnell say you thought we shouldn't be making assumptions?"

Quaid sighed. Connie was seeing flying saucers. Why not?

"Actually I just came out here to let you know that I, for one, thought you had a good idea."

Frank folded his arms and nodded. "But your delivery stinks."

"What the hell is that supposed to mean?"

Frank snorted. "Exactly."

Quaid turned to A. J.

A. J. was nodding as well. "Like it or not, we're in a political situation here. Personalities matter. There is a group of people here that sees things the way I think you do, and you're not helping us by rubbing people the wrong way."

Quaid backed away. "Now come on—"

"Son, you practically called two old ladies idiots back there." Frank had a grim expression. "You think that impresses anyone?"

"I just wanted you to think a little bit about

how people see you," A. J. said. "Did yelling at Louis solve anything?"

"He directly contradicted himself."

"Son," Frank bent over and lowered his voice. "Just don't go out of your way to piss people off." He waved at A. J. and led the way back to the hotel, leaving Quaid alone with Carlos.

"Well, that's fucking terrific," Quaid muttered.

"You *were* kind of harsh in there."

"You're taking their side?"

"Hey, I think you were right," Carlos said. "But you *were* harsh."

Thirteenth Move

The next morning, at dawn, Team D was sent off into the wilderness.

Behind the hotel was an abandoned greenhouse where a trail snaked off into the dense jungle toward the one mountain they could see. They all gathered there, at the greenhouse. Not just Team D, but the whole exile population to see them off.

The team was as well-prepared as they could manage. Each of them carried a backpack, or some other bag, weighted down with food and fresh water. A. J. carried Oyler's gun and a makeshift first aid kit that Dr. Yanowitz had put together. Gordon Hernandez carried a machete that had been discovered in a garden shed near the greenhouse.

The four members of the team, Eve, Bobbie, A. J. and Gordon Hernandez, were dressed for the expedition, wearing jeans and long-sleeved shirts. Bobbie's shirt was oversized flannel that she must have borrowed from somebody.

Team D spent their good-byes shaking hands

and whispering some final words here and there. Bobbie looked excited, where Eve simply looked determined. Gordon Hernandez, the one person of the four Quaid hadn't really gotten to know or talk to, kept looking over his shoulder at the woods, shifting his grip on the machete, as if searching for something. A. J. kept glancing at the sky.

A. J. hefted his pack and scanned the semicircle of people who faced the team. Sunlight was just beginning to dust the tops of the trees. "We better go, make the most of the daylight."

Gordon, Eve, and Bobbie moved up next to him.

Quaid couldn't decide which was more bizarre, the fact that they were sending four of their own into the wilderness, or the fact that it had taken this long to get their act together and send *someone* for help.

With team D gathered, A. J. took a last look at the rest of them. "I've got two signal flares for each of us, from the boathouse. We'll send one up if we find anything nearby. We'll send two up if we hit any kind of trouble."

A. J. smiled and Quaid wondered if the pilot had the same thought he had. *How long before they traveled too far for their flares to be visible?*

Then the four of them, with A. J. in the lead, walked off on the dirt path that led away from the rear of the old greenhouse. In a few seconds the jungle had hidden everything but their sound. Half a minute and that was gone as well. The rest of them stood there a bit longer.

Fifteen of them now.

That afternoon, Henry Sukomi took Quaid to the library.

Though abducted might have been a better term for it.

Quaid had been discussing something with Carlos and Frank down in the lobby when Henry swung by, grabbed his arm, and pulled Quaid after him. When Quaid asked him what was going on, Henry mumbled something about needing to see the doctor.

Henry had come straight in from the front doors, and Quaid didn't catch sight of who had been with him—if anyone. The sudden apparent violation of the buddy system disturbed Quaid, and Henry's nervous demeanor didn't help.

As he half ran up the stairs, Quaid followed him. Henry seemed distracted and distant. The man hadn't seemed quite right since finding Oyler's body. That gave Quaid an evil thought—

What if Henry's the one?

Was Henry freaking out because we found a body, or because we discovered the evidence?

The library was on the second floor, above the ballroom. The far wall was dominated by a huge stone fireplace, and the walls alternated windows with dark built-in bookshelves. Four pairs of red leather wing chairs took positions at each point of the compass. The floor was covered by an Oriental carpet with a detailed headache-inducing design. Above, surrounded by intricate plaster molding, a black ceiling fan from the twenties slowly rotated.

The room was occupied by Iris Traxler and Dr. Yanowitz.

Iris Traxler didn't quite fit the decor. Not that she wasn't pleasant to look at, her legs were as well sculpted as the molding above them, and her blond hair, spilling over her shoulder, upstaged the more somber colors of the room surrounding her. But, looking at her sitting in one of the wing chairs by the fireplace, Quaid couldn't help thinking that this room should be filled with crusty old men smoking cigars and reminiscing about their adventures in India or the Boer War.

Dr. Yanowitz, with his size and Oliver Sacks beard, was marginally more at home in the library. Though his Bermuda shorts seemed just as misplaced as Iris did. Henry grabbed him and whispered urgently. Dr. Yanowitz barely had time to set his book down on one of the chairs before Henry was dragging him out the door past Quaid.

Iris stood up and said, "Abe, where're you going?"

"It's all right," said the doctor. "Henry just has to show me something."

"Maybe you should take Quaid—" Iris said it in such a way that Quaid knew that she harbored the same evil thoughts that he did. And she had even less reason to give Henry the benefit of the doubt.

Henry hadn't stopped to debate; he was already halfway down the hall. "I'll be fine," said the doctor. "And I can't leave you here alone."

Then they were both gone, and Quaid was alone with Iris.

Iris looked up at Quaid, probably reading the befuddled expression that the whole situation had left on his face. "You're Mr. Loman," she said.

Quaid nodded. "And you're Miss Traxler."

"Iris," she said.

"Quaid."

"Is he going to be all right?" Iris asked him. There was a note of concern in her voice.

"I don't think you need to worry about Henry."

"Uh-huh." She sounded unconvinced.

He walked over to the chair that Dr. Yanowitz had left his book on. *The Paradox of Self-Amendment*, read the title on the spine, the author was Peter Suber. Quaid picked up the book and sat down. "So, have you found anything interesting here?" He pointed the book toward the shelves.

Iris glanced at the shelves. She could have been a model. She had that kind of face, the kind of flawless skin that made you think that someone had already taken an airbrush to her. "To be honest, that was just the most interesting thing I've seen today." She gestured toward the door, after Henry and the doctor. "What did he want with Abe?"

Quaid shrugged. "I don't know. I was just there for the sake of rule number eight. Henry just grabbed me and dragged me after him without explaining."

"I know the feeling." She saw his expression and shook her head. "No, Abe didn't drag me here. He's an all right guy."

"He didn't tell you what he was looking for here?"

"No." She gave him a wistful smile. "He was just so nice, asking me to 'accompany him.' He isn't married, you know . . ." She said the last part as if it was a defense. "He wears a ring, but he lost her—his wife—ten years ago. Cancer."

Quaid felt the hardness of his wedding band on his left hand. What made someone keep wearing it after the marriage was over? Denial? He looked at Iris and wondered at her interest in Dr. Yanowitz, couldn't fathom it really—but he'd been unable to truly fathom anyone's interest in anyone else since his marriage disintegrated. Any relationship beyond simple acquaintance seemed so self-evidently painful, Quaid had trouble imagining anyone else's motives. He was so alienated from the concept, that he hadn't even thought of one patently obvious aspect of their captivity.

People were going to attempt to pair off, and the only surprising thing about that was the fact he was caught by surprise.

"He didn't say what he was looking for?"

"No," Iris said. "Was he looking for something?"

Quaid chuckled to himself. "I don't know. I *guess* he didn't have to be looking for anything here." He opened the book he still held in his hands and glanced at a paragraph at random;

"One might say that citizens' failure to overthrow their constitution and government in revolution is a sufficient manifestation of consent to give the constitution and constitutional form of government legitimacy. Continuing failure to revolt would be continuing consent. But this view amounts to the proposition that a regime has legitimate authority if, and so long as, it successfully puts down and postpones revolution . . ."

"Rather dry reading," Quaid said.

"Actually, Abe seemed rather excited when he found that book."

Quaid looked down at the weighty tome. Dr. Yanowitz was excited over finding a copy of a textbook on legal theory? Though, upon reflection, from some of his arguments at the last vote, he did seem to be someone who'd be interested in arcane areas of knowledge. He could ask him about it later.

Quaid closed the book and said, "Can I ask you something?"

Iris leaned forward, resting her arms on her knees. She pursed her lips. "Now that depends on what you're asking, doesn't it?"

"Does the name 'Alphomeg Entertainment' mean anything to you?"

"Now where did you hear that name?"

"Madison Oyler carried their business card."

Iris looked down and shivered.

"What's the matter?"

"It's a little unsettling, I don't know why."

"The name's familiar, then?"

"I saw it in the newspaper." She looked up at him. "I'm not sure exactly when, just before the blank spot in my memory."

"What was the story about?"

She shook her head. "Not a story. I saw the name in the want ads." Quaid must have looked as if he sought more explanation, because she went on. "I had reached the point where I needed to be doing something other than what I was doing. I was getting kind of desperate . . ."

"What kind of job were they offering?"

"I don't know, the ad didn't say."

"Did you interview with them?"

"I don't know," she said. "I don't remember."

"Alphomeg," Carlos said. He chewed on the word as if it was a tough piece of meat. He was walking with Quaid along one of the white gravel paths that surrounded the hotel. The sun was setting, and the sky was deepening to purple as they talked.

"I think it might have something to do with us being here," Quaid told him.

"Okay, so Iris saw a want ad," Carlos conceded. "And Oyler had a business card. Does that mean anything?" *Why does the name bug me?*

"Connie's at least seen their logo . . ."

"It could be a huge company," Carlos said. "Have you thought of that? Would these connections mean as much if we were talking about Visa, or Coca-Cola?" *Come on, you've heard of them, where? Why can't you remember where?*

"It means something to you."

Carlos' expression must have been giving his thoughts away. He didn't like admitting it. "You're the one who gave the speech about not making assumptions, not jumping to conclusions—" Carlos shook his head. "I don't even remember why it's familiar. What would they have to do with all of this anyway?" Carlos waved a hand in the direction of the hotel.

"If we've been kidnapped, there have to be kidnappers. Someone had to set this all up."

"So we're test-marketing a new type of vacation getaway?" Carlos laughed. It was weak, and Quaid didn't join him.

Quaid didn't even respond. From his expression, Carlos believed that he was picturing Oyler's corpse. Suddenly, it didn't seem quite right to make light of their situation.

They rounded the corner of the hotel in the fading light and came across another pair of fellow "kidnappees."

Louis LeMonde was towering over the much smaller form of Erica Urquort. She sat on a stone bench on the edge of the small flagstone patio behind the hotel. Erica looked at home sitting on the edge of the garden, Louis looked grotesquely out of place.

Louis was making some grand statement, sweeping his arm with a force that sent ripples across his torso. He saw Carlos and Quaid approach and stopped gesturing. "Ah, welcome to two more exiles," he said. He reserved his smile for Carlos. He looked at Quaid with barely veiled suspicion. Erica's glance at him was almost hostile.

It's first impressions that linger, and Carlos thought that Quaid hadn't done well in impressing these particular people.

"Hello." Carlos waved.

"We were just discussing the topic of the day," Erica said. She looked at Carlos. "Feel free to join us." Carlos wondered if Quaid was excluded from the invitation.

"Topic of the day?" Quaid said. Either he was oblivious to the way they looked at him, or he had stopped caring what they thought—if he had ever cared. Quaid took a seat on a companion bench to Erica's.

Carlos walked over to the bench, standing next to Quaid. It was silly, but thoughts ran through Carlos' mind about making a united front. Almost as if they were on one side and Erica and Louis were on another.

We are *all in this together,* aren't *we?*

Carlos looked at the pair and wondered about Erica Urquort. She was by far the oldest among them, but she also seemed the most composed. By contrast, Louis seemed agitated—or excited, it was hard to tell. The heat didn't treat him well. The skin of his neck folded over the collar of his Hawaiian shirt, leaving sweat stains, as if he was melting and his flesh had turned semiliquid.

"So you seen any spooks about?" Louis asked him breathlessly.

Carlos looked at Erica, but her expression didn't provide him with any clues to what Louis was talking about.

"Spooks?" Quaid asked for him.

Carlos asked, "The men behind this— Right?"

Louis nodded, his flesh rippling like the ocean.

"I was under the impression that no one had seen anyone other than the twenty of us," Quaid responded.

"Nineteen." Carlos muttered.

"Ah, but that young woman, Connie, saw something last night," Louis said. It was almost triumphant.

And you haven't noticed the woman is crazy? Carlos thought. He looked at the expression on Louis' face and answered himself. *No, if anything, he sees her as a kindred spirit.*

If Quaid knew anything, he didn't say so. "She did?" he asked.

"Lights over the mountain," Louis said. "Hovering."

Carlos turned around. "Wouldn't surprise me. That woman's nuts."

"That's kind of strong—" Quaid said.

"She could've Tiffany-lamped someone to death if you hadn't stepped in."

"It's an understandable reaction," Quaid countered. "I'm surprised we've not seen more violent reactions to this—" Quaid looked up at Louis. "You were saying? Lights, spooks? You think she's seeing ghosts?"

Louis laughed, shaking his head. He clapped his hands. "No. Ghosts? That's rich." He looked over at Carlos. "I don't know her. But I did overhear that Mrs. Greenhart riding her to keep quiet about her 'hallucinations.' "

"See," Carlos said, "she is nuts."

"And Mrs. Greenhart," Quaid added, "has been in raging denial since I first saw her."

"I know what Connie saw," Louis said. "And it wasn't a hallucination, or UFOs, or ghosts—"

"What, then?" Carlos asked.

"Helicopters," Louis said. "Helicopters plain and simple. Unmarked civilian choppers have been their vehicle of choice since Vietnam."

"Whose vehicle of choice?" Quaid asked.

"The CIA, who else?"

"The CIA?" Carlos shook his head. "You're as crazy as—"

"Why do you think it's the CIA?" Quaid asked.

"Think about it." Louis waved his arm to include the hotel and the surrounding area. "The

Agency has a history of conducting experiments on civilians. They have unlimited resources that aren't accountable to anyone. And have you noticed something odd we all have in common?"

"Which is?"

"The whole lot of us are American. English-speaking American."

"That's odd?" Carlos asked.

"It means," Louis said. "Our keepers are probably Americans. Well-funded Americans. And this 'Game' is some sort of covert psychological experiment. Our amnesia— They have some sophisticated drugs at their disposal. . . ."

Quaid looked across at Erica. "What do you think about all this?"

"I think he has some good points—"

"You don't think it's the CIA, do you?" Carlos asked.

Erica shook her head. "No, that's what we were discussing before you came."

"Good," Carlos said, "At least someone has some sense—"

"I think," she continued, "that it is much more likely the Chinese."

Carlos started to say something, then just shook his head. Quaid leaned forward. "Why do you say that?"

"She thinks," Louis said, "that they would be the most likely to engage in some covert experiment on American psychology. Me, I don't think they have the technical expertise or the resources. It'd require some really sophisticated pharmaceuticals and one hell of a wide network to gather all of us and tweak our amnesia just right."

"Seems a strange sort of experiment for the government to pursue," Quaid said.

Louis wiped the sweat from his forehead. "These bastards have done stranger. They've hired psychics to target Russian missile bases, they tried to depose Castro by sneaking depilatories into his beard. It's not an Agency known for its sanity, especially when the doors are shut." The hand on his forehead clenched into a fist. Carlos noticed that Louis' cheeks were very flushed. "Comes down to business, whether the spooks running this show are CIA, Chinese, or Ethiopian. 'Playing' this Game is falling right into their hands. We shouldn't even be pretending to go along with it. Look at Oyler . . ."

Erica was leaning forward. "Are you all right?"

"I'm fine . . ." He turned toward the mountain, as if sensing something the rest of them weren't aware of. *"There!"*

The rest of them turned to face in the same direction. Louis was breathless when he said, "There, you see them, don't you?"

Lights. Bright white lights. At first Carlos thought they must be flares from A. J. and the others, but they were too low, and they *circled* the mountain, the lights not completely obscuring the dark shapes that carried them. There were three of them slowly traversing the base of the mountain, just above the tree line.

"There are the damn black helicopters. There're the bas—" Louis sucked in a breath. "Bastards . . ." The word came out in a rush of breath, followed by a sound like someone dropping a wet sack of flour.

Carlos turned around to see Louis on his knees, his clenched fist now holding onto his chest so tightly that it sank halfway into the flesh underneath his shirt. His face was bright red, and his breathing was coming in ragged gasps.

Shit! "Quaid, run and get the doctor!"

He took a step and Erica stood up. "I better go with you—"

Christ, can she be thinking about the damn rules?

Carlos didn't have any more time to think. Louis was collapsing, and Carlos had to spend all his strength to ease him sideways on the ground. He had to loosen his collar, and he ended up tearing his shirt open because he couldn't feel the button buried under the flesh of Louis' neck. "We're getting you help, Louis." He tried to sound reassuring, but he had a bad feeling about this. The feeling worsened when Louis' shirt was open and Carlos saw the deep nasty scars of a past surgery across his chest. Louis' fist clutched at the scar as if he was trying to tear the wound open again.

Louis was still conscious and must have seen

his glance. "Quadruple bypass," he said. "Fucker should have lasted more than three years."

"Save your strength."

"Light's going," he said quietly, shaking his head.

Carlos thought he was talking about himself, but when he looked over his shoulder, he saw what Louis meant. One by one, the three lights by the mountain disappeared.

BOOK TWO:

MIDGAME

Fourteenth Move

Louis LeMonde died sometime during the night.

Dr. Yanowitz couldn't do much of anything. His opinion was that, given his obvious ill health, Louis would've had only a fifty-fifty chance if he'd gotten to a hospital. Stuck here, with no real medical equipment or drugs, he didn't have a chance.

The news seemed to stun everyone, even more so than Oyler's death. Murder was threatening, but—perversely—more understandable. Louis' death was an ill omen. Quaid wasn't ready to start reaching for supernatural explanations for what was going on, but he got the feeling that some of the others weren't as skeptical.

Breakfast in the dining room was ominously silent. If people talked, they did so in hushed tones.

Quaid was at a table, eating cold cereal and wishing he had a beer, when Olivia Grossmann sat down across from him.

"Trying to save my soul again?" he asked. It

sounded more flippant than he intended it to, but she didn't seem to notice, or care.

"I wanted to know if Mrs. Urquort was right about what Louis said."

"He said a lot of things."

"He was talking about the Game right before he collapsed, wasn't he?"

Quaid looked up from his breakfast. He didn't like the way she was saying that. He could almost hear the capital "G." Whatever her line of speculation was, it made him uneasy and he didn't want to encourage it. "Like I said. A lot of things."

"About the Game?"

"Mostly about the CIA."

She smiled slightly. "The CIA?"

"U.S. Government black helicopters, the whole right-wing conspiracy song and dance."

"Technically, the black helicopters are United Nations . . ." she said, still smiling slightly.

"What?"

"The right-wing conspiracy theories you're referring to, the black helicopters in question are usually ascribed to the UN/Zionist occupational forces."

"I always thought the 'black helicopters' were responsible for cattle mutilations . . ."

Olivia shrugged. "That's a different set of conspiracies altogether."

"What Louis was saying, he thought that this whole game, our abduction and so on, was some CIA experiment in group psychology."

"While Ms. Urquort blames it on some other sinister foreign power."

"China," he said. He pushed aside his breakfast and looked at Olivia. She was wearing another suit, powder blue this time. From her face he couldn't really place her age. She was in that indeterminate area somewhere between thirty and fifty. Mature, not old. She watched him through thick-framed glasses that camouflaged her expression.

Quaid shook his head. "All it is, he got excited. That, combined with the heat, was too much for the guy."

"I know," Olivia said.

Quaid looked at her and started wondering. He kept thinking about her talk about God and the rapture . . .

"You don't think his death is some sort of sign?" he finally asked. "That he was struck down for denouncing this 'Game' we're playing?"

"Do you?" she asked in return.

Quaid didn't know how it happened, but suddenly he was the irrational one. Louis' sudden death seemed so pointless, especially in the face of the bizarre situation they found themselves in, it was almost comforting to try and connect his death to the game in some way. He felt a little embarrassed and asked her, "You don't?"

"I believe that everything, Louis' death included, is part of God's plan for us."

"And the game?"

"Especially the Game," Olivia declared.

"You think God struck Louis down for saying we shouldn't play this game?"

"God took him," she said. "We can't say why."

Quaid looked at her, trying to see what she was thinking. She seemed sincere, and she also seemed to have found a well of calm inside herself that seemed pretty incongruous given the circumstances. There was something about her that irritated Quaid—and that made him feel petty. The mixed cauldron of reaction was giving him a severe case of déjà vu.

"What do you think we should do about the game?"

"I liked your solution," Olivia said. "Everyone wins . . ."

"Should we even keep pretending—I mean isn't that what most of us are doing? Pretending? Appeasing our keepers?"

Olivia looked away. "Like life. It's something that each of us has to come to terms with." She stood, reached across, and patted his shoulder. "Decide what the right thing is, and go do it."

She left him there and he realized where his sense of déjà vu came from. The combined feeling of irritation and self-loathing was familiar. It was the same feeling he had for anyone who had ever tried to intervene in his drinking.

They gathered in the ballroom that morning. This time the familiar envelopes were waiting for them on the folding metal chairs. When Quaid came in, he could hear Duce telling Tage Garnell in a stage whisper, "I don't know *how* they got here! We had our patrol, but they must know where we are all the time."

Quaid took his now-traditional seat next to "his group," and watched as the others filtered in by twos and threes. Tage, Jarl, and Duce kept up their whispered conversation, though Quaid was pretty sure that everyone in the room could hear them—not to mention the fact that the envelopes on the seats were a pretty obvious sign that something had happened.

One small group of people seemed oblivious to the triumvirate of whisperers by the stage. Quaid saw Olivia Grossmann with an arm around the schoolteacher. It took a while for Quaid to connect a name—Susan—to the woman. He had never talked to her. Her manner seemed more reserved and suspicious than anyone. Right now, she seemed on the verge of breaking down on Olivia's shoulder.

Maybe she was upset over Louis. They both had been on the same team, which meant that they had spent some time together over the past few days. It was possible that they'd become friends—Iris and the doctor obviously had.

He returned his attention to the envelope that the "keepers" had left for him, tearing it open and scanning the contents. It was pretty much the same as the last one, except Louis' name had been dropped from the list of players. He thought of Connie's doodle, the page filled with eyes.

They were watching them right now, whoever they were.

After a few moments, Frank said, "I think we have a problem."

That got everyone's attention, including Duce and company. Quaid looked around to see what he was talking about. It took a moment for it to register.

Henry was gone.

Everyone else was here, Quaid counted thirteen people, including himself. He felt an involuntary shudder when he realized how quickly their numbers were dropping.

Carlos turned to Quaid and said, "He *has* been acting oddly. He must have heard about Louis and panicked."

Jarl Theodore took Frank's statement as a cue to climb up on the stage. "There's some bad news, if you ain't heard—" He waved Dr. Yanowitz up to the stage. The doctor looked somewhat deflated. Quaid wondered if the man was getting any sleep at all.

The doctor flipped the page on his legal pad and began going into detail on the death of Louis LeMonde. His report wasn't as graphic as the one on Oyler, since an autopsy didn't seem warranted—at least, he explained, he didn't have the capability here to learn any more from an autopsy than he could from examination of the body.

While the doctor spoke, Quaid saw Tage scanning the audience. It seemed that he had just realized that Henry was missing.

"They took him." He heard Connie whisper from behind him. He looked around and saw Connie looking disheveled and even less together than usual. Mrs. Greenhart sat next to her, seemingly unmoved over Louis' demise. He saw her mouth move. He couldn't hear what she was saying, but it was something like, "It's all right, child." He noticed Beatrice Greenhart's hand holding Connie's.

Connie repeated, *"They took him."*

Quaid didn't know if she was talking about Louis, or Henry. He looked over to where Olivia was still comforting Susan, and Quaid was surprised to see that Susan's attention wasn't on the doctor, but on the audience. She was staring at the place where Henry used to sit.

She'd just noticed it, too.

The doctor finished with his summary description of Louis' death, about as much eulogy as the guy was going to get here, and Tage spoke up.

"Does anyone know where Henry Sukomi is?"

From the reaction of the audience, only about half of them had noticed that Henry was missing. Dr. Yanowitz, still on the stage, looked surprised and started staring down at them, as if he expected to find Henry amongst them. Quaid found himself wondering what Henry had dragged the doctor off about last night.

"Anyone?" Tage repeated. "Any idea where he went?"

"Christ, man," Carlos spoke up. "This ain't a police state. Maybe he just didn't want to wake up for another meeting."

Tage glared in Carlos' direction. Quaid had a flashback to A. J's advice about not alienating people.

"We can't go off on our own," Tage said, "if we expect to survive this. Alone, anyone is easy prey for the person—or persons—who murdered Mr. Oyler. And what would we do if Team D came back here with help, a ride back home? How much time will we have to search for Henry before our keepers intervene?"

Everything he said made sense, but the way Tage said it made Quaid feel a little uneasy. It was a little too practiced, almost as if he had prepped the argument beforehand—

Which didn't make sense; Tage didn't know that Henry had run off.

The argument did have the effect of making Carlos shut up and return slowly to his seat.

"Who was with him last?" Tage asked. "Who paired up with him last night?"

There was an ominous silence. Quaid stared directly at Dr. Yanowitz, who didn't move to say anything.

What's going on here?

Quaid looked over at Iris, who was looking

at Dr. Yanowitz very intently. Something was definitely going on there, Iris had *seen* Henry go off with Dr. Yanowitz, she saw how agitated he had been—but she wasn't saying anything about it.

The only other person who had been there was Quaid. He saw Iris and Dr. Yanowitz cast furtive glances at him. Something in their attitude made him hold his tongue. He didn't know how long it was going to last, since Frank and Carlos both had seen him going off with Henry. Carlos might reserve judgment before saying Quaid was the last person to see Henry, but Quaid wasn't sure about Frank. There was something hard in Frank Pisarski, and he sat, nervously waiting to hear Frank's voice break the silence.

It wasn't Frank.

The schoolteacher, Susan Polk, stood up next to Olivia Grossmann, wiped her eyes, and said, "I think I saw him. When those lights were by the mountain." He noticed the relief on the faces of both Iris and Yanowitz.

"*Where?*" Quaid asked. He snapped the question, and after the words were out of his mouth he was cursing himself for betraying his nervousness. No one seemed to notice.

Susan faced him. She was blonde, youngish, and had blue eyes that seemed very distant and very cold. The flat way she spoke now made him think that she was having some deeper reaction to what was going on here, more than just Louis' death.

"I was in Erica's room. She was already asleep. I looked out the window and saw the lights. In the distance, near the trees, I saw a man standing out by the path to the green-houses. He was alone."

"Are you sure it was Henry?" Frank asked. There was a tone in his voice that was almost accusatory, though Quaid might have been imagining it.

"I don't know," Susan answered. Her voice remained flat, almost a monotone. "It was a man, and he wore a shirt and tie like Mr. Su-komi wore. Dark hair, and about his size. But I never saw his face. He was watching the lights."

Tage stepped off the stage and moved toward Susan. "Where did he go after that?" The prac-ticed air was gone from his words. He was firing the question at her as if Henry's life, or his own, was at stake.

Susan shook her head. "I don't know. There was a commotion below the window, I looked down and saw Mr. LeMonde collapsing. When I looked back, the man was gone."

"*It was one of them*," Connie whispered.

"No, it wasn't," responded Mrs. Greenhart, patting Connie's hand.

No monsters under the bed, Quaid thought to himself. *No alien body-snatchers, my child. And there are no evil UN Zionist helicopters mutilating their cattle* . . .

Quaid looked back at Connie, who was staring at her lap, being comforted by Mrs.
Greenhart. Who was more sane? The obvious
paranoid, or the one who firmly believed that
everything was perfectly rational, refusing to acknowledge—maybe refusing even to perceive—
the insane aspects of the reality they inhabited.

Quaid's head was throbbing, and his mouth
was dry. Sure signs that his body wanted a
drink, as if his six months of sobriety were as
many days. God, it would be such a relief to
just stop thinking about these things for just a
while. Just one evening.

Just one drink . . .

"We have to organize parties to find him,"
Tage said, snapping Quaid's attention back to
the moment.

"We need to vote," Frank said, standing.

Tage nodded and walked back up to the
stage. "Okay, we need to determine how we're
going to do this, who's searching where . . ."

"There's a question we have to address first,"
Frank said.

"Like what?" Carlos said. "Do we have that
much time?"

For the first time since the issue had come
up, Dr. Yanowitz spoke. "Yes. If he's injured
somewhere out there, time is of the essence."

Frank nodded and stepped forward. "Yes, I
know. But if we're taking this damn voting so
seriously—after yesterday, apparently we do—
there's an issue we have to deal with first."

Frank pulled out a slip of paper. "A. J. gave this to me before he, Eve, Bobbie, and Gordon left. Apparently, they had talked between themselves and didn't want to be left out—"

"Out of what?" Duce said. "They ain't even here."

"These are their proxies."

Duce snorted. "What the fuck is a proxy?"

"What do you mean their 'proxies'?" Tage asked. He was stroking his beard, the expression on his face unreadable.

"Since I was counting votes," Frank said, "they told me that they assigned their own votes to people who would be present for the duration of their absence."

"This is some fucking scam," Duce said.

"Hey, they can't do that," Carlos said.

"Isn't that against the rules?" someone he didn't see, probably Erica, said.

"The 'rules' don't address the question," said Dr. Yanowitz. "I would say that it is de facto permissible . . . granting we're using a permissive model for the rules."

"So much worry over a stupid game," complained Mrs. Greenhart. "I can't believe people are so worked up about it."

"They came to me with this. It's up to you all to resolve it." Frank said.

"What?" Duce said.

Tage nodded. "Put it to a vote, if people can assign proxies."

"I ain't voting on nothing until you tell me

what's on that paper." Jarl Theodore stepped up next to Duce. "Who's going to get two votes?"

Frank shook his head. "No, we vote on the issue first, on the merits."

"Doesn't that give you an unfair advantage?" asked Iris, "You know what's on that paper. Maybe that gives you all their votes?"

"No. I don't receive a single proxy," Frank said. "And I will abstain for this vote."

"Christ, I don't like this," Jarl muttered.

"You've got a vote just like everyone else," Frank reminded him.

"And perhaps two?" asked Dr. Yanowitz. "Exactly how do we deal with the ramifications of these proxies for this particular vote?"

"If it passes," Frank said, "the proxies count."

"That leads to a possible paradox," Yanowitz said. "If the straight vote differs in result from what the vote is with the proxies counted—"

"Oh, come *on*, people." Jarl was really looking frustrated. Quaid thought that his irritation was echoed throughout the rest of the players. There seemed little patience for procedural minutiae.

"—how do we resolve it?" Yanowitz finished.

"We can deal with that if it happens," Frank said. "Right now let's just vote on the damn issue, and leave the hypotheticals out of it."

Fifteenth Move

The proxy vote passed.

Two things decided the issue—at least for Carlos. First, the way things were going, it was becoming clear that *he* wouldn't want to lose his vote in what was going on in this half-assed democracy of theirs. Second, the folks in Team D were putting their own asses on the line for them, and it only seemed right to abide by their wishes.

Nine others agreed with him. Frank, as promised, abstained. Duce, Tage, and Jarl voted against it.

Frank had also told the truth, no one had given him their proxy. A. J. had given his proxy to Tage. Gordon Hernandez had given his to Susan Polk, the teacher. Carlos suspected that was because Susan was part of Gordon's "group," like Quaid was part of his. Bobbie had given hers to Erica Urquort—perhaps out of solidarity between two people who took the game seriously.

Eve, ironically, had given hers to Henry Sukomi.

When they started matching up search parties, Carlos ended up with Quaid, and Quaid seemed to make a point of accompanying Dr. Yanowitz to go search the greenhouse. For that matter, Dr. Yanowitz seemed to want Quaid on his search team.

There was some argument about putting their doctor in harm's way, but Dr. Yanowitz made a convincing argument that if Henry went off that way and did not come back, he might be in immediate need of medical attention.

The path to the greenhouse wasn't as obvious as the other paths around the hotel.

Everywhere else, the way was well-maintained and covered by a new layer of white gravel that was almost painful to look at in the morning sunlight. Behind the hotel the gravel turned into a geometric pattern of cobbled pathways that wove through the maze of the English garden. The garden itself was oblong, paralleling the rear of the hotel between the two backswept wings, not quite reaching either.

Central to the side facing the hotel was the patio where Louis had collapsed, right under the ballroom windows. The three of them stopped there a moment to get their bearings and find the way to the old greenhouse.

Carlos looked up at the walls above them, trying to find Erica Urquort's room, the place from which Susan had watched Louis collapse.

"Here it is," he heard Quaid say.

Carlos turned to see him standing by the far wall of the garden, about a hundred feet away where a low stone wall marked the end of the garden, and the end of the maintained area of the grounds.

Carlos joined him, and Yanowitz came over carrying a backpack of first aid equipment.

There was a break in the wall where Quaid stood, almost invisible because of a flowering vine Carlos couldn't identify. It covered the stone wall, as well as a significant portion of the gap, with yellow flowers the size of his hand. Their scent was heavy and sweet, like breathing syrup.

The path away was only really visible because prior explorers had trampled a good deal of the foliage flat.

Carlos looked back at the patio. He doubted he'd have been able to see Henry last night, not with everything else going on, not in the dark, as overgrown as it was back here. In fact, it seemed that Susan must have had excellent night vision to see anything back here last night.

Something isn't right about all of this. She was lying about Erica being in the room with her as Louis collapsed. What else was she lying about?

The three of them stepped out on the path of overgrown cobbles. They matched the ones in the garden, but weeds and creepers had claimed the spaces between them, and moss had claimed their surface. It made their footing treacherous and slippery.

The sun was starting to beat down in earnest, and a choking humidity clung close to the ground. All three of them were covered in sweat and a cloud of tiny black insects surrounded them like their own personal storm cloud.

Back here there wasn't a tree line as such. When the hotel had been built—or maybe when the plantation that had preceded it had been built—the land back here had been cleared, maybe for acres. The jungle had reclaimed it. Tall palms grew within a dozen feet of the garden, and the lush growth threw up more and more trees as the hotel receded behind them.

It wasn't until they reached a point where a tree had grown up nearly in the center of the cobble path, causing them to wade through the underbrush around it, that he realized they had completely lost the sky to green.

The greenhouse was iron, constructed of arches that reached above their heads for about fifteen or twenty feet. That was just the part of the building that pointed toward them. Beyond, past the entrance, a giant dome sat under the trees, half-hidden in creeping vines like some lost Aztec pyramid.

The sounds of birds greeted them, multiple calls that increased in volume until they reached the front of the greenhouse, and a cloud of multicolored wings erupted from the iron skeleton in front of them.

Dr. Yanowitz led the way into the structure. Quaid followed. Carlos brought up the rear.

Walking into the greenhouse was like setting foot on an alien planet. Decades of bird droppings and dead plants had made the floor a rich black soil in which grew seemingly endless varieties of fungi. Moss grew up the structure on the inside, softening the lines and making it less obviously man-made. Above, crawling across the old iron latticework, creeping vines dangled tendrils inside toward them.

The greenhouse's age had reversed its function. Now, instead of trapping light, with the overgrowth it provided more shade than any of the surrounding forest. It felt almost fifteen degrees cooler in here.

Yanowitz walked down the center aisle, toward the room of the massive dome, an area distinguished by being slightly lighter than anywhere else in the greenhouse.

Quaid followed. He stopped under the dome next to the doctor. "What happened between you and Henry last night?"

What?

Dr. Yanowitz turned to face Quaid. He looked uncomfortable, but he didn't look surprised at the question. "I don't think we have the time to get into this—"

"Cut the crap, Doctor," Quaid said. "You know what he was doing out here, don't you?"

Carlos caught up with them. "What are you talking about, Quaid?"

Quaid waved toward Yanowitz, who stood at the center of the ruined greenhouse as if he was on public display. "He's the last person Henry actually talked to. Henry was nervous as hell, wanted to see the doctor. Grabbed me to escort him last night." Quaid looked at the doctor. "Both you and Iris decided to not mention the fact at the meeting. What are you trying to hide?"

"Iris?" Carlos asked.

"The doctor and our entertainer from Las Vegas are an item," Quaid said.

"It isn't like that," Yanowitz protested. "I just need someone to talk to."

"So talk to us," Quaid said. "What are you hiding?" Quaid started walking along the perimeter of the domed room. With the high arched ceiling, dripping with vines, it was like a cathedral to some island nature deity.

"What are *you* hiding?" Yanowitz threw back at him. "You didn't say anything about Henry either."

"Because I wanted to hear from you, before I told *everyone* that you were the last person to talk to Henry. What was he scared of? What did he want from you?"

Dr. Yanowitz looked at Quaid, then at Carlos. "I kept quiet, because if Henry was—is—right, we all might be in a great deal of danger."

"We aren't now?" Carlos asked.

"Henry came up with a theory about Oyler's death . . ."

"I thought you pretty much explained it,"

Carlos said. "Someone ambushed him at the boathouse, right?"

Yanowitz looked at both of them and took a deep breath. "I thought so, too. Henry didn't."

In the corner, under the dome, sat some old cast-iron patio furniture. Yanowitz grabbed a chair that was cushioned by moss, and sat. Carlos heard the chair's legs scrape on the flagstones buried in the soil.

Quaid walked up and leaned on the table next to the doctor. "Why didn't you bring this up back there?"

"Think a moment, Quaid. Henry's *missing*. If he's right, one of us is probably responsible—in fact, the only reason I'm talking to you two now is because, if Henry's right, you're two of the three people who couldn't be involved in Oyler's death."

Quaid looked at Carlos.

Carlos was confused. "But we went through all this. Everyone was with someone else—"

"During the time Oyler was in the boathouse." The doctor looked at them both. "Everyone wonders what sane murderer would strike Oyler on the head and then wait around for him to wake up and struggle before slitting his throat." Yanowitz looked up at him. "What's the obvious answer?"

"You got me," Carlos said.

Quaid finished for the doctor. "The obvious answer is, the murderer *didn't* stand around. The murderer wasn't even there, probably not until about thirty seconds before Oyler's throat was slit.''

Yanowitz ran his hands over his face and nodded. He looked exhausted.

"That's what Henry came to you with?" Quaid asked. "There's got to be more to it. I came up with that myself."

"He came to me, because I was the doctor. I was the 'official' investigator. He wanted to know if his theory was plausible. He had managed to frighten himself badly with it, so badly that he could barely get the words out—"

Henry had grabbed Abe as he was absorbed in one of the appendices to Peter Suber's book. He yanked Abe's elbow, almost spilling the textbook out of his hands, whispering urgently, *"You have to talk to me, tell me I'm wrong."*

Abe's first impulse was irritation. This was the first real break he'd had since Oyler's autopsy, and he had found the reference he'd been looking for. He had wanted to reacquaint himself with the concepts it represented.

Abe turned to Henry, intending to say something sharp about interrupting him when it wasn't a medical emergency—

But when he looked into Henry's eyes, he saw that the man was quite obviously terrified. He was glancing around, as if he expected someone to ambush him any second. The look was so irrational that for a moment Abe considered that he might be looking at the man who'd killed Oyler.

Abe put the book down on his chair. He patted Henry on the shoulder. "Calm down," he said. "Tell me about it."

Abe thought their killer too subtle to be Henry. At least, he doubted Henry posed a current threat, in front of witnesses anyway.

"No," Henry whispered. "Not here, somewhere else, *alone*."

Alone?

Iris objected, and when Abe saw Henry's reaction—to start moving away, down the hall—he found his decision made for him. He reassured Iris and followed the man.

In retrospect, Henry seemed in such obvious turmoil about something that it was Abe's first reaction to help.

He followed Henry downstairs. Yanowitz expected him to stop once he was out of earshot of the library. He didn't. Henry kept them moving, through the lobby, the dining room, the kitchen, then down a narrow set of stairs to a dark, narrow wine cellar.

Instincts aside, Abe's paranoia was beginning to make itself felt. He wished he had stopped in the kitchen for something to defend himself with. . . .

The place was lit by a single incandescent bulb. The bulb dangled from a black wire attached to the arched stone ceiling by rusted steel staples.

Yanowitz finally said. "You can hold it now. We're alone."

"Just a little farther—" Henry pushed deeper into the cellar, past the reach of the single bulb. Yanowitz debated for several moments before finally following.

Is this being suicidal? I should turn back now—

He followed Henry down a long, narrow aisle, until he heard a door open ahead of him. He paused, and could see a strip of illumination beyond the door and Henry. A few moments later, a second bulb came on, washing the room beyond in dim yellow light.

Yanowitz walked into the room. It was long and much wider than the wine cellar. The floor was packed dirt; in one corner the root of a large tree had grown in at the base of the wall, dislodging some of the stonework. Above them were the timbers supporting the floor above. Wooden shelves lined either wall, perhaps they once housed preserves, but now they were populated by rusty cans of paint and cobwebs. There was a stone stairway leading up from the far wall and another, rectangular, wooden door leading off to some other part of the basement.

Yanowitz almost expected Henry to open that door and continue this follow-the-leader game he was playing, but he stayed where he was, standing between the stairway and the invading tree root.

"Okay," Abe said. "We're definitely alone *now*."

Henry nodded nervously. His hands were shaking. "You know, before yesterday I'd never seen a dead body."

I'm not a psychiatrist, Yanowitz thought. "Son, it's understandable that this has upset you—"

"This is the perfect place to talk, isn't it? If you don't want to be overheard . . ." At this point, Henry seemed almost to be talking to himself. He turned around and knelt by the root. At this point, Yanowitz noticed mud on his hands and on the knees of his pants, marring their crease.

"What did you want to talk to me about?"

"Had to grab Quaid, you know?" Henry looked up, real fear in his eyes. "If I go anywhere where they might *see* me, can't let them see me alone, breaking the rules." He looked back down at the root. "I think I can trust Quaid, maybe Carlos and Frank. Anyone else . . ."

Abe walked up next to him. "Anyone else, what?"

"Could be one of *them*," Henry said. "Even you, Doctor. You don't know the chance I'm taking, telling you this."

Abe knelt down next to Henry. With his old knees he couldn't squat, so he bent carefully, resting his bare knee on the cold earth next to the root. He placed his hand on Henry's shoulder and said, "You haven't told me anything yet. What do you mean, 'one of them'?"

"The people who killed Oyler," Henry said matter-of-factly.

In the silence after that, Yanowitz was uncomfortably aware of the sound of his own pulse. The silence stretched a few moments.

"Why are we here?" he finally asked Henry.

Henry reached down and touched one of the stones that had been knocked free of the wall by the invading root. The walls down here were of rough stone, covered with niter. Where the root had made its way, the parts of the wall it had claimed had returned to the scattered jumble of pieces that they had been before man had intervened.

Henry touched one of the stones. "Doesn't this look familiar?"

Abe felt a hollow in the pit of his stomach. This was the same sort of stone that had been responsible for knocking in Oyler's skull. "I see what you mean," Yanowitz said, "but this was probably made with local stone. The rock by the boathouse didn't necessarily come from here."

"Am I remembering wrong?" Henry said. "Wasn't that rock covered with this white, flaky stuff?" He peeled off some of the niter with his thumbnail.

Abe simply nodded; he was remembering picking out pieces of that niter from Oyler's head wound. At that time he'd been worried solely about matching the fragments to the rock that'd been found there.

Henry continued. "Did you see any other rocks like that around the boathouse?"

Abe shook his head. It wasn't something that he had worried about at the time, but there hadn't been. He couldn't recall coming across one other example in the area around the boathouse. "Okay," he said. "You've convinced me. The rock came from here. But it could have gotten there fifty years ago. What's gotten you so upset?"

Henry picked up one of the rocks and hefted it. His hand was shaking. "The doors up there," He pointed the rock up the stairway. "They lead outside. We're under the west wing of the hotel. The boathouse is that way. It's overgrown, but the doors have been forced open, tearing the vines—forced from the *inside*, recently."

"Now what are—"

"—let me get through this, please?" Henry's words were rushed and shallow. "You examined him. Tell me it didn't happen this way. He's not in the boathouse," Henry said. "He never went to the boathouse. Not under his own power. He was standing here," Henry stood and walked over under the light. "Where I am right now. Before everyone teamed up and started searching for whatever it was we were looking for." Henry looked toward the ceiling, the words coming faster, almost tripping over each other in a rush to be said. "I've been picturing it, over and over. He's here because it's private. He's talking to someone, maybe more than one person, talking alone. They don't want to be overheard. They're angry, shouting maybe. Very angry. Oyler, he's the one who decides to leave. He heads for a door, away from the other—others. His back is to them—him—her—and the other is angry, furious, maybe even panicking that Oyler is leaving. Maybe he's going to do something, say something that the other can't let be done or said. The other sees Oyler turn his back and decides to stop him. Maybe grabs him first, by the arm, and gets shrugged off. Angrier now. Lethal anger. Grabs one of the rocks here. Runs up. Slam." Henry brought the rock down on the wall next to the door to the wine cellar. It struck a spark and a cloud of niter. He dropped the rock. It thudded to the dirt floor.

Abe thought the sound was similar to the noise Oyler's body would have made when it fell.

The soil embedded in the abrasions in his face, under his fingernails . . . It *could* have happened here.

Henry turned around, facing Yanowitz again. "You can see it, can't you? The rock slamming into his skull, the body falling at the attacker's feet? Might not even know he's still alive. Anger's probably spent now. Over a dozen people will soon be wandering all over the place once they get their shit together. The attacker's one of those people. Got to get back before anyone notices someone's missing. But what to do with Oyler? Can't leave him. Can't drag him back through the hotel where all the people are. Only a few minutes."

Abe felt his mouth go dry as he listened to Henry. The rush of words was like an assault. Almost as if he was hearing the confession of the killer himself. He stood and took a step back from Henry, until he felt the cold, damp stone on the back of his legs, and on his bare neck.

Henry went on, oblivious. "You start looking around. What now? You see the stairs. If you have some sense of direction, you realize where they go. Even if you don't, you know they're a way out. Away from the body, maybe a place to take the body, hide it. Run up, slam into the vine-covered doors. Panic maybe. Push. Force them open through the vines and rusty hinges. There you can see the path down to the boat-house. You can take that, only fifty feet away is the woods and cover. You can make it with the body. If you're lucky, no one will see you. At some point you realize that he's still alive. And you come up with a plan."

Henry picked up the rock. "You take this, the weapon. You drag the body to the boathouse. Fifteen, twenty minutes if you don't have any help. Half that if you do. Bash the lock open with the rock and drag Oyler inside. He's still out cold, but by now he's moaning, moving maybe. You haven't come to your final decision yet, so you restrain him. Use the nylon rope you find there. Truss him up so he can't go anywhere . . . You're back before people start going out to to look at the grounds."

Henry looked at the rock in his hand. For a moment, Yanowitz was afraid that he might strike him with it. Instead, Henry walked back to the root and allowed it to roll out of his hand and join its brethren.

"I see," Abe said. "Later on, while people are in groups, he only needs to slip away for ten minutes or so, before you and the others reach the boathouse."

Henry nodded.

"By then, though, Oyler had already struggled half-free." The frightening aura had left Henry, and Abe stepped forward to place a hand on his shoulder. "But there weren't any defensive wounds. Why's that?"

Henry looked up and said, "Can't you see why?"

"Well, I can't," Carlos said.

"The murderer was someone else," Yanowitz said. "Oyler only knew the person who struck him. Anyone else steps into the boathouse—"

"And Oyler asks them for help," Quaid shook his head. "Christ. The evil bastard—whoever it is—walks in on Oyler trussed up and the guy thinks he's there to help him out."

Yanowitz looked pale and sunken, more so after telling what he'd been through with Henry. "He described it like this. The murderer walks in. Oyler calls for help. The murderer runs in, and fusses, gets Oyler to sit up so he can reach the knots. While he's behind Oyler, he slips out the knife, and opens up his throat from behind. No defense wounds because Oyler never got a chance to defend himself. He must have struck the water before he fully realized what had happened."

"Christ, it could be anyone now . . ."

"Any two people," Quaid said.

Sixteenth Move

Connie thought looking for Henry was pointless. They had taken him, and Henry would be found the moment they wanted him to be found, no sooner.

Soon enough they would come for the rest of them. Connie was so frightened by the prospect that she had gone numb, following her "team" dumbly through the corridors of the hotel looking for signs of Henry Sukomi. Connie didn't *look*, she simply wandered after the other two women of Team C, frightened of being left alone—fear that ran deeper than any worries about breaking their rules.

"He broke the rules," Erica Urquort said as they entered one of the dozens of unoccupied, and unlocked, rooms in the hotel. "We won't be finding him alive."

"There's no call to talk like that," Mrs. Greenhart chided as she followed the old woman into the room. She cast a backward glance at Connie, checking to see that she was all right.

Mrs. Greenhart was once Sourpuss to Connie, but Connie had come to realize that there was something much more sour, and harder, in the heart of Erica Urquort. The old woman seemed to almost revel in the game their keepers had set up. As if Henry's demise would be some sort of personal vindication for her.

Evil was the word that came to Connie's mind.

Erica could very well be one of them. If she wasn't, it was even worse, because she *wanted* to be. Connie felt a hand on her shoulder and she winced, jerking her gaze up from where it had been locked on the carpet between her feet.

"Are you all right, child?" Beatrice asked her.

Connie laughed, shaking her head and closing her eyes against the forming tears. "No. Yes. Go on and join the treasure hunt. I'll be right here for all the gory details, God forbid we miss a part of this grand drama, God knows *they* aren't—" Connie sucked in a breath. "I'm fine."

She looked unsure but followed Erica into the room.

Connie brought up the rear as Beatrice reengaged the evil old woman in their argument. Connie turned away from both of them and walked to one of the windows.

She opened it to escape the pile of words the other two were leaving in their wake. The fresh air that blew in was comforting.

"Stop badgering me!"

The shrill voice was coming from below. Connie looked down and saw another of the search teams rounding the path around the hotel. The person yelling was blonde, hugging herself.

The teacher, Connie thought. She'd been crying at the meeting, and she looked even more upset now.

She was yelling at the leggy woman with the huge boobs. *Team A*, Connie thought, though instead of the doctor, the trio was completed by the bald, hulking form of Frank Pisarski.

Yes, they swapped places, didn't they? Quaid insisted on taking the doctor out back. . . .

"I was just asking about Henry," said Legs.

"Stop it."

Frank walked up to the teacher and put a hand on her shoulder. She winced. "We didn't mean to upset you, Mrs. Polk—"

"*Miss*," she almost spat.

"What's the matter?" he asked.

Miss Polk leaned against the wall of the hotel, shook her head, and looked up—

Connie withdrew from the window, embarrassed at eavesdropping. She still listened, with difficulty since the outside voices were competing with the argument between Erica and Beatrice.

"Have you ever seen these garish little tracts?" Miss Polk's voice. "About the size of your palm, little fundamentalist Christian comic books? No. The story's always something like this. The main character walks through life, gets a chance to accept salvation, but blows it by listening to some smooth character, gets hit by a train, goes to hell where he finds out the smooth character is the Devil."

There was a long silence before Connie heard Miss Polk again. "Of course, I'm not all right."

"We're going to get through this." Another woman's voice, must be Legs.

"You don't understand . . ." The voices were getting harder to hear, and Connie leaned out again to catch what Miss Polk was saying.

The other team had resumed their obit around the hotel, and they were almost gone around the next corner. Connie caught one last fragment of the conversation, it sounded like Miss Polk saying, "Something unforgivable."

"Connie," Beatrice's voice called her back to the room. "We're done here."

Connie nodded and followed, thinking about smooth characters and the Devil.

"Do you think Henry was out here last night?" Quaid asked Yanowitz.

Yanowitz stood, shaking his head. "I don't know. He could have been."

Somewhere above them an unseen bird called for its mate. To Quaid, it was a distant, alien sound.

"We've wasted enough time, though," Yanowitz said. "I was serious when I said he might need medical attention."

"You think he panicked and ran?" Carlos asked.

"I *hope* he panicked and ran," Yanowitz said. "If that's the case, he's probably still alive."

No one needed to spell out the alternative.

The three of them checked the greenhouse for signs of recent activity. They did find their share of footprints, but there was no way of telling if they were Henry's or from a couple of days ago when Team C was tramping through the woods here.

Why would Henry come here?

Maybe he was looking for something. He had just finished his tirade with Yanowitz, providing the scenario for Oyler's death. The doctor hadn't denied the possibility of Henry's theory. In fact, Yanowitz seemed convinced that it was the most plausible explanation.

It explained everything but a motive.

Why come here, then? Was Henry running. . . ?

Or was he still figuring out how Oyler was killed? Maybe figuring out who killed him?

"Where now?" Carlos asked. There was nothing in the greenhouse giving any sign of Henry. The direction of their search was arbitrary now. But Quaid was starting to have an idea of what Henry might have been doing back here.

"Southwest," he said, pointing.

The three of them exited from a different wing of the ruined greenhouse, into undergrowth that didn't even have a hint of a path. "Why this way?" Carlos asked, kicking some of the vines that tried to ensnare his feet.

"It's toward the boathouse," Quaid said. He started walking away from the greenhouse. "We'll need to spread out if we're going to see anything." He motioned to his left and right. "Fifty, sixty feet—just keep in sight."

"Why are you thinking he went toward the boathouse?" Yanowitz asked.

"Alibi 101," Quaid said. "He was figuring how long it would take someone to cover that distance. He talked to you, and convinced himself how. He still needed to know *who*."

They all spread out and started moving toward the north end of the lagoon. The way was slow going, not because of the footing, but because they were keeping a careful eye out for anything along the way down.

They were about midway between the greenhouse and the boathouse when Carlos said, "Oh, holy fuck . . ."

Carlos had almost stepped on him.

Lying there, facedown on the forest floor, Henry almost seemed to blend in, as if he was melting back into the earth. Yanowitz confirmed the pretty much obvious. He was dead, and had been for most of the night.

Yanowitz turned him over to examine the body.

Quaid felt his gut wrench when he saw his face. Henry had suffered the same fate as Oyler, and the cut that slit his throat had nearly decapitated him. His shirt was black with blood and the soil that adhered to it. Worse were the ants.

They covered him from the neck down like a living blanket.

"Damn. Three bodies in four days?" Carlos asked. "It's not going to be too long before none of us are left."

Quaid crouched next to Yanowitz, and tried to keep from being sick to his stomach. "Can you tell if it's the same weapon that killed Oyler?"

"Best I can say is that it could be." He looked at the corpse. "I don't like guessing like this— but we don't have any defensive wounds, and the neck wound is severely distended. It looks as if the attacker surprised him from behind, one hand pulling back while the other made a single cut across the neck."

Yanowitz bent over the ant-covered wound, and Quaid looked away as he brushed off the insects. "No hesitation marks, clean. One powerful stroke."

Yanowitz stood up. "He was walking *away* from the boathouse. He was facing this way when he fell."

Quaid looked down at Henry again. He had a nasty feeling. Whoever did this was very good at it. Unlike Oyler, here the victim wasn't bound. Henry had been moving, and had good reason to be paranoid about pretty much anyone approaching him. The killer had to sneak up on him, and finish him off with one stoke.

"We wouldn't have heard anything back at the hotel, would we?" Quaid asked.

Yanowitz shook his head. "Not with that kind of wound, that quickly. He wouldn't have managed much more than a wheeze."

Quaid stood there, wondering if Henry had made it all the way down to the boathouse, or if he had seen or heard something that made him start back to the greenhouse.

When Oyler had been killed, the people at the greenhouse were Tage, Duce, Jarl, and Olivia Grossmann. . . .

"Did you tell anyone else about Henry coming to you?"

"No one," Yanowitz started, then corrected himself. "Well, Iris. Nobody else."

"Do you know who else Henry might have talked to about this?"

Yanowitz shook his head. "I don't know that he told anyone."

Quaid looked down at the corpse. "Well, somehow, the killer found out."

"Come on," Carlos said, "We found him. Let's go tell everyone the 'good' news."

It was becoming frighteningly routine. The gathering, the death announcement, then the tentative postmortem by Dr. Yanowitz—this time without his dirty legal pad. There was the initial silence, followed by the snowballing debate on what exactly they should do.

The three of them didn't volunteer what they knew about Henry's suspicions, or any of the conclusions they'd drawn from them.

They had a couple of compelling reasons not to.

Quaid's main concern was that if the killer was in the audience—which seemed most likely—once he or she knew what they knew, it would be that much harder to determine his or her identity. Yanowitz was afraid that revealing what Henry had said might panic the killer into more bloodshed. The motive for killing Oyler was uncertain, but Henry had unquestionably been killed because the murderer thought Henry was getting too close to identifying him or her.

However, the debate among the captive population led to a different conclusion.

Erica Urquort led the faction that believed that it was the "keepers" who had finished Henry off. He had forfeited the game by breaking Rule Eight: *"All Players must stay in groups of two or more people at all times."*

Quaid was shocked by how many people muttered that Henry should have seen it coming, breaking the Rules like he had. Jarl Theodore made a comment almost to the effect that the poor bastard had it coming.

Tage managed to encapsulate the whole mood of the ballroom, "I think we can assume that we're taking a lethal risk if we fail to abide by these Rules."

As the meeting broke up, Quaid intercepted Olivia Grossmann on her way out. He tapped her on the shoulder. "Can I have a few moments of your time?"

She turned and faced him with her thick-framed glasses. For once, that well of faith and calm that he'd seen within her seemed shaken. The recent debate, or something else, wasn't sitting well with her.

She seemed surprised at him being the one to initiate a conversation. "I suppose you can . . . There are chairs in the lobby—"

"I'd prefer to go outside, if you don't mind."

Almost reluctantly, she nodded.

They walked down the white gravel path, taking the branch that led down to the beach. By now the sun was setting, and the white beaches had turned golden in the evening light. Above them, the hotel sat, incongruous lord of its tropical surroundings.

Olivia didn't look at it.

"What's disturbing you?" Quaid asked.

She laughed, almost a sigh. And hugged herself as if she was cold, though the temperature was probably in the low seventies. "Remember what I said about this Game being a test?"

"Yes?"

"I think I was wrong."

"It's not a test?"

"It's not *God's* test." She rubbed her arms. "There's something evil here. Something dark."

"I thought you said everything was God's test for us—"

"We live in the Devil's world, Quaid. Sometimes the tests are his . . ." She turned to face him. "What is it you wanted to talk to me about?"

"Henry."

She bit her lip and turned, walking a few paces toward the lagoon. "You have no idea how sorry I am, the way he died."

Quaid looked at her back, the way her shoulders drooped. He had taken her aside on a hunch. Henry must have talked to more people than just the doctor last night. He had to have tipped his hand to the killer. It was a stab in the dark, but he suspected that Henry would have tried to talk to members of the various teams who'd searched the grounds the day Oyler was killed.

Especially, he thought, the team that covered the greenhouse.

Olivia, Jarl, Duce, and Tage. He would have wanted to talk to somebody, just to find out who had enough time to escape to the boathouse and do the deed. Nervous as Henry had been, Quaid thought the least threatening member of the quartet was his most likely target.

"Did you get to know him at all?" Quaid asked.

The back of her head shook. "No, but for someone who wears her faith on her sleeve, I was terribly *un*-Christian to him."

"I'm not here to accuse anyone—"

"Aren't you?" Olivia spun around and gave him a look that was despairing and accusatory at the same time. "You're following in his footsteps, aren't you? Not just for Mr. Oyler, but for Henry as well, now."

"I misspoke," Quaid said. "I *am* trying to find out who their murderers are. But I'm not here to be judgmental to you."

"Unless I am a murderess, I suppose?"

"Are you?" Quaid had never been one for subtlety in tense situations. And he was pretty tense. He kept thinking that he needed a drink to calm his nerves, and that thought made him tense up even more. He'd blurted out the question before he'd really thought about it, and afterward, once he'd said it, he expected her to slap him or just run away.

To his surprise, she did neither. She just shook her head and said, "No, I'm not."

"You talked to Henry, didn't you?"

Olivia nodded. "Or he talked to me. I thought he was raving. I wanted him away from me. From us."

"Us?"

"I've stayed with Erica and Susan the past few nights. Rule number eight."

Quaid nodded. "I understand."

"Apparently Henry didn't, did he? He seemed to be ignoring that rule. At least he came to our door alone."

"When did he show up? What did he say?"

Olivia sucked in a breath. "He showed up an hour or so before Louis collapsed. He just showed up in the doorway, without even knocking . . ."

*   *   *

Susan was in the bathroom taking a shower, and Olivia was leaning back in a chair next to the open window. She had been reading a Bible she'd found in the library, but at the moment she had drifted into quietly smelling the tropical breeze and listening to the occasional sentence fragment from the conversation between Erica and Louis downstairs.

"Olivia, Olivia Grossmann, I need to talk to you."

Olivia turned to see Henry Sukomi standing in the doorway. His hair was disheveled, and sweat was dripping from his face, though Olivia thought the night here was somewhat chilly. Mud streaked his pants, and his hands were black with grime.

Olivia slammed the Bible shut and said, "What do you mean, storming in here like that?"

"This is important—" Henry said. "I need to ask you something."

"Whatever it is," Olivia stood, and placed her hand on the door, "can wait until morning." She endeavored to force the door shut on Henry.

A grease-streaked hand, fingernails black, caught the door an inch from the jamb.

"No," he said, voice muffled by the door. "This can't wait." He was trying not to raise his voice, Olivia could tell. And he was out of breath, as if he had just run all the way here.

She tried to push the door shut, because Henry's manner was beginning to frighten her. She asked God for strength, but Henry pushed the door back open, against her.

"You have to leave, now." Olivia backed away from the newly open door. "You shouldn't be here."

"I'm here about Madison Oyler," Henry's voice was low and shaky, almost overwhelmed by the sound of his breathing.

The moment Henry grabbed her arms, she was convinced that he was the murderer. She gasped in a breath to scream, but a dirty hand clamped over her mouth and all she managed was a choking gasp.

"No," Henry said. "They can't find out. They've killed once, right? They'll do it again. One of us did it. Walked in on him while he was tied up. Oyler didn't know till it was too late . . . Only a few minutes. Only a few people close enough to the boathouse to do it."

Olivia struggled, tried to free her mouth.

Henry said, "Shhh."

She slowed her struggles, and Henry nodded. "You have to tell me. You were up there. Who was left alone, out of sight? Twelve minutes. That's all they'd need." Henry caught his breath, his voice was near a whisper. "Nod if you understand."

She wasn't really hearing him. Her thoughts were filled with a frantic prayer that she would get out of this alive. She was now certain that

Henry was deranged and the killer himself, whatever he was saying.

Still, she nodded so that he would remove his hand and allow her to breathe.

"Please be quiet. They could be listening. I need to know for sure who they are. When you were at the greenhouse, who spent that much time away from the rest of you?"

Olivia sucked in a breath, saw something out of the corner of her eye, and said, "Susan?"

Henry let go and turned to see Susan Polk standing in the doorway wrapped in a towel. Very quietly, she asked, "Are you all right, Olivia?"

Henry didn't wait for the answer. He ran out the door without another word. Olivia rubbed her face where Henry's hand had gripped her, the skin felt greasy.

She wondered how long Susan had been watching them.

"How long *had* she been watching you?"

"I don't know, I didn't ask her."

Quaid looked back up at the hotel, trying to think of what had been going through Henry's mind. He had seen Susan and run. Was that his overwrought—though justified—paranoia? Something more?

"Could she have heard Henry's ranting?"

"I suppose so—" Olivia sighed. "You have no idea how bad I feel believing he'd been the murderer. It doesn't even make sense in retrospect. He was with you and two others when Mr. Oyler—"

Quaid turned around and patted her on the shoulder. "He frightened you badly, barging in and grabbing you. You aren't expected to analyze things when you're in the middle of a situation like that."

"I should have been more—"

"More what? Accommodating? The man was roughing you up. No one needs to accept that kind of treatment, whatever the motive." The sun had almost set. The purpling sky began to come alive with unfamiliar constellations. At the moment he couldn't decide if they were in the southern hemisphere or on another planet.

"Thank you."

"I have the same question," he said. "You never answered him."

She bit her lip and shook her head. "Do you really think—"

"I don't know yet. But I need this information to find out."

Olivia nodded. "I was with Jarl Theodore the whole time. Tage and Duce split from us when we reached the greenhouse—to circle around and check the woods. They might have been gone fifteen, twenty minutes."

Quaid found himself looking around the empty beach, as if the killer might materialize then and there now that he'd heard the crucial bit of information.

"Let's go back," he said.

"Yes."

They'd walked a few dozen paces up the gravel walkway when he asked, "When Henry turned up missing, why didn't you tell everyone this?"

There was a long pause. "I don't know. The news shocked me dumb until Susan spoke. I thought she did it to protect me."

"Did what?"

"Told that story about seeing Henry out the window."

"She didn't?"

"We weren't even in the room when Louis collapsed."

Seventeenth Move

Carlos had taken Yanowitz and Iris Traxler up to the library straight from the meeting, at Quaid's request. Most of the time they waited was spent catching Iris up on what was going on around here. She frowned a lot, but apparently the doctor had told her enough for her not to be surprised or shocked about the rest of it.

About fifteen minutes later, Quaid entered the library, a woman in tow.

Carlos had to struggle to remember the woman's name. Olivia, he couldn't remember the last name. Iris remembered for him. "Mrs. Grossmann."

Yanowitz gave Quaid a look that asked, "What is she doing here?"

Quaid told the doctor, "I've talked to Olivia here, and I think someone needs to keep an eye on her while me and Carlos check some things out."

"Fine," Carlos said. "What are we checking?"

Quaid drew him aside, leaving Olivia with the others. As they left, Quaid gave him a hurried whispered description of the further adventures of Henry Sukomi on the last night of his life.

"Damn," Carlos said, more than a few times.

"Here's the main thing, though," Quaid said. "Susan Polk *lied*. She was downstairs in the dining room with Olivia while Olivia was trying to shake off the scare Henry had thrown into her. She wasn't anywhere near a window overlooking the garden when Louis collapsed."

Carlos nodded. "That woman has been off all day, at least. Iris asked her about Henry earlier today, and the woman went on about unforgivable sins."

"She did?"

"Yeah," Carlos said. "Iris mentioned it while we were waiting, talking about how Miss Polk said she was in the room with *Erica,* when Erica was out on the patio with Louis until he keeled over."

"What'd she say?"

"Nothing concrete. She got very upset over questions about Henry—but she never admitted why."

"Maybe Henry's strong-arming of Olivia?"

Carlos shook his head. He didn't think so. "She seemed to feel she had done something 'unforgivable.' "

They walked in silence for a few long moments before Carlos said, "What gets me is that it was such a completely stupid lie. Anyone who thinks about it for more than a few moments knows she was lying. Why bother?"

"Good question," Quaid said.

They started their search for Susan Polk at the room she had shared with Erica Urquort and Olivia. Some of Henry's paranoia must have rubbed off on the two of them, because they skulked down the corridors silently, watching for other people. Carlos thought the whole thing would be ridiculous if people weren't dropping like flies.

Down the hallway from Erica's room, Carlos asked the question that they both seemed to have been avoiding. "If it *is* one of us, or two of us, and we find out who. Then what?"

"I don't know. Restrain them, keep them away from the rest of us?"

Yeah, right. And we'll probably have to vote on it.

After a few minutes Quaid shrugged. "It might not come to that."

"Yeah," Carlos said. "If it comes to my life or his, you know which I'm choosing."

They stopped in front of Erica's door and knocked.

No one answered.

"Hello?" Quaid called out. "Anyone there?"

"No one home," Carlos said.

Quaid nodded and tried the door. The knob moved freely, unlocked. He pushed it open.

"What are you doing?" Carlos asked.

"Quick look around, make sure everything's all right." Quaid stepped in.

Carlos watched him from the doorway. Skulking around the hallways, talking trash about some possible murderer, that was one thing.

This was another.

The room looked the same as all the others, though the women had found a rollaway bed somewhere. "I don't think we should be doing this," Carlos said from the doorway.

Quaid waved a hand at him, as if dismissing his little invasion of the women's room.

Quaid peered out the window. It was open, and let in a breeze that carried the floral scents of the garden below. He had a view of the patio where Louis had collapsed. The sky was dark and the only lights were those from the hotel.

Quaid looked down, and with the hotel lights blazing against the night, the unlit wilderness beyond the garden wall was almost impenetrable blackness—even with the moon shining down on them.

Why was she lying? Did Henry suspect her? Is that why he ran? Or was Henry so stressed out at that point that anyone's sudden appearance would have provoked his flight? Quaid himself had told Olivia that fear and rational analysis didn't go together.

Henry had been, by all accounts, terribly frightened. Maybe Henry *wasn't* thinking rationally.

And Quaid Loman? Here *he* was, rummaging

through someone else's drawers. Maybe he wasn't thinking rationally either. He searched quickly, hampered by the fact he was unsure what exactly he was looking for.

Quaid did find something, and it definitely wasn't what he was looking for. At least not on a conscious level.

Erica had an antique flask stashed away in a bureau. Unlike him, she had obviously taken time to unpack. It lay on top of a folded stack of bedclothes that filled the left side of the otherwise empty drawer. It was an expensive, heavy-looking piece, silver, not silver plate. Black threads of tarnish traced a floral engraving. A coat of arms graced the top front of the flask, and also the cap.

Quaid's hand brushed it. The metal was cold, the touch almost intoxicating in itself. His hand shook as he picked it up and felt the telltale shift of liquid within it. Almost full.

Carlos cleared his throat. "Are we just going to stand here and wait for someone to walk by and ask what we're doing?"

Quaid turned around with a fear closer and much more immediate than the killer in their midst. He slowly slid the drawer shut and said, "No, there's nothing more here. We should see about Susan's original room."

Carlos sighed. "How'd I know that one was coming?"

They shut the door behind them and were halfway down the Victorian-clad corridor before

Quaid realized that he had taken the flask. It rode cold and heavy in his hip pocket.

Susan wasn't in the room their keepers had assigned her.

There was one difference though, the door was locked.

"Okay, so much for that," Carlos said. "Let's go downstairs and actually *look* for the woman."

"Wait a minute, Carlos," Quaid turned to him questioningly. "Do you have a key for your room? Because I don't."

Carlos looked at him and then at the door. "Hell, the keys could have been left somewhere—"

"We've been in these rooms how long? Has one key turned up?"

Carlos looked down at the lock. It was scrollwork wrapping around an antique keyhole. If he remembered right, there would be a small thumb-knob to lock the door from the other side.

"She's got to be there. The door has to be locked from inside." Quaid pounded on it. "Susan? Susan Polk?"

"What're you doing?" Carlos tugged on his arm. "I thought this was supposed to be low profile."

Quaid kept pounding. And Carlos felt an ominous sensation in the pit of his stomach.

"What's going on here?" Jarl Theodore opened a door about twenty feet down the hallway. He was in boxer shorts and a pair of white socks. "Some people are trying to get some fucking sleep."

Carlos faced him. The guy seemed oddly out of place without the mirrored sunglasses and checked shirt. Carlos hadn't seen him without them until now.

Quaid kept pounding. "I think Susan's in trouble, I can't get her to answer the door."

Duce appeared behind Jarl. His outfit hadn't changed. As far as Carlos could tell, he probably slept in those jeans and that leather jacket. "Christ, man. She's bunking with the old bitch. Cut the noise."

"She's locked the door from the inside," Quaid said.

Jarl took a few steps forward and said, "Shit," and looked down at his feet.

Carlos looked down as well.

The carpet in the hallway was soaked. When Jarl lifted his foot, the sole of his sock was stained faintly crimson. "*Fuck*," he whispered.

Quaid looked at Jarl, then he slammed his shoulder into the door.

Carlos was suddenly unworried about appearances. He joined Quaid, running at the door. The solid wood sent a shivering shock all the way through his body.

On the third try, the door burst open, swinging wide and spilling him down, face first, into a soggy carpet. He took a moment to catch his breath. For a few seconds, the only sound was running water.

Carlos pushed himself up and saw that the water spilling across the carpet was streaked with red. The four of them reached the bathroom almost together. No one said anything.

There was nothing to say.

Water spread across the hexagonal tile, alive with tendrils of red that gathered and intensified in the uneven crevices of the old floor. The water rippled from the edge of the tub, down its white enamel sides, breaking into streams that either dripped from the bottom or rolled across the clawed brass feet—the redness of the water giving the brass more the color of old bronze.

The only part of her that remained above the surface of the water was her face, a white oval that only extended from the point of her chin to her forehead. Everything else was submerged in the cloudy-red water, nearly invisible.

Nothing moved, except the water dripping from the faucet. Susan Polk wasn't going to tell them why she had lied.

Quaid shook his head, went over, and shut off the water.

Eighteenth Move

Olivia was right. Some tests belong to the Devil.

Quaid didn't remember when he first went to the flask at his hip. All he knew was that by the time everyone had gathered in the ballroom, his hand wasn't shaking anymore when he raised it to his lips. The liquid burned down his throat, but that was a well-worn passage and soon all he felt was the warmth. For the first time in a while, the raw, painful edges of his mind were soothed.

It was a relief to feel a little numb. A little easier to bear the chaos that was brewing around him. That's what his drunken mind told him anyway.

Twelve of them left. He thought to himself that it was just enough for a jury. The irony forced him to stifle an inappropriate burst of laughter. He sucked in a breath and snorted through his nose, the scotch stinging his nose, making his eyes tear.

There was no preamble this time, just Tage

stepping onstage, saying, "This time it's Susan Polk." There were gasps from a few people. All Quaid could manage was disgust at him. Even now, the guy was cleaned and pressed, the goatee immaculate. How could the guy look so clean after everything that had happened? Looking at Tage's condescending stare from behind those rectangular glasses, Quaid became certain that it was him and Duce. . . .

"We can't deny, now, that there's a killer in our midst." Tage looked everyone over. "Susan's death might have *looked* like a suicide. But nowhere in the bathroom with her body was the blade that cut her wrists."

Quaid was standing, slightly dizzy. He didn't remember getting out of his seat, but he knew that he was about to lay into Tage with what he knew about Henry, and everything else. But Tage's revelation caught him off guard. Susan's death a murder, too?

Quaid was only half aware of the others staring at him.

Tage strode across the stage. "We've seen the evidence in the rules. Our keepers, listening to us, watching our every move. They even write down our Rules for us. And those who stray from that Rule set, those keepers demand the ultimate penalty of—but how? How do they move among us without us ever seeing them?"

Tage stopped and looked directly at him. "Because there is one of *them* here, in our midst—"

Quaid pushed the chair in front of him aside

and approached the stage. "What are you say-ing, Tage?"

"Someone who's been present at every death. Someone in a position to—"

Quaid charged the stage, "Like hell you say—" Something large and solid blocked him from connecting with Tage. He thought it was Frank. Quaid tried to shout past the obstacle. "Henry knew it was you, didn't he? I bet you know how to use a knife." He couldn't get past Frank, so he hurled the half-empty flask at Tage.

It skidded harmlessly on the stage. And when Quaid heard Erica gasp, he knew, even in his inebriated state, that he had screwed up.

Badly.

Erica stood and stared at the stage, then at him. Quaid felt all the strength leave his body, and suddenly it was Frank keeping him upright. "What are you doing with my father's flask?" she asked him.

As Olivia said, some tests are from the Devil.

Sober, he might have said something coherent in his defense—a pointless observation, since if he'd been sober he never would have pulled such a damn fool stunt. Instead he tried to get his traitorous feet beneath him and said, "You don't understand, he's—" Quaid stopped, be-cause now even he could hear the slur in his speech.

"You were in my room!" Erica said. The color drained from her face when she asked, in a hushed voice, "You were looking for Susan?"

Again, the alcohol did its best to bury him. He spoke without thinking, "Yes, but—"

Quaid never got the chance to say the part after the "but."

People started shouting all at once. He couldn't make sense of any of it. He pushed against Frank, and maybe he said something conciliatory. Frank knew him, right? They were in this from the beginning. Frank was one of "his group."

Frank grabbed him and shoved him roughly into a chair. He got the distinct impression that Frank didn't consider Quaid part of *his* group.

Tage picked up the flask and made a great display of wiping it off with a handkerchief. Then he walked off of the stage, down the aisle, and presented it to Erica. "I apologize for that display."

"Why, you bastard—" Quaid snapped.

"Quiet, Quaid." Frank had forced his hands down on his shoulders. The guy might have been past middle age, but he was powerful and more than a match for Quaid in the state he was in. Quaid had sobered up just barely enough to realize that. Frank kept talking. "You don't want to make this worse than it is."

That he didn't. Though how things could get worse at this point was hard for him to tell. He had managed to make Tage look rational and reasonable by sheer contrast. Quaid could even see a cloud of doubt cross Olivia's face—and she knew as much about what was going on as he did.

Frank had to know that Tage's implications were dead wrong. Frank was with Quaid at the time Oyler was being killed. But Frank was looking at Tage, and Quaid was afraid the expression he wore wasn't one of disbelief.

"We need to protect ourselves," Tage said. "Where he's gone there have been four deaths."

Dr. Yanowitz spoke out in Quaid's defense. "You can't *prove* any of this. You're right. There might be one of our keepers here, in this room right now. But you have no more basis to believe it's Quaid than me—or you." Quaid heard the emphasis on the last syllable.

"No?" Erica replied harshly. She was glaring at him with pure hatred. The flask shook in her hands . . .

"I think we do, Doctor," Tage said. "And I believe that it is in the best interests of our group to vote on dealing with him."

"I won't be a party to mindless vigilantism," Yanowitz insisted.

"No," Tage said. "We're civilized, even if our keepers aren't. I'm simply suggesting a house arrest. For the safety of the rest of us." Somehow, again, Tage had turned things so that his proposal was the sound, reasonable one.

Quaid knew how the vote would go even before Frank started counting. The proxies from the outside team gave Tage and Erica two votes apiece, and it was no surprise where Duce and Jarl Theodore voted.

In the end, the only votes for him were Carlos and Doctor Yanowitz.

Connie could count, so by the time it was her turn to vote, she did so out of fear, and not out of any belief that Quaid was one of *them*. She could see the byplay between Tage and Erica, and she could *feel* how wrong everything was.

Susan's death was just wrong, too wrong. What Rule had she broken? Going alone to her room? Then why enforce their rules by making it look like suicide?

Connie's head was throbbing with the effort of piecing it together. Wheels within boxes within conundrums.

She needed to talk, but when she turned to Beatrice, she saw her face set in the hard mask that said she wasn't going to discuss the situation. She had been like that ever since the word suicide was mentioned, and when the Grand Master Tage said that the keepers had staged the event, practically pointing at Quaid, Connie heard old Sourpuss mutter *"bastard"* under her breath.

Someone here had to tell her—someone who wasn't *them*.

How could you tell? Erica and Tage, she knew, they seemed to feed off of the vibes this Game gave off. But Frank? He was hard and stony. Olivia? Maybe, Connie had seen her with

Susan, but she was on the same team with Tage, Duce, and Jarl. . . .

Carlos? She felt she might trust him, but he was already following Tage, Jarl, and Frank as they dragged an incoherent Quaid away.

Connie looked across the room where the leggy woman with the boobs was sitting near the doctor. *Why not?*

She stood up and started weaving through the chairs toward the pair. She heard Beatrice say, "Connie?"

"I'll be right back—" She almost said *Mom.* She did think it, and strangely enough it wasn't in a sarcastic or condescending way.

Legs was just about to leave the ballroom when Connie caught up with her.

"Wait," Connie said.

The pair turned toward her. "It's Connie, right?" Legs asked. She had the tone about her, the one that said that she knew Connie wasn't normal.

For once, Connie didn't care. "It's not right, is it? What he said. You feel it, too, you know it—"

"What are you talking about?"

"—I saw you with her. This morning. Searching for Henry. She was upset."

Legs looked at the doctor, and he put a protective on her shoulder. "What are you asking?" the doctor said.

"Why would they do it like that? Kill her? It doesn't make any sense, not that anything they do makes sense, really, but it doesn't fit the pattern, does it?" Connie looked at the doctor. "She did kill herself, didn't she?"

The doctor looked back toward the stage, where Tage, Jarl, and Duce were standing. "I can't say for certain—"

"But that's what you think, isn't it. But why? Why was she upset? Why was she talking devils at you? What was she trying to say?"

Legs shook her head. "You heard, obviously. She felt guilty about something, but she wouldn't say what—"

Connie had a growing hunch. "She knew."

"Knew what?" asked the doctor.

Connie turned around and headed back toward Beatrice. "She knew," Connie repeated.

Susan Polk knew that Henry was already dead. She had known it when he turned up missing. *She wasn't killed because she was of us, she killed herself because she was one of* them.

Quaid dreamed that night of a chess match.

Quaid stood on a board that covered an infinity of squares, each square four feet on a side, black and white from horizon to horizon. He was marching forward with his army of pawns toward a black, unseen enemy.

Each move, more of his ranks would fall, headless, to roll off the board. Every step forward, more would die, until he stood alone. Then he realized that something was wrong with the board. It was no longer square. It would change colors and shapes under his feet.

Pieces suddenly could move at random, and an army of blackness that had been safely across the board descended on him.

Quaid could hear someone laughing.

Nineteenth Move

Quaid woke with an aching in his head, and a fiery craving for drink that was as bad as all his prior episodes put together. *Christ,* he thought, *that bastard Tage did me a favor locking me in here.* The way he felt, he knew that if he had his freedom, nothing would have kept him from straying off the wagon permanently. It only took one slip, and last night was one hell of a slip.

For a long time he just lay on the couch that served him as a bed, unmoving, feeling sorry for himself. After about half an hour of that, he opened his eyes for variety.

Quaid stared up at naked rafters arching up over his couch. The rafters were hung with cobwebs and light came from tiny leaded octagonal windows. Quaid's prison was the hotel's attic. There were broken items of furniture, rolled up carpets, tables, chairs, and piles of boxes that fought for floor space.

Quaid felt filthy.

It wasn't just awakening from a drunk—al-

ways good to give yourself serious thoughts
about personal hygiene. No, it was, most of all,
sweat and dust. Sweat, because the attic was old
and unvented and managed to trap the hottest
air of the hotel all through the night, keeping it
probably close to a constant ninety degrees, if
not hotter. The sweat was also the perfect me-
dium to attract the thick layer of dust that
coated everything, including the couch he'd
made his bed.

The dust had become a gray slime that covered just about every part of his body.

Fortunately, the throbbing of the pulse in his
head kept his mind off of how dirty he was.

Quaid didn't really remember much of the debate about where to stash him for his house arrest. He just had this hazy impression of Frank
leading him up a set of stairs to a darkened
room. Then he sort of fumbled around in the
dark until he found an appropriate piece of furniture to collapse upon.

"Lord, would you make a crappy PI," he muttered to the eaves. Talking made him aware that
the dust had even coated his tongue. He tried
to spit it out on the floor and only succeeded in
making himself dizzy.

Slowly, after the vertigo passed, he sat up.

An envelope tumbled down off his chest.

Quaid stared at where it had fallen, a brown,
oblong manila envelope. Very familiar. He
stared at it, wondering who had laid it on his

chest. Did Tage himself come up here? Or did one of their mysterious keepers do it?

Quaid was afraid to bend over and pick it up.

It wasn't a rational fear, but then he wasn't feeling particularly rational at the moment. He was a ludicrous man trapped in a ludicrous situation. Whatever force ran this game, God, Devil, CIA, or UFO—must really think him pretty damn pathetic right about now.

Damn rules delivered right on top of his chest . . .

Duce, he thought, *he must've delivered it.*

After a few long moments he bent down and picked the thing up. There were changes in the list of players. He saw Louis, Henry, and Susan were no longer on the list.

There were also some new rules:

9: **A Player may grant their vote by proxy to another player by giving signed written consent.**
10: **The Player Quaid Loman shall be kept under "House Arrest," isolated from the remaining Players for their own safety. This rule takes precedence over rule number eight.**

There was something darkly amusing about the fact that he was still, somehow, playing this diabolical game by sitting up here. He shook his head at the idea.

11: A guard (or guards) shall be posted to prevent Quaid Loman's escape. These guards shall be on duty for six-hour shifts. This rule takes precedence over rule number eight.

The guard was probably posted outside the door to the stairs. Rule twelve listed the players who were on guard rotation. It was a short list; Tage, Jarl, Frank, Duce. No women—which wasn't much of a surprise, the most capable woman they had left was Olivia, who was probably—despite her vote—too sympathetic to him to be trusted as a guard. He assumed the same was true of Carlos and Doctor Yanowitz.

"Hello? Anyone up there?"

Quaid lowered the sheet of rules and called out, "I haven't escaped yet." He immediately regretted the volume of his voice.

Quaid heard the sound of footsteps coming up the stairs. He smelled something that tied his stomach in a fist of nauseated agony.

Ham and eggs.

"How're you doing up here?" asked Iris Traxler. She stood, holding a tray of breakfast.

Quaid rubbed his forehead and tried not to think about the food. "How do you think I'm doing?"

"I brought you breakfast . . ."

Quaid nodded without looking up. He waved over at some of the larger boxes. "Set it over there. I'll eat later."

She walked over in the general direction he'd indicated. "Do you need anything else?"

Quaid drew his hand over his face. He could feel the grooves his fingers left in the coating of dust and sweat on his skin. He looked at Iris. She wore a T-shirt and a pair of tight denim shorts. The ensemble left little to the imagination. "Why are you here?" he asked.

"Someone has to bring you food, Mr. Loman."

"You think I killed Henry? Oyler?" He stopped and looked down at the rules that he still held in his hand. "Susan?"

"I don't know."

Quaid laughed. It turned into a hacking cough that made him dizzy. *"You don't know?"* The rules crumpled in his hand as his body shook with the coughing laugh. "You weren't so uncertain when it came to voting me up here."

"Have you thought about how that happened, Quaid?" Iris said. *"That* was decided when you attacked Tage." She folded her arms and shook her head. "Anyone who could count would've seen it coming."

"But you voted—"

"With the majority, Quaid." She came over to him. "I don't make waves. I'm sorry."

"Great," he whispered. "Nice to know I have your support."

"Get over it," Iris said. Her voice was suddenly very hard. He looked up at her and she was frowning at him. "Let me clue you in to

some reality here. Four people are dead, Quaid.
Has that filtered in through that self-pity of
yours? *Dead*, Quaid."

"You don't think I know that?" He stood, almost toppling from weak knees and vertigo. "I
saw their bodies. I fished Oyler out of the fucking ocean. I nearly drowned—"

"And you don't get it. *Still*. You're feeling
sorry for yourself because someone locked you
in the attic? You have no right, especially after
what you did to put yourself here."

"Me? What did I do to deserve—" He could
feel the slow rusty gears of rationalization moving already. It was easy, like riding a bicycle.
All you had to do was hang on to that single
golden thread—believe with all your heart that,
whatever happened, it was not your fault. It was
everyone else, they misunderstood, or were ac-
tively against you. If they really cared, they
would listen to your explanation. How it was
that you didn't really do what they thought you
did. That you didn't say what they thought
you said.

It was so easy, so familiar, that he surprised
himself when he stopped in mid-sentence. At
the height of his alcoholism he could wallow in
that kind of lie and actually believe it himself.
He didn't have that kind of sincerity anymore.
He wanted to believe what he was about to
say—he really wanted the comfort of that kind
of self-delusion.

Quaid couldn't do it sober.

Quaid was filthy, and hungover, and he was gagging on his own bullshit. He was left, shaking with anger that had no focus but himself.

"Damn it," he said, and turned away. "Just get out of here, will you?"

"What gives you the right to be sorry for yourself?"

"You don't think I know how badly I screwed up?" he said. "Christ, you have no idea how badly I screwed up."

Iris sighed. "No, I suppose I don't."

Quaid hugged himself. "Why *are* you here?"

"Because someone has to bring you food, and no one's going to trust your friends up here."

Quaid turned around. "Friends?"

"Abe and Mr. DeVay. They supported you in that vote, remember? However pointless it was." She looked him up and down. "I'm going to bring you a bucket of water and a washcloth. Some fresh clothes, too."

"Uh-huh." He looked at her and realized how slimy his teeth felt. "This would be easier if they just kept me in a hotel room. There's no shortage of them."

"You were out of it last night, weren't you?" She shook her head. "You don't remember any of the debate? They're afraid you'll dive out the window or something."

"I guess so." He sighed. "Then you better bring me a toothbrush, and another bucket."

"Another bucket?" She looked around and after a moment said, "Oh."

Now that he was standing, he was starting to feel the pressure of his bladder. "If you could bring it quickly . . ."

"Sure," she said, and vanished down the stairs.

It was astounding how quickly things could go to shit. Carlos had never thought of himself as particularly naïve. He'd lived inside the Detroit city limits long enough. He should be a fairly streetwise individual. He had no grand illusions about people's good intentions, he knew that self-interest was a pretty universal yardstick.

But when the shit hit the fan with Quaid, he'd been completely blindsided. As recently as twenty-four hours ago, Carlos had seen them all as being in the same boat. Sure there were these votes and this Game, but everyone's goal was pretty much the same, they were all on the same side.

It had just been dawning on him that there might be more than one side when the vote on Quaid made it clear that Carlos was on the losing one.

"*Christ,*" he muttered over breakfast. "*The poor bastard probably does deserve it.*" Getting drunk on an old lady's stolen liquor wasn't top in Carlos' list of classy moves. He stirred his spoon in uneaten oatmeal and looked across at his new "buddy," Frank Pisarski. The bald bull of a man didn't acknowledge Carlos' comment.

He was tempted to yell at Frank, "But he didn't kill Oyler, and you damn well know he didn't!" He refrained. He had already gone that route last night. He and Frank had gotten into a shouting match—

More accurately, Carlos had shouted at Frank for nearly an hour.

Frank had been irritatingly civil. They had set up a means to deal with this shit, why didn't Carlos use it? Hell, why not, after it had worked so well prosecuting Quaid.

Frank had remained unmoved. Quaid's display seemed to have impressed him almost as much as it had impressed Erica Urquort.

Carlos had spent the evening contemplating bringing up the whole sordid mess up in front of everyone, killer or no killer. Problem was, he saw the political fault lines now. He had one vote, and that was pretty much it. His vote against Quaid's imprisonment had cost him whatever pull he might have had with the people who were left.

He looked up and saw Dr. Yanowitz walking into the kitchen. Carlos dropped his spoon and followed him. Frank started to get up, but Carlos waved him back, shaking his head.

The doctor was the only one in the kitchen. Carlos caught up with him as he was putting his hand on the door of the large walk-in refrigerator. Carlos could see his own reflection in the chromed surface as he walked up behind him.

"So, what do we do, Doc?"

Yanowitz tuned around and shook his head. "Can we *do* anything?"

"You're telling me we just let them lock Quaid up?"

Yanowitz rubbed his temple and sighed. "You know, that may be the safest course for all of us."

"I don't believe this . . ."

"Think a moment," he said. "Henry was nosing around about Oyler; he was killed out of panic. With Quaid locked up as a scapegoat, there's a chance our killer won't be prompted to kill again. We can wait it all out until real authorities come here with a real investigation. Quaid's in no danger, and if the killer feels safe, the rest of us may be safer."

Carlos stared at the man and narrowed his eyes. "Do you actually believe that line of bull you just fed me?"

Yanowitz opened the refrigerator door. The sound of a compressor hum filled the kitchen, and a harsh white light spilled out from the open door. In the rear of the refrigerator were four oblong shapes made of black trash bags and duct tape, they averaged about five and a half feet long.

More trash bags sat along the right wall, the one opposite the shelves that held most of the food.

Carlos stepped in after Yanowitz, trying not to think about the contents of the trash bags. "I asked you a question."

Yanowitz nodded. His voice was a whisper. "We're in a dangerous game here. And I don't refer to that set of rules we keep voting on."

"Damn straight we are—"

"If we misstep, it isn't just our own lives at stake." Yanowitz opened one of the smaller trash bags that sat by the wall. "We're dealing with someone who has shown no reluctance to kill anyone who threatens him . . ."

"Or her."

"Him," Yanowitz repeated.

Carlos nodded. There wasn't much doubt where Henry's suspicions had been leading him. Quaid had practically called it down from the stage. "Okay, him."

"Murder," Yanowitz said. "But only indirectly."

"Huh?"

"Susan Polk," Yanowitz said, still rummaging. "She slit her own wrists. It's obvious, the hesitation marks, no defensive wounds, she got in the tub fully clothed . . ."

"What about the—"

"The weapon? They took it before I got there. That and the suicide note."

"How do you know there was a note?"

Yanowitz tapped his breast pocket. "Ink stains. She had it in her pocket. They could take the note, but the note bled enough to leave a mark."

"Why would someone want to—"

"Frame Quaid?" Yanowitz finally seemed to

find what he was looking for. He pulled out a Ziplock baggie with a folded sheet of paper in it, it looked like a receipt for something. "I suspect that she killed herself because she felt responsible for Henry's murder. That's why I think she lied about seeing him where she said she did."

"Why?"

"I think she told Henry's killer about his visit to Mrs. Grossmann, and his suspicions. Maybe she saw him as a leader, or maybe there was a deeper relationship. She had been fully seduced and only realized her mistake too late."

"Uh-huh, and the note would have said as much, you think?"

Yanowitz nodded.

"So what've you got there?"

He showed Carlos a water-stained boarding pass for a Delta flight from New York City to New Orleans, one way, coach. "Does the name 'Steven Coombs' mean anything to you?"

It took Quaid about two hours to feel completely human again. It involved the toothbrush, both buckets, a fresh change of clothes, and the breakfast that Iris had brought up—after his stomach could stand him looking at it.

After that, his options about what to do seemed fairly limited. He contemplated escape, which amusingly didn't seem to be against the rules. The question remained, if he managed that, then what? Where would he escape to?

Quaid's only real hope was that A. J. and company would find help, and then whatever authorities had jurisdiction over this place would step in and make a real investigation of all the deaths here.

During the day the attic got hotter and hotter. He tried to open some of the tiny windows for ventilation, but they were nailed shut.

There was a slight draft from the stairway. He decided to make the most of it. He edged down the narrow staircase until he was sitting just on the opposite side of the door.

It wasn't much, but it was a little cooler here.

Quaid sat there for about fifteen minutes. Long enough to hear the guard outside whistle tunelessly.

Well, no one said he couldn't talk to the guy. "Hey?" he asked. "Who's out there?"

"What you care?" A sarcastic voice came back. Duce.

"Just curious." After a few minutes he added. "Six-hour shift. That's a long time."

He made a disgusted noise. "Fuck you, too. I get to go home after it."

"None of us are home, Duce. Haven't you noticed?"

Another disgusted noise, and he heard chair legs scraping.

"You know," Quaid said. "I wouldn't tell anyone if you left."

"Yeah, right. You'd like me to end up breaking the Rules. Make your day, wouldn't it?"

Interesting. When it came down to it, Duce was *not* the epitome of the law-abiding citizen. Quaid didn't see him giving much credence to authority of any stripe. Of all of them, Duce should be the least interested in following a set of arbitrary Rules.

Why was he one of the ones most supportive of this Game?

"Hey," Quaid said. "What's that matter? You got me locked up. The 'keeper's' enforcement agent. No one has to follow these Rules anymore, right?"

"You'd like me to believe that, wouldn't you?" Duce said. "You'd like it if I wasn't around to win this Game. Fuck you. I'm looking out for number one here."

"What's to win, Duce?"

Duce laughed. "Don't give me that crap. You know. You *all* know."

Quaid had a feeling of dissonance that he got when talking to someone whose worldview differed fundamentally from his own. Someone whose unvoiced assumptions were at odds with his. He got the feeling that Duce was, at least partly, in a completely different reality.

Quaid looked up. He could see a narrow slice of the rafters above the stairwell, cut by a few beams of sunlight from unseen windows. Plaster wrapped the walls halfway up before they gave way to naked lathe.

Outside that door, Duce sat, or stood, on an

Oriental-patterned carpet in a hallway of garish wallpaper and dark wood moldings.

It was like talking from one world to the next.

"What do you think the Game is, Duce? Why do you think you're here?"

"That supposed to be some trick question? I'm here to play the Game. I'm here to win."

"The last person not to forfeit?"

Duce chuckled. "Whatever the Rules say at the time."

"Then why'd you vote against my proposal? Everyone would've won."

"Neat idea, but you think I wanted to share with eighteen people? Come on."

Quaid wondered how much of this Duce actually knew, and how much he had invented, or had had invented for him.

"Alphomeg," he said, mostly just to hear the kid's reaction.

There was a long silence before Duce said, "Where did you hear that name?"

That was a better reaction than he had expected. "Where do you think?"

"Christ almighty, you *are* working for them."

The pulse was throbbing in Quaid's temple, and his throat was dry. There was a very delicate balance. He couldn't fumble. He needed subtlety even if it wasn't his forte.

"I was under the impression," Quaid said quietly, "that was what you believed, Duce. That and the fact that 'we' were responsible for—how many deaths, was it?"

"Fuck, fuck, fuck." Duce sounded agitated now. "No, you ain't going to fuck with me like that. I followed the Rules, right? I'm due, corpses or no fucking corpses."

"What about Mr. Oyler, Mr. Sukomi—"

"*Fuck*, the way you got this place wired, you know I didn't kill anyone."

"And you know I didn't."

"Look, that's—" There was a pause. "Fuck, man. You think I'm *stupid*?" Something slammed into the door. He heard splintering wood, and the door shook violently. It must have been the chair.

Quaid backed away from the door.

"I know what you're trying to do, Quaid. It ain't working!" The door vibrated again. "You ain't fucking this up."

So much for subtlety.

"You ain't one of them." Slam.

"Why are you doing this, Duce?" Quaid asked. "What do you think you'll win?"

"You shut the fuck up." Slam.

"Alphomeg. That's who set this up."

Slam.

"Why, Duce?"

Slam.

"Is it Tage?"

Silence.

"Did Tage tell you about Alphomeg?"

Nothing. Duce had stopped attacking the door, and now he heard nothing, except what might have been Duce's ragged breathing.

"Did Tage—"

"Stop talking and go upstairs," he said.

"I deserve an answer from you." Quaid said. "You *know* I didn't kill anyone."

Nothing.

"You know!" Quaid pounded on the door. No answer.

Quaid tried a few more times to get a rise out of Duce, but he wouldn't react, even when he accused him directly of killing Oyler, Henry, and Susan. . . .

Eventually, he retreated back up the stairs.

Twentieth Move

The library was extensive, if somewhat limited in subject matter. Carlos hadn't paid attention to the books the few times he'd been here, he'd been thinking about more important matters. Now he stood behind Yanowitz as the doctor ran his finger along the spines arrayed on the bookshelves.

Carlos looked at the reading material their keepers provided. Books on game theory, go, chess, military strategy, legal theory . . . *Christ, great supply to play this damn Game, if corpses didn't keep turning up.*

Yanowitz seized on something near the bottom shelf. He drew out a thick hardback with a white dust jacket. The cover showed a hand of playing cards, and the title read *Busted Flush*. Beneath that Carlos could read, "The Mafia, the Gaming Industry, and Atlantic City."

"I knew I saw this somewhere," Yanowitz said, handing Carlos the book.

"What?" Carlos said, taking the book. It fit the gaming/strategy theme that permeated the library, but otherwise he couldn't see the relevance to their situation. "You think the Mob set up this game?"

"Look."

Carlos looked. The doctor's point was so blatant that it hit him like a sledge when he finally saw it.

"*Holy shit.*" Carlos' voice was little more than a hoarse croak.

The author of *Busted Flush* was a Mr. Steven Coombs.

Carlos looked up from the book. "Can't be the same guy, can it?"

"Look at the back cover."

Carlos flipped it over. At first he couldn't see it. Older man, full beard, lighter hair. But after staring a while he could picture him cleanshaven, with a dye job. It could be Oyler. "What's going on here?"

He opened the back flap and read, "About the Author: Steven Coombs is a Pulitzer prize winning journalist whose work has appeared in *The New York Times*, *Newsweek*, *Rolling Stone*, *Playboy*, and *The Village Voice*. He has investigated the gaming industry and organized crime for the past fifteen years . . ." Carlos flipped through the book.

"The name on the boarding pass has bothered me," Yanowitz explained.

Carlos shook his head. "This guy was a reporter."

"I suspected something like that."

Carlos kept flipping through the book. "Have you looked through this? This guy posed as a dealer, a limo driver—John Gotti tipped him a C-note."

Yanowitz nodded. "I hunted that up this morning. I saw it about the time Henry dragged me out of here, and I didn't have a chance to stop and think about it until now."

Carlos shook his head. "You think they know?" Carlos and the doctor understood who "they" meant. It wasn't their keepers.

"That Oyler was Coombs? I think that might be what got him killed."

When Iris came up with lunch, Quaid asked her, "What does 'Alphomeg' mean to you?"

"Where did that come from?" she asked as she set the tray down. She glanced in the direction of the two buckets and wrinkled her nose.

"It means something."

"Is that what you baited Duce with?" She stood up and looked at him. "And don't look shocked. Do you think anyone in the building missed that little episode between you and that kid?"

"He's old enough to be responsible."

"Yeah, and you didn't answer my question."

"He thinks Alphomeg Entertainment is behind this Game of ours."

Iris nodded. "And you think?"

"A lot of people here seem to have at least a subliminal connection to them—" Quaid gave her his current rundown, from the business card, to his own uneasy feelings about it, to Connie's doodles.

"The name is familiar . . . Don't you remember, I told you I saw it in the want ads. But whatever it is, it's part of my memory that's clouded over."

"Does it trigger any kind of memory? An image? Anything?"

Iris closed her eyes in thought for a few long moments. "More than before. I think I see an office. And a logo, like you described. A man handing me a piece of paper, to sign it maybe—" She shook her head and opened her eyes. "I'm sorry, it's just a flash, I don't even know if it's a real memory."

"Ask Dr. Yanowitz about it for me, would you?"

"Okay." She turned to go.

"Wait—"

"Yes?"

"I just want to tell you that I'm sorry about this morning." He felt the urge to say more, try and explain himself. But a rationalization wasn't going to be any better than a flat apology. "That's it," he said.

"Accepted," she said. She went down the stairs without looking back.

The door slammed, and he was alone again.

Carlos sat next to Doctor Yanowitz at the next meeting. They were an exiled group of two, just this side of pariahs. Most of the others refused to sit next to them, and the only ones who'd deign to talk to them were Iris and Olivia Grossmann.

He and the doctor still hadn't come up with any reasonable way to make their case. They certainly had a few points in their favor, and even a small bit of physical evidence. But when it came down to it, they were a distinct minority, and it was hard to see how they'd convince the others of their theory.

Frankly, it was easy to see that Oyler being an undercover reporter might actually give *more* credence to the idea that their "keepers" had done him in. And after Quaid's display, Carlos thought that accusing Tage directly might be a dangerous thing to do.

Yanowitz was right, at least, about being cagey and not spooking the villain into doing something everyone would regret.

Even so, the debate this time just about washed all thoughts of subtlety from Carlos' mind.

"I think," Jarl said, "we need to do something about these damn votes."

"Like what?" Frank asked from up by the stage, his station as half vote-counter, half security guard.

"We need someone to run this crap. We can't keep having a debate on every single shitty thing. We're spending more time in this room talking than we're spending trying to get ourselves out of this mess."

"You have a proposal?" Frank asked.

"Hell, yes," Jarl said, hooking his thumbs in the loops of his jeans. "I say we need to elect a leader."

Carlos felt his stomach sink a few notches, especially when he saw nods of approval from Mrs. Greenhart and Erica Urquort.

"We can vote on changing the damn rules, but who looks for what where—stupid crap like that, just have one of us make those decisions. Save a shitload of time."

"Who did you have in mind?" Carlos heard Dr. Yanowitz ask from behind him.

When Carlos heard the nominee, he stood up and called out, *"Are you people nuts?"*

When Iris brought Quaid's dinner, the sky was beginning to darken.

Quaid had just come to the decision that either everyone had forgotten him, or they had voted that he had been given enough food for one day already.

Quaid was lying on the couch staring into the fading light. There weren't any light fixtures up here, the only light came from the windows, so when the sun set, there wasn't much left to do but stare into the growing shadows.

Quaid smelled dinner before Iris reached the top of the stairs. Unlike this morning, he was ravenous. He stood up, walked over, and freed the tray from her hands before she had cleared the top step.

She watched him grab the tray and said, "You're welcome."

"It's a little past dinnertime," Quaid said.

"We had a long meeting tonight—"

"I bet you did." He shook his head. "What did they vote on now?"

"On Tage."

"Oh?" he said between mouthfuls. "Locking him up as well?"

Iris shook her head. "No."

"What then?"

"Jarl said things were too chaotic, someone needed to lead these meetings—"

"Tell me they didn't."

Iris shrugged.

"They elected Tage?" He almost spit up the food he was eating. "Don't they—don't you realize that he—"

"It was a lock, Quaid." She shook her head. "With Erica behind him with her extra proxy, Tage has the votes to do anything he wants."

"Votes? Iris, this is just a game, an arbitrary set of rules—it's nothing."

"Is it?" She shook her head. "We'd be in the same place if there was no 'game.' These people are in a life-and-death situation." The room was silent for a long time. Iris finally added, "I asked Abe your question."

"What did he say?"

"He has nightmares. Bad ones."

"About Alphomeg?"

"He isn't sure." Iris sat down on the couch

next to him. "He says that he dreams of a demon coming to him with a game."

"Alphomeg reminds him of this?"

"He thinks it's the demon's name. Anyway, the demon brings a game. Sometimes it's cards, or dice, or chess. The stakes are always the same. If he loses, the demon takes his life. If he wins, the demon takes the life of a dozen strangers."

"What if he doesn't play?"

"He says, in the dream, he doesn't ever have that choice. The demon already has his soul."

"Does he win or lose?" Quaid asked.

"It never gets—" Iris stood up. "What's that?"

The outline of one of the small windows, the one facing the mountain, was suddenly carved out of the rafters in crimson red. The image slowly traveled up the timbers, giving a rose cast to the room. As they watched, it was joined by another outline, brighter and lower.

Quaid stood up and made it to the window behind Iris.

Outside, drifting over the forest between the hotel and the mountain, was a pair of red flares.

Team D was in trouble.

"Where are they?" Quaid groaned. He could pretty much guess the answer, even looking through the tiny window. The flares had gone up near the side of the mountain, about where the lights had been the night that Louis had collapsed.

"I better go," Iris said.

"Wait . . ." He turned after her, but she was already going down the stairs.

Quaid looked back out over the forest. The flares were descending slowly toward the tree line. What kind of mess was happening out there?

Quaid lay on his couch, trying unsuccessfully to get some sleep. He couldn't help thinking of A. J., Gordon, Eve, and Bobbie. In retrospect, with what Iris had said about Tage electing himself leader, he wondered if the selection of those four people had a darker purpose to it. He didn't know about Gordon at all, but Eve didn't strike him as someone who'd allow that sort of thing. Even if A. J. gave Tage his proxy, would he have handed the reins over to him? He seemed too much the leader himself.

Quaid had no proof, but he knew it was Tage behind the killings. It all fit together too well. The way Oyler's death made everyone paranoid about their keepers and serious about the Game at the same time. That was the way Tage seemed to want things.

Tage wanted the Game to be serious, and he wanted to control it.

Duce had acted as his lieutenant all along. Duce even passed out the mysteriously appearing rules.

Henry had gotten too close to what was happening, and somehow Tage got wind of it. How?

Quaid began to think about Tage, and it began sinking in that he had been quietly amassing allies since this game began. Duce and Jarl Theodore were solidly in his camp. Quaid's drunken tirade had managed to push Erica toward him, if she needed a push.

What if one of those people had been Susan? She was in a position to hear what was going on between Henry and Olivia. And if Henry had known her loyalties, then with the way his own suspicions were drifting, of course he'd panic and run when he saw her.

Why slit her wrists, then?

Maybe it *was* suicide?

Quaid came up with an ugly scenario.

She's in with Tage, but doesn't know that he's responsible for Oyler. Only Duce knows at this point—he had to alibi for Tage when he slipped down to the boathouse to finish off Oyler. Susan tells Tage about what Henry suspects, maybe even accuses him.

Tage reassures her, tells her Henry is nuts. Easy enough to believe, the way Henry was acting.

Then, that night, Henry's throat ends up cut.

Susan doesn't *know* yet, but when Henry turns up missing, she suspects. She can't bring herself to say exactly what happened, she's too frightened of Tage. So she comes up with the story about seeing him out Erica's window—the direction she believes Henry went.

When Henry turned up dead, Quaid thought one of two things must have happened.

Possibility one, Susan confronts Tage, and he finishes her off.

Possibility two, she couldn't accept her own unknowing complicity in Henry's death and slits her own wrists. It would have been easy enough for Duce to have removed evidence from the scene to make it look like murder.

To Quaid, it didn't matter which it was. Tage was responsible for her death, either way.

It still didn't answer the big question.

Why kill Oyler in the first place?

Twenty-first Move

Quaid woke up without realizing that he had nodded off.

The attic around him was a web of ink-black shadows pierced only in a few places by moonlight from the windows. He lay there, eyes open, wide awake, unsure of what had awakened him. Fear was an ice-cold wire wrapping his chest, and he hadn't been awake long enough to realize what was frightening him.

The door.

It was opening slowly, almost silently. But the old oak door was too old and too warped to open without making some sound, however slowly it moved.

Quaid had been half-expecting this all along. It was his turn to receive the knife to the throat.

The door stopped opening, and he heard the first soft tread on the steps up to the attic.

Well, at least the bastard wouldn't take him completely by surprise, like Henry and Oyler. He was going to have a fight. Quaid held his breath, afraid his breathing might betray him, and rolled off the couch on to his stocking feet. He felt huge and clumsy, afraid every move he made might alert his attacker.

Quaid grabbed for the one weapon in reach, the fork from his dinner tray. He didn't have much of a choice. He didn't even have a butter knife, his keepers had seen to that.

Quaid inched around the opening of the staircase. He crouched under the eaves, so that when the guy emerged, he would be facing away from him.

Now Quaid had to figure out what he was going to do when this guy reached the top step. He didn't know the first thing about fighting, and if this was Tage, he had—according to him—special forces training that would probably best any fork-armed civilian in hand-to-hand combat.

Christ, he was in deep shit.

Quaid felt dizzy and finally allowed himself to breathe.

Quaid's only chance was to incapacitate Tage before he had a chance to react. Quaid's thoughts over the next thirty seconds were incredibly vicious. He considered a blow to the base of the skull, but he doubted that a fork could manage a disabling amount of damage there. Tearing into the throat, ripping the carotid or the jugular, that would be disabling, but he was afraid that it wouldn't be nearly immediate enough.

Quaid began regretting his impulsive choice

of a weapon. Something blunt and heavy would have been much better. But he was committed now. Tage was halfway up the stairs, and there was nothing immediately around him that would serve better as a weapon.

A few more cautious steps up the stairway.

The eyes, Quaid concluded. That would be the one vulnerable area he was sure he could get to. Even if he didn't completely disable Tage, if he was partially blind, that would give Quaid at least some chance of getting back down the stairs and away—

Quaid's throat went dry when he thought of the guard down there. It would have to be one of Tage's men, Duce or Jarl. He prayed it was Duce; he thought he'd have a chance of bowling past the kid if he had to. Jarl was bigger, and probably more competent in a fight. At least he looked like he would be.

Quaid's speculation ended when a man-sized shadow stepped out onto the floor in front of him. It turned toward the couch and raised a hand.

This was it.

Quaid sprang.

In his imagination his attack had been a lithe jump from his hiding place, landing on Tage's back. Quaid was going to tear into him before he realized what was happening.

In real life, Quaid's attack was slow, clumsy, and his victim had a chance to hear a commotion and turn in his direction before Quaid was

266 *Steven Krane*

on him. Instead of an unobstructed blow to the back, taking him down, Quaid tackled into his shoulder, an arm already rising to block Quaid's blow to his face.

They both tumbled to the ground. As they fell, Quaid half-turned so that his side took most of the impact from the fall, knocking the wind out of him. The fork went sailing into the darkness. He heard it clatter into the eaves.

Quaid's victim rolled on top of him, pinning his arms. Quaid had the first unobstructed view of his face.

"*Carlos?*"

"Nice to see you, too," Carlos whispered harshly. "Keep your voice down. What the hell did you think you were doing?"

"I thought you were Tage."

"Yeah, lucky for you it was me." Carlos slowly got up off of him. Then he reached a hand out and helped Quaid up. Carlos looked down at Quaid's feet. "Get some shoes on."

From Carlos' perspective, once these idiots elected Tage glorious leader, everything that followed was inevitable. He could barely work up a significant level of shock when Tage explained, in very precise, reasonable terms, that they weren't going to send anyone out after A. J. and the rest of Team D.

Carlos watched as the will of the people went along with Tage.

Dr. Yanowitz had protested strongly, insisting

that a rescue party be assembled. Tage informed him that they wouldn't risk any more lives. When the doctor insisted that he'd go himself if no one else did, Tage informed him that he was too valuable to spare.

"Just in case we need another autopsy?" The doctor's words had dripped with acid, and Carlos had watched as his only ally was placed under house arrest. For his own protection, of course.

Tage hadn't called it that. He'd just made the reasonable suggestion that the doctor go to his room and get some rest. It was the implicit threat of Tage, Jarl, and even Frank, watching Yanowitz that had made it more than a suggestion.

Later on, Carlos walked up to the doctor's room with Iris. Jarl had been sitting in the hallway, in sight of the door. Carlos had ignored him. He'd gone in and had a whispered conversation with the doctor about what he planned to do.

Once Quaid got his shoes on, Carlos practically dragged him toward the stairs. "What are we doing?" he asked as he pushed him ahead, down the stairs.

"Shhh," Carlos told him, and kept pushing.

The door at the bottom was open wide. And when Quaid stepped across the threshold, he saw the slumped form of Frank Pisarski, lying in the corner next to the door. The lights in the hallway were dim, but he could see several trickles of blood running down his scalp.

Quaid bent over to see if he was all right.

Carlos grabbed him. "We don't have time for that—"

"Hey, wait, it's Frank." *One of their group.*

"I don't care if he's the King of Denmark," Carlos whispered harshly. "He's thrown in with this insanity."

"He's bleeding—"

"A knock on the head," Carlos said. "Move."

Quaid didn't feel as if he had a choice. Now that he was a fugitive from whatever authority Tage represented, Quaid suspected that he would be subject to a punishment a little more severe the next time around.

Quaid followed Carlos through the darkened corridors, wondering if he was really better off with Carlos "rescuing" him.

The hallways took on a twisted, sinister cast in the darkness. There was only the occasional light to lead their way, and behind every corner was the fear that someone would see them.

It looked, however, like Carlos had picked the right time for the jailbreak. They didn't see a single soul.

Carlos wouldn't say a word until they reached the greenhouse. They stopped there for a few moments while he pulled some debris from out of a corner of the central atrium. Quaid sat on the old cast-iron chair that Dr. Yanowitz had sat in when he told them about Henry.

"What's going on?" Quaid asked him.

From the pile of debris, Carlos pulled out a backpack and tossed it by his feet. He had swiped them from a stockpile that Yanowitz had been building.

"You know what that bastard did?" Carlos said.

"Tage?"

"Yes, Tage."

"Iris told me about it when she brought me dinner—"

"No, after that."

Quaid shook his head.

"He's got a lock on this so-called democracy," Carlos said. "I think there's only one or two people who can distinguish our so-called decision-making from the damn Game." He pulled another backpack out of the hole. "You saw the flares."

Quaid nodded.

"You know what he's going to do about it?"

"I don't—"

"*Nothing.*" Carlos shouldered his pack. "Let's get moving, grab that." He indicated the pack at Quaid's feet.

Quaid grabbed it and slipped it over his shoulder. "What do you mean, nothing?"

"Just like it sounds. The four we sent out to get help are in some sort of trouble—no rescue party."

"I can't believe it."

"Believe it." Carlos started out the end of the greenhouse opposite the hotel. The sky above them was lightening with the dawn.

Quaid followed. "I can't believe people went along with that."

Carlos snorted. "Half of them are panicked. Erica won't do anything that someone convinces her is against the will of the keepers. Jarl and Duce do pretty much what Tage tells them to. Connie's a fruitcake, but she follows Beatrice's lead— And Frank, the poor bastard, decided that he had to support Tage as our 'elected leader.' Iris—"

"Won't make waves," Quaid said.

"Someone's got to go out after them," Carlos said. "I don't give a shit about Tage and the fucking Game."

Carlos led him through the underbrush now where there was no real path. There were no clues to what direction they were moving in, the light of the dawn was, at the moment, directionless. Carlos had to take it all on faith that this was the direction that Team D had followed.

When they stopped talking, the only sounds were of their feet dragging through the underbrush, their breathing, and the sound of insects in the greenery around them.

"Do you know where we are going?" Quaid asked.

"Northeast, near the base of the mountain."
I hope.

"Carlos, do you realize how far that is? It's got to be at least a couple days' hike from here."

"We sent those people out with a promise, Quaid. No one said it, but we knew that if they got in trouble, someone would help them." He turned toward him and said, " 'Someone's' us, Quaid."

"Did you tell anyone else about this?"

"Dr. Yanowitz."

"Why just us?"

Carlos hung his head and told him about the doctor's confinement. Then he added, "This shit *is* dangerous." He looked across at him. "I figured you're already on his hit list. I didn't want to risk more people than I had to."

"Thanks."

"Does it help to say that you're the one guy I think I can trust in all this?"

They went along for a few more minutes before Quaid asked him, "Why do you think this is happening? Why this game?"

"I try not to think about it, Quaid." He looked up at the sky as if an answer was in the treetops. "I try not to think about it."

Twenty-second Move

Connie did not believe that they had escaped. She knew that they had *taken* Quaid and Carlos.

And she knew why.

The purpose of the game had been slow to dawn on her. At first she had been sure it was a prison for the folks that didn't fit their mold. A repository for square pegs. But that didn't make sense with the brutally aggressive normalcy of some of the people here. There were too many suburban minivan types, cubicle workers . . .

A test, then, like a social worker's questions. What would they be testing for, though? With the social workers, the psychiatrists, the cops, the doctors . . . their games had a purpose. They wanted to find out how far across their boundaries you'd strayed. Evaluate you for their own specially tailored confinement . . .

This game was different. They were already imprisoned, and the losers were killed off.

Connie didn't realize the purpose until she understood that Susan Polk had become one of *them.* That was it. *They* had created this game for the express purpose of creating more of *them.* The secret masters, the ones who controlled everything, the ones who decided that Connie wasn't normal—those people had to come from somewhere. Their attitude bred. Their thoughts molded.

How better than to take a group of people and place them here. *They* hadn't killed anyone; all *they* had done was give their prisoners the chance to become *them.*

Tage was right; their keepers walked among them, and always had.

Connie spent the whole day after Quaid's and Carlos' disappearance, watching the people who were left, deciding who *they* were.

Erica, Duce, Jarl, Tage—Connie knew that they had all become *them.* She saw it in the afternoon meeting, the way they grouped together now, the way Tage gave the orders, the way the others nodded and were perfectly reasonable. They didn't question, didn't break the mold.

This was it, came Connie's realization, *this is how they define the normal.* Those four had become a knot of power that no one else seemed capable of breaking. The doctor spoke out, and now he was a virtual prisoner. Iris Traxler—Legs—and Beatrice seemed too dumbfounded to do much of anything but go along. Connie knew how they felt. She had been too scared herself—with all *their* eyes on her—to act against what the group was doing.

Frank, Connie didn't know, but he seemed to be loyal—if not to Tage—to the system they had in place.

Connie might have imagined it, but she thought that, under his bandaged and bloody head, she saw some glances of skepticism toward the quartet that had taken over.

That left Olivia Grossman. She had dissented, fruitlessly, over the decision not to go after Team D. Connie had been afraid of her because she'd been on the same team as Tage, but with so many people dead or missing, the teams didn't seem as important anymore.

More important, she was sitting by herself—watching the quartet with eyes narrowed behind thick-framed glasses.

"Where are we going?" Beatrice asked. Her voice sounded small and somewhat frightened.

"We're going to make friends," Connie said. "We need to talk to people. Networking, the kind of thing the good old boys do. You don't want to have to face all this crap alone now, do you?"

"If you think so . . ."

There was something about Beatrice that Connie had found out rather quickly. Her exterior was hard and willful as iron, but the moment someone stepped inside that shell, she was as soft and pliable as silly putty.

They found Iris and Olivia together in the library. Connie had known that these two would be together from simple elimination. Rule eight was helpful that way. The doctor was under Duce's guard, everyone else was down by the bar.

"Mind if we join you?" Connie asked the pair. She walked in and took a chair without waiting for a response.

"Hello again," Iris said.

"Please don't give me the 'she's nuts' look. It's getting kind of old." Connie stood up and held out a hand to Olivia. "We've not been in-troduced—really—funny how we've been here six days and there're still people who've haven't been introduced face-to-face. You're from Washington, right?"

Olivia nodded. She looked as if she hadn't had any sleep. She glanced over Connie's shoulder. "I'm Mrs. Thomas Greenhart," Beatrice said. "I don't really know why I'm here—"

"Come on, Sourpuss," Connie said. "You're here because you're my friend, and I wouldn't think of going off and doing this sort of thing without you. Have a seat, we might be here a while."

Iris was still giving her the "crazy woman" look, but Connie ignored it. "Now," Connie clapped her hands together. "Let me guess. You're both comparing notes on what happened to Susan Polk, and you've come to the conclusion that Tage is full of shit."

It was hard to tell if the looks they gave her

were variants on the "crazy woman" look, or simply expressions of surprise.

"Well, ladies," Connie proclaimed. "I'm here to tell you that if we don't get our act together, *they* are going to steamroller over us."

The meeting of Connie's quartet lasted most of the night.

The calculus of the rescue effort was frustrating. Team D, hiking through dense jungle, had gotten three days of daylight travel in, before they sent up the flares. The terrain was uneven, and dense with vegetation. The butcher knives that Carlos had liberated from the kitchen were no substitute for a machete, and while they found Team D's trail in the daylight, when night fell, they lost it again.

It seemed almost suicidally stupid to move at night, moon or no moon. But Carlos drove them both mercilessly, stopping only for two breaks that lasted about an hour apiece. The motion was frantic, obsessive. Quaid was having trouble deciding if they were running toward A. J. and the others, or if they were running away from the hotel.

So, by the second morning, they had been hiking nonstop for over twenty-four hours, and maybe had covered half the distance. A lot of the progress they'd made in the night seemed to be lost in the time they spent searching for Team D's machete-hewn trail again in the daylight.

They found the trail at a clearing in the jungle that had the remains of a campfire, a small pile of cans and food wrappers, and cuts in some of the trees where they would have hung some makeshift shelters.

They stopped there, and Quaid collapsed on the soil next to the old campfire. He was exhausted. "Stop," he called out when it looked like Carlos was going to move on after making a cursory examination of the clearing. "I need some rest."

"We're gaining on them—"

"Carlos, we're making at least twice the time they did. We can afford a rest. We won't be of help to anyone if we collapse on the way there."

Carlos turned to look at him. For a few moments Quaid thought he would argue, but he could see the fatigue on Carlos' face. If anything, he looked worse than Quaid felt.

Carlos unshouldered the backpack and sat down opposite the dead campfire from Quaid. Carlos looked into the ashes and asked, "How close do you think we are?"

"This is their second campsite. If they made the same time up the slope, halfway. If they moved slower, we're closer."

Carlos nodded and pulled a can out of his backpack. Spaghetti-O's. The doctor had packed canned goods and bottled water, but it wasn't gourmet cuisine.

While he ate his Spaghetti-O's, Quaid opened a can of tuna for himself, wishing that Dr. Yanowitz had thought to raid the spice rack—or had just put in a salt and pepper shaker. But Quaid was as ravenous as he was tired, and the lack didn't slow him down at all.

"Carlos," he asked between mouthfuls. "What are we going to do when we find them?"

"I don't know."

"What do you mean, you don't know?"

Carlos tossed his empty can into the ashes. "You think I had the time to plan this out in detail?"

Quaid rubbed his temple; a headache was coming on. "You don't know? That's just great. What if someone's seriously injured? We just have half-assed first aid kits. I only know of the one doctor—are we going to take them *back?*"

"I don't know— There *were* helicopters, something, out here, too.

"You want to bet that they're friendly?"

"What choice have we got?"

"Great," Quaid grumbled.

"We can't make any decisions until we find them."

Quaid tossed his own can into the ashes and said, "I suppose not."

That night Quaid dreamed again about the mutating chessboard.

This time he saw some of the black pieces before they descended. He recognized the knight as Duce. He carried a banner that bore the logo of Alphomeg Enterprises.

*   *   *

Carlos prodded him awake.

Quaid opened his eyes and saw a strip of night sky through the break in the trees above him. There was something wrong about it, though.

"What?" Quaid muttered, sitting up.

"Look," Carlos said.

Quaid sat up. He could see what was wrong now. There was light coming from the east, toward the mountain. It hit the tops of the trees around the clearing. He could hear it now, too, the sound of a helicopter. It was a subsonic throbbing that seemed to sink into the ground around them.

"Do we run," Carlos said, "or try to signal it?"

That was a good question. They didn't have any way to know if it was the people who had kidnapped them, or if it was a rescue party. He stood up and looked toward the light.

Quaid couldn't see the helicopter. Their view of the sky was too narrow from this clearing. It felt close by, though. "Signaling it?" he asked, "Do we have any flares?"

Carlos shook his head. "These were only half-packed before the doctor was locked up, and I didn't have a chance to go by the boathouse. That's where the flares were."

The light swept by the trees above them, and the noise began to fade. Carlos' question seemed a moot point. He didn't think the helicopter knew where they were, whether they wanted it to or not.

Aware of them or not, their visitor spurred Carlos on to resume their trek. It was predawn, the sky barely lightening, and they were pushing out after A. J. and his team.

Also, coincidentally, they were heading in the direction the helicopter noises had come from.

After Quaid had shouldered his pack and they had both stepped off into the woods, he asked, "How do we know when we reach the area where the flares went off?"

"I was hoping for another pair to guide us—" Carlos looked skyward and shook his head. "If we don't get that by the time we reach the foothills we can start doing a search pattern."

"Maybe one of those helicopters picked them up."

"I sort of hope so."

Quaid nodded. There were a number of other, less pleasant, reasons they would have stopped signaling.

They went another two hours before the sun actually started to rise. During that time they felt the first angling of the ground toward the sky. Large rocks began to reach through the thick black soil, and the trees began to move away from each other. The trees themselves seemed to change character, becoming thinner, coarser. The underbrush became less verdant, hugging close to the ground. Impassable terrain became more common—most often a sheer wall of earth that had shrugged itself out of the ground, to face them with a vertical serrated face.

The first orange rays of dawn were beginning to reach them through the dappled shadows when they caught sight of something. It was visible at a distance as a patch of sunlight that cut through the woods ahead of them like a glowing dagger.

At first Carlos thought it was a river; since the greenhouse, the only signs of human habitation in this place were the remains of A. J.'s campsites. He was about to say as much to Quaid. Quaid had stopped still, facing the light, unmoving.

Carlos stepped up next to him and realized that he was wrong.

First off, the clearing marked by the sunlight was above them, and running perpendicular to the slope of the land. Common sense told him that rivers didn't do that. Rivers also made noise. This didn't.

Carlos knew something that did hug a hillside like that.

"A road," he whispered.

"I think so," Quaid agreed.

Carlos' hopes started to rise. Where there was a road, there was civilization. There would be people who could pull them out of this bizarre situation they found themselves in.

Carlos ran the rest of the way up the hillside.

As he stumbled through the underbrush, he pulled himself up using an old stump that the architects of the road ahead must have cast aside when cutting their way through.

Carlos broke through the woods and into the sunlight. He blinked and shaded his eyes. It was too bright after spending so long shaded by the trees.

The road came into focus. A gravel track wide enough that he thought two cars might be able to pass each other. Two ruts marked the center of the path, and he could see relatively fresh tire tracks in the mud.

Quaid followed him. "I think we found it."

Carlos nodded. But he was feeling a vague unease. The same sort of anxiety that last night prompted the question of whether to hide or attract attention.

Quaid was walking down the center of the ruts. "This might not be the Ohio Turnpike. But it goes somewhere—"

Carlos nodded. *Yes, but* . . . "We're looking for A. J. and the rest of them."

"I know," Quaid turned around and shook his head. "But you admitted that we have no clue what to do if we do find them." He kicked the tire track. "This road goes from A to B. Someone at either A or B will be able to help us find them, and will be better prepared to deal with injuries."

"We don't know that."

"I know that anyone's better prepared than

we are right now." He looked up. "And they have helicopters. They'll be able to find them quicker."

Carlos walked up to him and grabbed his arm. "What if it's *them?*"

"*Them* who?"

"You know." Carlos felt an empty pit in his stomach. *What if they're right?* "Alphomeg, or whoever set up that madhouse in the hotel in the first place."

Quaid said, "Bullshit."

"Huh?" Carlos stepped back.

"Just what I said." Quaid spat on the ground. "*Bullshit.* You know what I think? I think Tage, on whatever murderous power fantasy he's on, has a vested interest in us believing that there are evil 'keepers' out there."

"Then who set this all up?"

"I don't know, but every theory—the CIA, the Chinese, UFOs, God, the Devil, and Carnival Cruise Lines—has all been just so much smoke blowing out of people's asses. We don't *know*, Carlos. And no death we've suffered has a reason that extends outside that damn hotel." Quaid stepped up and grabbed the strap on Carlos' backpack, pulling him closer. "Now, by God, you have the right instincts. There are people who're in trouble here. But if we start playing with people's lives because we believe some hokum someone pawned off on us, we're no better than everyone who sat on their hands back there."

Carlos felt a little ashamed, but that didn't make the uneasiness go away. He shrugged out of Quaid's grip. "Okay," Carlos pointed down the road. "I think that's the direction the helicopters were going."

He started down without waiting for Quaid to catch up.

BOOK THREE:

ENDGAME

Twenty-third Move

They had been on the island for nine days. The population of the hotel had dropped by half. Ten left. Five of them had decided that Tage Garnell was bad news.

For the first time in a while, Doctor Yanowitz felt reason to be optimistic. Iris had visited late the prior day with, of all people, Connie. They had spent most of the evening with him explaining how the quartet of women, Olivia, Beatrice, Iris, and Connie, had become a unified block against the ascendancy of Tage Garnell and his cronies.

"It's how *they* operate," Connie had said. "First *they* make you feel like you're alone, that you're the only one who can see what *they're* doing. They cut you off so you think if you so much as hint that *they're* out there, the so-called normal people will lock you up and call you crazy. And *they're* the ones who are defining normal, and real, and reasonable, so even the ones who aren't *them* have to believe, have to fit in, go along, or they're the crazy ones, right?"

It was a measure of how grave things had become when the textbook worldview of a borderline paranoid schizophrenic was a cogent and reasonable interpretation of the situation they found themselves in.

Somehow, Connie had brought these four disparate women together. Abe was impressed, especially that she had convinced Iris that some sort of overt action was required. Outside, Iris seemed unflappable, but Abe knew that she was deeply frightened. He suspected the reason she'd been attracted to him was because she saw him as the only man here she could trust—or, less complimentary—he was the least threatening man here.

This morning they were going to attempt a coup.

One moment Quaid was walking with Carlos down the jungle road. The next they were washed by a demonic wind and deafened by a thrumming roar above them. Quaid felt his chest tighten as the noise resonated in the back of his jaw.

The helicopter appeared with no warning from behind a rise as if thrust up by the ground ahead of them. Wind-torn foliage whipped toward them and small stones and gravel bit into Quaid's skin. The damn thing felt close enough for him to touch it.

Carlos yelled against the wind and the noise

of the engine. *"Please, tell me we aren't in deep shit!"*

Quaid squinted at their visitors. The helicopter wasn't black, it was more of a gray-green color. It was close enough to see the rivets in its underbelly, and the face of the pilot behind the windscreen. It filled the strip of sky above the road ahead of them. Quaid hoped they didn't have intentions of landing that thing here, the road was too narrow, wooded on both sides.

A voice, painfully loud and distorted by amplification, called down to them. *"Put down the backpacks and step away from them."*

"Say what?" Carlos yelled at the helicopter.

Quaid was getting a bad feeling from this, but he did as the voice asked. He shrugged out of the pack and let it drop to the ground.

Carlos followed his lead, but he was looking around as if he expected someone to jump him at any moment.

The PA called down to them again. *"Put your hands behind your heads and step back to the center of the road."*

"This ain't happening." Carlos didn't yell this time, and Quaid barely heard him. He had to keep his eyes slitted because of the dust the rotors kicked up.

In a moment Quaid could hear a new sound, another engine, closer to the ground.

A gray-green Hummer abruptly appeared over the rise. It bounced over the hill and pulled to a stop twenty yards down the road from them, almost directly under the helicopter.

Four men got out of the vehicle in front of them, all dressed in similar khaki jumpsuits—a uniform without any markings or insignia other than a name embroidered on the left breast. They all carried rifles.

The PA above them told them to lie facedown on the ground.

That was too much for Carlos. He ran.

Before Quaid was aware of what he was doing, he was running after Carlos. After the sunlit road, the jungle was a dark green shadow where he could barely see where he was going.

"Please give yourselves up. We cannot allow you to go."

"Carlos," Quaid called out. "Carlos, you dumb fuck! What do you think you're doing?"

Quaid's only answer was the PA telling him to give himself up.

Somewhere behind him he heard something suspiciously like gunfire. He redoubled his efforts at running, now concerned for more than just Carlos.

The inevitable happened.

Quaid tripped over something in the shadows and fell face first, twisting his ankle. He had been running fast enough that the breath was knocked out of him. He lay there a moment, stunned, listening to the sound of the helicopter and the tramp of feet close by in the woods.

"Carlos, damn it!" he cursed.

Quaid pushed himself upright, using a tree for balance.

It was a mistake. Behind him, as he stood, he heard the crack of a rifle, followed by a dull impact in his shoulder, like a sledgehammer wrapped in cotton. He fell against the tree. His left arm was numb and wouldn't move.

Quaid reached up for the wound, expecting blood and a ragged crater where his shoulder had been. But his shoulder was still there, intact, as numb as his arm.

There was something sticking out of his shoulder. Quaid pulled it out. It took two or three tries. His good hand seemed to be falling asleep, and his fingers couldn't feel much of anything. He yanked the object free.

His legs refused to support him anymore. Leaning against the tree, he started sliding to the ground. He blinked a few times to focus on the item in his hand. His vision was blurred, and he couldn't see what it was. He shook his head. He was tired, and found it very frustrating that he couldn't see what this thing was.

Quaid's knees sank into the soil, and he couldn't feel his hand anymore. It had fallen to the ground in front of him. On his palm rested a small thing that resembled a hypodermic needle.

His brain lost connection with the rest of his body. He didn't really notice that he had toppled over. He couldn't manage to be too distressed at this. It was as if he were watching a movie. A boring movie at that.

Quaid's awareness faded in and out, granting him more and more disconnected views of the world around him.

Three or four guys. Khaki uniforms without insignia. Carrying the wicked-looking rifle that must have shot him. Talking without looking at each other, but Quaid couldn't hear them.

The Hummer on the road. Mud-covered, diesel smokestack, the rear converted to a canvas-covered truck. Being strapped on a stretcher that they slid into the back.

Carlos laying next to him staring blankly at the canvas above them. Quaid trying to say something. The words coming out in low moans and drool.

The feeling of the truck stopping. Sliding them out.

Glimpses of buildings, corrugated steel, antennae, more people.

The Alphomeg logo spray-painted on a pile of wooden crates.

A long unbroken darkness.

They held the meeting after breakfast, as usual. Abe wondered how much of the tension he felt in the room was real, and how much was his surging adrenaline. When Jarl led him in, there wasn't any of the usual chatter. The four women of the counterrevolution were sitting in the back, and when Jarl walked forward to Tage's coterie, Abe walked over to the women.

Even Tage's group was subdued, as if they had some sense of what was coming.

Olivia was whispering to Iris as Abe approached. "No, Frank isn't evil, once we say what's happening, he'll be with us."

"I'm scared of what they'll do," Iris whispered back.

"We'll outnumber them," Olivia said.

When Abe walked up next to them, Tage got up on the stage and said, "There are a few items I think we need to vote—"

Olivia Grossmann sucked in a breath and said, "No."

Everyone in the front of the ballroom looked in her direction. Abe thought he saw surprise in Jarl's eyes and Duce's. Frank and Erica looked confused, as if they'd been caught unaware by the schism. Tage, of all of them, looked unsurprised and unmoved. He simply said, "Mrs. Grossmann, you have some sort of objection?"

Abe stood up next to her, "Yes, we do."

"We? Which 'we' is this?"

Connie stood up next to Olivia. Iris took Abe's hand and stood next to him. Last to rise was Beatrice Greenhart.

"And your problem is what?" Tage asked.

"It's you," Connie said. "What you've been doing, to us, to this game, to everything—"

Jarl stood up. He was scowling. "You don't have to take this shit—"

Frank stepped in from his position, alone at

the far side of the stage, "No, Jarl, let them talk."

Tage nodded. "Yes, I want to hear as well, since they voted me into this position."

"A vote that was rushed, with no real debate," Abe said. "You've made the pretense of being reasonable, while at the same time you've been demagoguing the issue of the 'keepers' as bad as Erica—"

"There's no call to be insulting," Erica said. "You have no right—"

"Abe has every right," Iris said. "That *man*—" She pointed at Tage, and her voice caught.

"—a vote," Abe continued, "that you called because you knew that the people you didn't have in your camp were panicked and disorganized and prone to vote with what they saw as the majority."

Tage shook his head. "You're merely making the argument that a leader was necessary. Are you all objecting because I was a good politician?"

"No," Beatrice said, for the first time. Her voice was strained and very subdued. "It's because you're a murderer."

"That's enough," Jarl stepped forward. Frank put a hand on his chest and pushed him down into his chair.

"Sit down," Frank said, "and shut up."

"The crazy bitch's catching," Duce said, but the words seemed forced to Abe.

"Do you know what you're saying?" Erica demanded. She was shaking her head. "It's our *keepers.*"

"*He's* our keeper," Connie accused, pointing at Tage. "He left the greenhouse to go slit Oyler's throat. Henry was about to figure it out, maybe he did, and he had to die—"

"And who killed Susan?" Tage asked. "When she was being killed, I was down here with Frank and Erica—"

"She killed herself," Abe said. "And you know that. She was behind you—I think she might have been pretty close to you. That was why she came to you with Henry's suspicions. What did the note say? That she couldn't live with her role in Henry's death, or that she couldn't live with having been involved with you?"

"Interesting theory, but there wasn't any note—"

"Jarl took it, and the knives that slit her wrists. The water made the ink run. I saw the stains it left when I examined the body."

Tage nodded. "I suppose this does call for a vote—"

Olivia stepped forward. "We're not playing the game anymore. This is real." She turned to Frank. "We have to lock him up before anyone else gets hurt."

Tage was walking along the side of the stage, looking at the knot of his supporters. "We're proposing to relieve me of duty and place me in custody. Who's against the proposal?"

Abe stepped forward. "This isn't accomplishing anything. This isn't a game anymore. It never was. No, please, let's do this quietly."

Jarl, Duce, and Erica raised their hands. Tage did as well, and turned toward Frank. "Well, Frank, how many votes is that?"

Frank looked at him as if the man had just gone insane. He shook his head. "Tage," he said. "That's not the issue here— Are they *right?*"

"Count the votes, Frank." Tage's voice had become cold and hard. "It's your job. You don't want to forfeit, do you?"

"Jesus Christ, man," Frank said. "These people are accusing you of killing two people. *Did you do it?*"

Frank took a couple of steps toward the stage.

"The vote," Tage said.

Abe looked at Tage and felt a firm certainty in the pit of his stomach. The man was insane.

Frank mounted the stage and grabbed Tage's jacket. *"Deny it, you smarmy little twerp!"*

Frank was a bull of a man, and seemed to tower over the smaller form of Tage Garnell. Tage raised his arms and took a step to the side. Suddenly, Frank was on his knees and Tage was behind him, holding his arm up between his shoulder blades.

Abe took a step forward, but Jarl and Duce stood up and put themselves between Abe and the stage.

It wasn't supposed to go like this.

"The vote." Tage said quietly, and jerked upward.

Abe heard the sickening pop as Frank's shoulder dislocated. *"Oh, God!"* Frank's voice came out in a low moan.

"Count."

"Bastard. Know, yourself. Six."

"What was that?" Tage asked.

Frank's face was white and sweat gleamed on his skin. He was hyperventilating and his body was tilted, so it seemed he was only supported by Tage's grip on his dislocated arm.

"Six. Votes. Against."

"Good," Tage said, and lowered the arm. "Was that so hard? For?"

For a long time no one moved.

"For?" Tage repeated.

"Count. Your. Own. Votes."

Tage jerked and Frank groaned. Beatrice ran forward and yelled, "Stop it!"

"Vote, then," Tage said.

Stared down by Tage, the rest of them voted.

"How many?" Tage asked.

"Six. For." Frank said, counting his own vote.

Tage nodded. "With a tie vote, the measure fails." Abe started walking toward the stage, but Jarl grabbed his arm.

"We're not done here," Tage said. In front of him, Frank appeared to be on the verge of unconsciousness. "Frank's job tallying votes seems to be taking a toll on him. He put a measure on the table that I become the vote counter."

Olivia walked forward. "Stop this. This is pointless."

"Frank's given his vote for, haven't you?"

Frank groaned.

"For?" Tage asked.

"*Yes*," Olivia said, "if it will make you stop torturing him."

There was a chorus of agreement. For Abe's ineffectual group of revolutionaries, the spectacle of seeing Frank brutalized seemed to make any point about the Game seem trivial. No one was willing to deny Tage such a pointless issue if it meant he'd let go of Frank.

"That's unanimous, isn't it, Frank?"

"Yes." Frank gasped, barely choking the word out.

"Thank you," Tage said. Then he reached his free arm around Frank's neck and grabbed his chin. He pulled, and there was a sickening crack.

The room fell silent as Frank slid lifeless to the stage.

"*No*," Connie whispered.

Olivia and Abe tried to rush the stage at the same time. Jarl managed to twist him and he slammed face first into the ballroom floor. He heard Iris scream something. There were the sounds of a struggle.

Tage called out, his voice echoing through the space. "There's one last issue, and please don't make me force it."

Abe craned his neck up to see him. Tage had

Olivia in a headlock, and was pushing her head forward. She was struggling, but she couldn't break his grip. *Oh, God . . .*

"Now all this voting is becoming tiresome," Tage said. "I propose we get rid of it entirely. In favor?"

The Game, what is all this about this Game that he's following the rules even now?

"That's me and Duce and Jarl for." Tage looked down at Erica, over Olivia's head. Olivia's struggles were becoming weaker.

Erica was alone at the foot of the stage below Tage and Olivia. "Now," Tage said, "do you want to go against me now that the 'keepers' are at our threshold?"

Erica looked as white as Frank's corpse. Something inside made Abe yell, *"Erica, no!"*

But she had already raised a shaky hand. "Six votes for," Tage said. "Do the five remaining players vote against?" A sick smile crossed Tage's face as he said, "I'll take the silence as an affirmative? Any objections?"

The ballroom was silent.

Twenty-fourth Move

"*F*uck," Quaid muttered as he came to his senses.

Whatever they had doped him with left him with a worse hangover than a fifth of Southern Comfort. His head was throbbing, as if his brain was a wounded animal that was trying to claw its way out of his skull so it could find someplace dark and quiet to die.

He opened his eyes a slit, expecting to be assaulted by the light. To his relief, he was lying alone in the darkness.

Quaid was sprawled on a hard, uncomfortable cot that sat along one side of a small, square room. The walls were plywood, and the roof was corrugated steel. There was one fluorescent light fixture, currently unlit. There was no window in this room, so he had no idea if it was day or night.

It took him a while to gather the strength to sit upright.

"Christ," he muttered, "Even sober, everything you do turns to shit."

He hoped Carlos was all right.

What possessed him to run? What possessed me to chase him? Neither of them had been in any shape to outrun anyone, not after nearly forty-eight hours of almost continual hiking. The muscles in his arms and legs throbbed to let him know just how badly he had abused them.

Quaid curled up on the cot and waited for the pain to go away.

It didn't go away, not completely.

He imagined Iris Traxler's voice telling him what a lousy bastard he was for taking the luxury of feeling sorry for himself.

It was a bad habit from his drinking days—perhaps more accurately, from his end-of-drinking days—to allow self-loathing to paralyze him. He had gone into AA convinced he was the most worthless, most pathetic drunk ever to cross their threshold. . . .

"Get a grip Quaid," he ordered himself sternly, rubbing the throbbing out of his temples. "Following the road wasn't a mistake. It might have turned out wrong, but it wasn't a mistake."

It wasn't.

Quaid kept telling himself that. It had been the only sane thing to do, whatever the risks might have been. All the risks they knew had been manufactured by a bunch of confused people trying to explain an insane situation.

Quaid sat up again, and tried to stand. His legs were weak beneath him, but they supported his weight. He found a light switch, shaded his eyes, and turned on the lights.

The tubes flickered a couple of times before coming on with an ominous hum. He blinked a few times, getting a better look at his surroundings.

The cot looked like it had felt. Heavy, metal and hard. The walls were whitewashed plywood. The floor unpainted plywood. He felt as if he were in a shipping crate. There was a folding metal table next to the bed. On it sat a tin cup and a metal pitcher. He used it to pour himself a glass of water to wash the fuzz out of his mouth.

The door opened behind him. He turned around to face a pair of guys in the nonuniform uniforms. "If you're ready, we'd like you to come with us, sir."

They took him outside, which gave him his first lucid view of where he was.

Midday sun was beating down on them now. Heat ripples gave everything a shimmering, otherworldly quality. He walked through the center of a cluster of buildings. Some of the structures appeared old, and might have dated from World War II. There were several buildings of plywood and corrugated steel, like the one he had emerged from. There were also a few buildings of whitewashed cinderblock across a courtyard of crushed white gravel.

Quaid saw several Hummers parked here and there. Away from the buildings, in a clearing

torn from the jungle, squatted a gray-green helicopter that had the yellow logo of Alphomeg
Entertainment on its side.

They led him into one of the larger cinderblock buildings, one that had a nest of antennae and a satellite dish on the roof. The door
slid aside, and he felt a wash of coolness. He
realized how much he had missed central air-
conditioning.

They led him through a large room that took
up most of the first floor. The place was filled
with desks piled with computers, radio equipment, and video monitors.

Quaid caught sight of a number of screens
which showed views of the hotel. Some even
seemed to be tracking individuals. He didn't get
much chance to stare. They pushed him through
to an office in the back.

They sat him down facing a long mahogany
desk. Carlos was here already, sitting in the
other chair facing the desk. Quaid's two khaki
companions left, closing the door. He turned to
Carlos and asked, "How're you doing?"

"Not so great . . ." His speech was slurred,
as if he was still partly drugged.

Quaid didn't have the time to get any more
details because the door on the other side of the
desk opened. A tall, elderly man stepped out.
He had a thin face, a hawkish nose, and the eyes
of a predator. His hair was silver-gray and he
wore a white suit and a tie that was the purple-

crimson shade of blood that was just starting
to clot.

"Welcome, gentlemen. I am Angelo Diomedes, owner of Alphomeg Entertainment." He
sat down in the leather office chair on the other
side of the desk. He folded his hands in front of
him and leaned forward, smiling slightly. "You
probably don't remember me."

Connie could still picture Frank, unmoving,
on the stage. She had never seen someone die
before. And despite events during this game,
she'd never seen a dead body before. It had been
such a shock, that it wasn't until Jarl and Tage
had been dragging them out of the ballroom
that she'd realized what had happened.

They were going to win.

She almost choked on the thought. The only
consolation was the fact that she wasn't going
to become one of them in the process.

It seemed small comfort now, confined in a
hotel room with Iris, Beatrice, and an uncompre-
hending Erica Urquort.

"What are they doing with Abe?" Iris whispered. It was probably the eighth time she had
asked that question.

Connie stood by the window. Jarl had nailed
it shut, leaving the room sweltering, even with
the ceiling fan spinning above them. "I don't
know what they're doing," Connie said. "I've
never known what they're doing."

"It doesn't make sense," Beatrice insisted. "No one is making any sense."

Connie glanced at Erica. The old woman seemed to have collapsed. She hadn't said a word since they'd been locked in here. Connie could imagine. It wasn't pleasant to think that you'd played into their hands, and had a part in something evil. Susan Polk had certainly felt that way.

Connie was feeling that way right now.

I can't fight them. I've known that most of my adult life. What made me try now? Did I think I'd win simply because some people actually believed me? Understood me?

She had been a fool, and her foolishness had gotten Frank killed.

Beatrice shook her head and rubbed her hands over the top of her unwrinkled skirt. "What are we going to do?"

Connie looked out the window and saw an ominous darkness on the horizon that mirrored perfectly her sense of impending doom. "I don't know." She knew in her gut that they were finished with them. Whatever usefulness this collection of people had borne for them was exhausted. Any moment now there was going to be a knock on the door—

As if in response to her thought, the doorknob rattled.

"Jarl?" Iris called out. Jarl Theodore had been the one guarding the door when Tage had thrown them in here. Not that a guard was necessary, Tage had Abe and Olivia as hostages to their good behavior.

"Ladies," Tage Garnell said as the door swung open. He was alone, and for a few moments Connie felt the urge to attack him, just grab something and leap swinging at the man's face. Images of Frank and Olivia flashed through her mind.

For Iris, the impulse was a little farther than mere thoughts. "You bastard—" she said as she grabbed for him. The words were brought short by a grunt as Tage grabbed the approaching arm and twisted.

"Not a good idea, Miss Traxler." He held her arm, wrist twisted upward, until Iris' incredibly long legs buckled under the effort of holding herself upright. Tage held her a moment more, as if for emphasis. Then he let her go. "Your friend the doctor is alive. Don't make me change my mind."

Connie wrapped her arms tightly around herself. The man's aspect hadn't changed one bit. He still was the same man who had brought them all together the first day. A little short, wearing an expensive looking black shirt and pants, and glasses that were little gold rectangles.

It was a sickening thought that the physical manifestation of such evil could be so mundane.

"Change your mind?" Connie's voice caught on the words. Her throat was trying to constrict around them. "Aren't you going to finish us off?"

"Finish you off?" He actually said it as if he didn't know what she meant.

"Like Oyler," Connie said. "Like Henry—" She could almost feel the blade across her own throat as she said it.

"Why would I do that now?" Tage asked. "After I've won the game?"

Carlos shook his head. His brain was still fogged by their drugs. Next to him, Quaid stood up, yelling, *"You're behind all this?"*

Quaid's voice made Carlos' head throb.

"You engineered this insanity? This goddamned Game?"

Carlos rubbed his forehead. This was the bastard behind it all, that was one thing that was sinking into his fogged brain.

Diomedes was leaning back in his chair. Carlos raised his head to get a good view of the man. He was old, with skin ridged and knotted like a weathered piece of driftwood. The outburst from Quaid did not seem to move him.

"Let me assure you," Diomedes said, "you *agreed* to this insanity, gentlemen."

"Agreed?" Quaid shouted. It looked as if he was about to leap across the desk. Carlos put a hand on his arm to restrain him. He kept thinking about the room full of men outside. This man wouldn't be half as assured if there wasn't adequate security in this place.

They didn't need a squad of the khaki-clad tough guys storming through the door right now.

"Yes," Diomedes said. "Agreed."

The old man reached into a drawer next to him and pulled out two fat folders and laid them on the desk in front of him. "It would take a few hours to go over the minutiae of these papers. The agreements are quite lengthy."

Carlos could see his name and Quaid's on the labels. Quaid reached over and grabbed his. He started pulling papers out of the thick folder, looking at the long, legal-sized pages with narrowed eyes.

"All twenty of you signed contracts with Alphomeg Entertainment to be participants in a game. A unique game." Diomedes nodded slightly toward the folders in front of him. "A condition of this agreement was preparatory psychological conditioning to remove your memories of the agreement, and of Alphomeg Entertainment."

Quaid looked up from the papers. His voice had a hard edge to it. "Pardon me, Mr. Diomedes, if I don't believe that I would willingly part with a few months of my memory."

Carlos felt an empty hole in his gut. "I don't know many people who would." But even as he agreed with Quaid, he had the sick sense that Diomedes was telling them the truth.

"Perhaps," Diomedes said, "you'll understand better if you knew what motivated you?"

"That would be a start," Quaid said.

"Your fee for your participation," Diomedes said, "amounts to two hundred and fifty thousand dollars."

Quaid dropped the folder in his hands. Its contents scattered on the floor by Carlos' feet. Carlos stared at Diomedes—

—a flash of memory, corporate office, Alphomeg logo hovering over the desk, some flunky explaining details, nodding, thinking, a quarter mil cash would finally get him out of debt, own the shop free and clear, all he had to do, play a game—

"A quarter million," Diomedes repeated. "Win or lose."

Iris was still cradling her wrist, but her voice was hard. "There's no game," she said. "It's been *you* all along. No keepers, no watchers, no evil presence detecting a forfeit. Just your own insane little manipulations."

Tage actually smiled. He turned and stepped across the threshold.

Connie thought that he might close the door and leave with no explanation at all. But, instead, he wheeled a room-service cart into the room. It was piled with food from the kitchen. "I came down here to bring you dinner." He glanced down at the cart. "Probably breakfast and lunch as well. I don't think we're going to cross paths again."

"Going somewhere?" Iris said. "It better be far away."

Tage smiled and shook his head. "Like I said, the Game is over—"

"There's no game!"

Tage squatted to look Iris in the eyes. "Oh, there is a Game. The ultimate, purest game—"

"Why?" The voice of Erica Urquort was small and dry.

Tage looked down at her. "Why?"

Connie shook her head. "She wants to know why you betrayed her."

"Such a loyal ally?" Tage stood up. "Despite her belief in the Game, I doubted that her commitment would extend toward what was necessary to win."

"What is the Game?" Connie asked. "What the hell have you won?"

Tage rubbed his chin. "You, I don't owe any explanations." He turned to face Erica. "Erica, though. You should know who the keepers were, what the Game actually *is*."

It began over a century ago, a private club for young men with ivy league educations, too much money, and too much time. A private retreat that grew the Game as an exercise in social dynamics. The members would isolate themselves from the world, and create their own unique society from scratch. The "games" could last for weeks, and "winning" became a badge of honor among the group.

As years passed, the members of this exclusive club began to find that prior experience with the game eventually contaminated the experience. Players would repeat "moves" that worked beforehand, the same problems would come up—voting, ties, adjudicating disputes—and would be resolved in the same way. The games, once unique, began to look alike.

That was when the members decided that they should recruit new players each time. The players received a nominal fee, and the club had the opportunity to watch as a fresh game unfolded each time. No longer playing the game, the men who'd founded it did the next best thing. They began wagering.

Old money gave way to new, and the membership in the club expanded. After World War II, the number of people with interest in the game, and the amount of money being wagered, led to the creation of an impartial third-party organization, Alphomeg, to administer the games, the rules, and—by now, most important—the wagering.

By the turn of the Century, Alphomeg Entertainment had become a very profitable enterprise.

Now, Alphomeg Entertainment selected their players from a massive database pool accumulated from public records, mailing lists, and overt solicitation. To be considered, the players had to fulfill two simple criteria. None of them could know any of the others, even by reputation, and none could have any knowledge of

Alphomeg Entertainment, the Game, or the people behind it.

The criteria assured the purity of the Game, and—increasingly important—confidence in the fairness of the outcome. Enough was riding on each game that it was crucial that Alphomeg could assure that none of the players would have their gameplay unduly influenced by external factors.

For that reason, after confidentiality agreements were signed, and secrecy was assured, and the player had agreed to participate, Alphomeg introduced a new wrinkle to the old game, the amnesia. It provided extra insurance against outside influence, and created the assurance of the "purity" that the first players had as a goal. No player would have prior knowledge of Alphomeg, or of the Game. All they knew would be what was given them on arrival.

"A single rule sheet?" Quaid said. "That's adequate explanation?"

Carlos was thinking, *It was insane. It was a game, all someone's damn game.*

"No, of course not," said Diomedes. "It was one of several papers giving everyone an equal background."

"Like hell," Quaid said. "You're watching, you know we got no such thing—"

"Because," Diomedes said, "Mr. Garnell systematically removed them."

"Good lord, what's the point of it?" Carlos couldn't believe still, that it *was* just a game.

"Those who win," Diomedes said, "Receive something substantially more than the quarter million due you for participating."

"Like what?" Carlos asked.

"An equal share of twenty-five million."

Carlos was dumbfounded. "This whole place, it's just for this—*Game?*"

"An island purchased from the British Commonwealth in 1948. It had the hotel and—"

"What do you mean, Tage removed them?" Quaid asked.

Diomedes cleared his throat. "I'm afraid Mr. Garnel emptied your orientation packets of everything but the initial Rule set."

"What?" Carlos felt as if he were half a beat behind. He was still getting a handle on what Alphomeg was.

"I'm here myself, in fact, to deal with some of the irregularities that have occurred in this particular game."

"Irregularities?" Quaid asked incredulously. "There are people dying back there."

Diomedes' face took on a grim cast. "I am quite aware of everything that has happened since the Game began. Much of it is unfortunate." He waved a wrinkled hand at the folder that was still on the desk. "Everyone signed a waiver acknowledging that the Game was potentially dangerous—"

Quaid stood. "That's bullshit."

Carlos stood up next to Quaid and put a hand on his shoulder. "He's right there, man. I don't remember what you told us then, but by God I swear that you didn't warn anyone about getting their throat slit."

"Sit down, both of you. What's done is done." Diomedes steepled his fingers in front of him. "We have made the decision to allow the Game to play out, without interference."

"Pardon me," Quaid said, "but one of your players is *killing* people."

Diomedes nodded. "A grave situation, but we will not interfere in the players' actions until the Game is resolved. Nothing Mr. Garnel has done is outside the theoretical limits of the Game—"

"You're just going to let him—" Quaid started to say. Then his hands clenched. "How much is it?"

Diomedes stared. His expression was still unmoved. He didn't answer, perhaps deliberately not understanding Quaid's question.

Quaid slammed his hands on the desk and leaned in toward Diomedes. "How much money is riding on this one Game?"

"I'm not authorized to reveal that."

"Come on—I bet you're setting some sort of record for this one. Your rich folks are probably getting off on the bloodlust. Anyone start a pool on who's next to die?"

"*That's enough*—" Diomedes finally let some anger show. The lip turned in a sneer and he almost spat. "*Sit down.*"

Quaid sank back down. Carlos followed his lead.

"Please do not allow the courtesy of my meeting with you to give you the impression that you are entitled to any justification. You were advised about the situation before you agreed to participate. Anything is in bounds until established otherwise by the rules, and there will be no interference until the Game is over and a winner is decided." He stood. "I permitted some liberty because of the state of your memory, but I have no more patience."

The door behind them opened and a quartet of khaki-clad security goons flanked Quaid and Carlos.

"Be thankful," Diomedes said, "the adjudication committee ruled that you two are still participants in the Game, even though you left the geographic boundaries of the play area. You're still entitled to your fee, and any winnings." He folded his arms. "However, now that you are here, it is my decision what to do with you. Letting you back into the field will be tantamount to allowing external interference into the Game, so I will have you taken off the island."

"Christ," Carlos said, "what about A. J.?"

Diomedes shook his head and waved his hand in a dismissive gesture.

Carlos stood up, and his escort grabbed his arms. "External interference? What the hell was Oyler?"

Diomedes turned and left the room.

Carlos called out to him, "What about

Coombs? Does the name Steven Coombs ring a bell?"

The door shut behind Diomedes, and the khaki guards hustled them out of the office.

They were shut in another room, this one was in another cinder-block building with air-conditioning. This place had a pair of beds, a television, and a bathroom.

Once they were alone, Quaid turned to Carlos and asked, "Who the hell is Steven Coombs?"

"Oyler."

"What?"

Carlos told him about what he and Yanowitz had found. Steven Coombs, investigative journalist. Late of the Atlantic City underbelly.

It made sense to Quaid. Coombs heard about Alphomeg somehow, and managed to replace one of their recruits, Oyler. He doubted that Diomedes mourned his loss.

But why was he killed?

"He's not going after A. J." Carlos said.

"I know, 'no outside interference.' "

"So, what do we do?"

"I wish I knew."

There was nothing much left for either of them to do but clean up and wait for their escort off the island.

Carlos fell asleep almost instantaneously, but Quaid, while exhausted, couldn't even close his eyes. He lay back on his cot and stared at the ceiling as afternoon dimmed.

Two hundred fifty thousand dollars.

It wasn't an amount that real people dealt with. Not all at once. The enormity of it had taken a while to sink in.

All he had to do was walk away, and it was his. It was more than enough to rebuild the life that his drinking had destroyed. Enough so he could stop treading water, pay off his debts. What did he owe anyone, to give that up?

What did he owe anyone, to go through any more of this?

"Some tests belong to the Devil," he whispered.

Perhaps he had spent so much of his life seeking the easy way out that he knew it for what it was. Another rationalization. This time without even the excuse of the drinking to hang his mistakes on.

If he went along now, it would be an order of magnitude worse than any of his drunken screwups. It would be a conscious decision to accept evil. Doing nothing would be as bad as if he had wielded the knife himself.

He had no illusions. He knew what he was capable of, and what he was likely to accomplish. He didn't know how far Alphomeg, or its employees might go, but he had a pretty good idea how far Tage would go.

The best outcome was probably his failure and the forfeit of the quarter million that Diomedes said was due him. More likely, he was going to end up as dead as Steven Coombs.

However, something about making that choice, in the face of everything, brought him a measure of peace. He wasn't frightened anymore, or angry at himself. He wasn't cursing all the bad decisions or mistakes that had led him to this point. All that was left was to figure out what he was going to do.

Twenty-fifth Move

The evening turned gray-black, lit by the occasional blue-white flash. Quaid was still awake, thinking.

A storm was coming, and they were going to want to evacuate Quaid and Carlos as soon as possible. Quaid didn't think Mr. Diomedes would be comfortable with them sitting the weather out here. The two of them were potential disruptions to the Game.

The concern wasn't unfounded; Quaid had his own plans about disrupting the Game. Most especially, Tage's role in this manufactured reality. But first he had to get away from this place, get to A. J. and Team D.

From the looks of the clouds, they were going to fly out at dusk. Quaid expected that Alphomeg must make a habit of night flying to be as circumspect as possible, using lights only when necessary.

So he had until dusk.

What then?

Alphomeg was treating them like willing players, but Quaid doubted that they were very trusting. Even if the Game hadn't resulted in a cascade of deaths, enough money was at stake here that standard operating procedure would require a healthy suspicion of the players.

They weren't going to be naïve about security, and Quaid wasn't going to get away with snagging any obvious weapon from this room, especially since they were probably under video surveillance.

However, Quaid knew from long bouts of hiding the extent of his drinking, paranoia was a two-way street. While it can keep you safe from real dangers—in Quaid's case the inevitable danger of the world finding out what a lush he had been, in Alphomeg the danger of their precious Game being corrupted—it made it very easy to see danger in logically improbable places.

What Quaid needed was a *threat* of a weapon. No matter how closely watched he was, how impossible the threat might be, their own paranoia would make the threat credible.

He needed an unobtrusive weapon. Something that no one would either realize was missing, or wouldn't figure out the significance of.

The idea that came to him was so ridiculous that it would probably be missed by any sane person watching them.

Quaid sat up, and Carlos mumbled something and turned to face him. When he stood up, Carlos muttered, "Where you going?"

"Bathroom. Get some rest."

"Uh-huh," Carlos said, and closed his eyes.

Quaid looked at him for a moment. Strangely, he felt as if he was getting his second wind himself. He could still feel fatigue in his muscles but it was a distant thing. He didn't feel tired anymore.

Maybe the decision to *do* something helped.

Quaid stepped into the bathroom to fetch his diabolical instrument. It took him a while to do it, moving his hands to hide what he was doing. He sat on the john the whole time, hoping that the bathroom wasn't wired for video. As he got up, he sat the toilet paper on the sink in a gesture he hoped was completely natural, just in case someone was watching.

Quaid returned to bed with the diabolical device safely in his pocket.

In the darkness, before they came for them, Quaid whispered, "Carlos?"

Carlos was half-asleep, the fatigue of the last few days was a suffocating pressure on his eyes and on the back of his skull. He mumbled a response. "Yeah?"

"You've done all anyone can expect of you already," Quaid told him. "Just remember that."

"Uh-huh." Carlos raised his palms to his eyes and tried to press the sleep from them. *What you're saying is we did our best and royally screwed everything up*. The sentiment did little to make

Carlos feel better. After a few moments, Carlos said, "I don't know why I ran."

Carlos heard Quaid turn on his side. He didn't look in Quaid's direction. He knew what Quaid was probably thinking. It was time to cut their losses. They'd made it to civilization, they did what they could to bring help. . . .

"What?"

"I've been going over it in my head," Carlos said, unsure why he was confessing. It was such a *minor* point, as if anything since would have changed if he hadn't run. "I don't know *why*. Sure I was scared, but I was moving before I *thought* about it."

"It's all right."

"No!" Carlos slammed his fist on the bed, angry at himself for running, for joining this damn game in the first place, for lying here unable to do anything but let these bastards ferry them back to real life while others were mired in this insanity. Carlos turned to look at Quaid. The guy still wore his glasses and they threw reflections from the window back at Carlos. Quaid had blind white holes for eyes.

Carlos sucked in a breath and said, quietly, "It was a damn fool thing that could've gotten us both killed—all of this was. I'm sorry."

"You don't need to."

"Yes, I do, and another thing—"

"What?"

"I meant it when I said you're the only one of the whole sorry bunch I trusted."

*   *   *

When the door opened, Carlos looked at Quaid. Quaid was staring at the pair of men in khaki who came into the room, and Carlos noticed his right hand move toward his pocket, and then stop.

The men announced that their flight was leaving in fifteen minutes.

Carlos watched Quaid, who seemed more nervous than the occasion called for. He wondered if their visitors noticed it, too.

What are you thinking, Quaid?

If it was escape, Carlos wondered how in the hell he was planning to do it. They were camped in the middle of a small army—an army that probably had more than tranquilizer darts at their disposal.

The pair led Quaid and Carlos out into the night.

The sky was black, completely. No stars, no moon, just a thick blanket of cloud cover. The air was heavy and humid, and ominously still. Carlos could feel the coming storm in his joints, a pressure that was just becoming an ache.

In the distance, toward the ocean, the undersides of the clouds rippled with blue flashes of lightning, and thunder was a constant background rumble.

Again, as they walked toward the helicopter, Carlos glanced at Quaid and saw his hand reaching for his pocket. In the dim light, Carlos thought he saw something, a bulge.

What have you got there?

The clearing with the helicopter was set far back from the buildings. They walked down a path that passed by most of the complex. Carlos saw people moving crates into the buildings and rolling steel shutters down over the windows. It looked like they expected a hell of a storm.

When they reached the helicopter, their escort slid the door aside and waved them into a large area for cargo, slung with empty webbing. One of the khaki-clad men stepped inside and swung a small bench down from the wall.

"Sit down," he told them. "I'll help you strap in."

A flash of lightning blue-lit the interior of the helicopter and for a fraction of a second, Carlos saw an expression on Quaid's face that looked like panic. For a moment he thought Quaid might run for it.

Then the flash was gone and he sat next to Carlos, allowing the khaki man to pull webbing down over both of his shoulders. Both straps buckled into the center of a regular lap belt. Then he did the same for Carlos.

"Now to release it," the guy said to both of them, "just hit it here." He indicated a red button on the buckle. Once he received nods of understanding from Carlos and Quaid, he left the helicopter and slid the door shut.

Carlos heard the pilot talking on the radio, and the engine began to whine. He looked over to Quaid and saw him finally put his hand all the way in his pocket, fumbling around the straps. Then, he turned to face Carlos and said, "If you don't want to go through this with me, there's time to bail now."

Carlos' thought was, *What kind of crazy stunt are you about to pull?* He said, "Whatever you're planning on, count me in." At this point in the choice between doing something and doing nothing, Carlos' self-respect was riding on *something*.

Carlos watched as Quaid pulled something cylindrical out of his pocket.

Is that what I think it is?

Carlos didn't know whether to laugh, or take Quaid's advice and bail. Quaid held in his hands the spring-loaded shaft from a toilet paper dispenser. As the engines gained in pitch, Quaid pulled it apart. The cheap plastic snapped, any sound lost under the roar of the rotors. The two halves slid aside, spilling a short black spring onto the floor.

Quaid pocketed the wider half, and gripped the narrower half in his hand.

Carlos stared dumbfounded as Quaid hit the release and his restraints fell away. He stood up, armed only with a cheap tube of plastic.

I don't believe he's doing this.

Quaid looked at Carlos and nodded to the door. He must have read Carlos' bewildered expression. Saying wordlessly, *There's time to bail.*

Carlos didn't move, and he didn't know if it was because he trusted Quaid, or because of a perverse curiosity about what he was going to do next.

Carlos shook his head.

The floor shifted under Carlos' feet. Quaid hung onto strapping in the wall as they became airborne. Once they'd been aloft about half a minute—an agonizingly slow half minute— Quaid jumped into the cockpit and rammed the plastic tube into the pilot's side, right over the kidney.

Carlos almost felt sympathy for the pilot. Quaid had jammed it *hard.*

Carlos could see what Quaid intended now, and Carlos hoped that Quaid's hand was enough out of the pilot's line of sight, and pressing through enough layers of fabric, to keep the pilot from calling Quaid's bluff.

"Don't move!" Quaid yelled. "Don't even fucking breathe."

"What the hell!" The pilot made a move toward the controls beside him.

"Don't try it! This baby will open you up to the *bone*, one shot." Quaid was yelling like a madman. "Give me a reason. Any reason."

"What do you w–wan—"

"Shut up!" Quaid yelled in his face.

Carlos was impressed. He never would have figured Quaid, who was a thin, nerdy-looking guy, to be able to pull this crap off. But if Carlos hadn't seen the toilet roll himself, he'd be on the verge of pissing his pants. It was hard to believe that Quaid wasn't armed and completely nuts.

It seemed as if Quaid had managed to distill the whole bizarre situation into a single crystalline vision of pure insanity.

Quaid was hunched over, inches from the pilot. Invading his personal space and, incidentally, hiding the guy's view of his fake gun. "You say nothing," he ordered. "You just listen. And you nod. Don't shake your head no, because that might upset me. Do you understand?"

Carlos saw a bead of sweat running down the pilot's forehead as he nodded.

"You're taking us to the four players who sent up the distress flares," Quaid whispered.

"I can't—"

"Don't make me kill you, motherfucker!" The sound of it made Carlos wince. Quaid was strung tight, shaking. Carlos thought that, if it had been a gun in his hand, Quaid might have shot.

"How many pilots you folks got?" Quaid yelled at him. "Two? Three? Your *job*—aside from running supplies to the Emerald City back there—is to make sure nobody gets too close to Oz's curtain. You know exactly where they are, if only to keep you from flying close enough they can read the logo on the chopper. Here's the news. That's where we're going."

"The storm—"

Quaid hit him with his other hand.

To look at Quaid, physical aggression was way out of his league, but he appeared on the

verge of frenzy. Carlos was wondering if it was
an act, or if he'd really gone off the deep end.

*Christ, if I'm thinking that, what's the pilot
thinking?*

The back of Quaid's left fist smashed into the
side of the pilot's mouth. Blood splattered the
windscreen in front of them and the helicopter
took a sickening lurch to the right and down
when the pilot's hands momentarily left the
controls.

Carlos saw panic in the pilot's eyes, especially
as he looked at the blood on the window in
front of him. It didn't seem to matter that most
of the blood seemed to be Quaid's. Carlos saw
the back of Quaid's hand bleeding, and Quaid's
face breaking character to show a wince of pain
as he shook his injured hand.

The pilot didn't see Quaid's lapse; he was
busy struggling to control the helicopter before
it plunged into the mountain.

Quaid composed himself and managed to re-
capture the manic gleam in his eyes. "That's
where we're going," he said.

This time no words, only a nod.

Twenty-sixth Move

"I can't land there!"

They were hovering over the area where Team D was supposed to be. Quaid had the pilot turn on the spotlight so he could see the area—the night seemed to be getting even darker, except for the occasional lightning flashes.

The jungle below them seemed to have collapsed in on itself. Tree trunks were tossed aside, down the slope of the hillside, like so many broken matchsticks. The land looked sunken in on itself.

"There!" Quaid said.

"The land's unstable! We land there and there could be another mudslide."

"You're going to land there," he said, "because that's your one chance of living through this."

The pilot muttered, "Fuck," but he headed toward the clearing below them. As they descended, Quaid saw what had caused the distress signal. This mudslide, which might have taken out a square mile of hillside, was very recent. The trees upended by it were still green under the spotlight. Team D must've got caught in it.

If they had, it was hard to believe that anyone would still be alive down there.

The helicopter lowered itself very gingerly. Quaid began to appreciate the pilot's fear. The space they were landing on was a relatively flat, clear area next to a river. The clearing overlooked the river from a thirty-foot-tall cliff that, he could see now, was made of a mix of dirt, trees, and other debris. It *wasn't* stable.

But, if Quaid let up now, gave the pilot a chance to breathe, to think, his act would be over. He couldn't let that happen.

So the helicopter lowered itself.

They set down like an overweight matron on a delicate antique chair. They touched, and settled down on the landing gear little by little. Quaid was impressed with the pilot; he didn't think you could have that fine control over this thing's movement.

When it seemed their weight had finally settled fully on the ground, Quaid told him to shut down the rotor. "Get up," he ordered the guy. He was going to back him into the cargo area and restrain him. He couldn't believe his luck. He was going to pull this off . . .

Quaid's self-congratulation was premature.

The pilot turned too quickly as he got out of his seat. Quaid couldn't move fast enough to hide his plastic tube. When he faced him, Quaid saw his gaze glance down at the tube in his hand. Realization dawned in the pilot's eyes.

Quaid saw what must have been the deepest fury he'd ever seen in the eyes of another human being.

"You bastard." The pilot's fist seemed to come out of nowhere—as if Quaid's face hit a wall chin first. Suddenly Quaid was looking up at the roof of the helicopter's cargo compartment.

Quaid's eyes were still blurry from the impact when he felt a boot slam into his kidney with an impact that made him feel that he'd piss blood for a week.

Before the pilot got a chance to get another blow in, Quaid heard the sound of another impact. Something solid striking something metallic, or vice versa.

Quaid felt a weight drape itself across his legs. He opened his eyes, the left one was already swelling shut.

The pilot was slumped across his legs, and Carlos was standing above both of them holding the metal box of a first aid kit. The kit had a large dent in one side.

"Are you all right?"

Quaid nodded, though the movement gave him waves of vertigo, and he sat up. Carlos started to pry the kit open and he shook his head. "Don't waste that on me until we see what A. J. and the others need."

Quaid looked down at his feet. The pilot was

facedown in a growing pool of his own blood. Carlos had hit him *hard*. He didn't blame him, but looking at the unmoving pilot, eyes half open and partway crossed, he couldn't help saying, "Please tell me that you know how to fly a helicopter."

Carlos frowned and shook his head.

Quaid pushed the pilot off of him and got to his feet, wincing at the pain in his side where the pilot had kicked him.

"Tie him up." Quaid had uncomfortable visions of Oyler as he said it. "Don't want him leaving while we're out looking for the others."

Carlos looked down at the guy. "How're we getting out of here if he can't fly?"

"We'll cross that bridge when we come to it."

They trussed up the pilot safely in the cargo netting, even though it looked like it would be quite a while before he would be up and around. The crease Carlos had put in his head looked real nasty, and it had bled all over the place. At first glance, it looked like the guy was dead.

Fortunately, he was still breathing, and Quaid looked into his eyes and saw his pupils still reacting to light—both equally. He was pretty sure that was a good sign.

Quaid didn't like leaving him alone, but he didn't think they had much choice. "I don't know how long we have before that storm hits," he said. "But we better get out of here before it does. This whole area is a mudslide waiting to happen."

"Great," Carlos said. "We don't even know that they're around here."

Quaid hunted around until he discovered a flashlight, some flares, and other emergency supplies. "If they are, I doubt they missed us landing. They'll either be making their way here, or trying to signal us."

Outside, the atmosphere had changed. It was still humid, but the temperature must have dropped ten or fifteen degrees, and a strong wind was coming in from the north.

Quaid lit one of the flares at either end of the helicopter. The last thing they wanted to do was lose it in the darkness.

Carlos came out after him and asked, "Where do we start?"

That was a good question. They were almost in the center of the flattened area of mud and timber. Broken trees and soil marked the hillside for about two or three hundred yards above them, and, below their temporary cliff, on the other side of the river, the devastation continued downslope for about twice that far.

It was too large an area to search in the time they had. Their only real hope of finding anyone was to pray that Team D had heard or seen the helicopter land—if they were anywhere near here, they must've—and hope they could see the flares now.

All they needed was some sort of sign from them.

Quaid walked as close as he dared to the edge of the cliff, moving around facing out from the helicopter and the glow from the flares. He shone his light out into the darkness, trying to pick out some movement, some patch of color, something to tell him where they were.

Quaid circled the helicopter twice, searching in vain for some sign of life.

"Over here," Carlos called out to him from the other end of the clearing. Quaid rushed there, slipping in the mud. "Shut off the flashlight," Carlos said to him as Quaid slid up next to him. He was looking north of their position, past the river.

When Quaid shut off the flashlight, he saw what Carlos was seeing. There was a very weak glow at the edge of the woods. It was dim and yellow, but obviously artificial. "That's them," Carlos said.

As Quaid watched, the light shut off.

"They've been turning it on for just a few seconds every minute or so," Carlos said. "Batteries must almost be dead."

Quaid shone his light in that direction, trying to identify landmarks that they could recognize once they came off of the high ground. While he was looking, the light came on again and waved back and forth. He waved his flashlight as well, to let them know they'd been seen.

"Carlos, go back in the helicopter, see if you can find any rope."

While Carlos looked for some rope, Quaid tried to plot out a safe course to the others. The problem was, he couldn't see one. Where he stood, for one reason or another, the sliding ground decided to approximate a flat, level surface. Between here and there was an obstacle course of deadfalls, washed-out mud, and a fast-flowing river that occasionally carried past a branch the size of his thigh.

Quaid began to feel the first mists of rain on his cheek.

If they had a pilot, they could hunt down a site that was closer—at least more easily reached. As it was, he didn't know how they were going to leave at all.

"One thing at a time," he cautioned himself. "Don't get ahead of yourself."

Carlos came back with a coil of rope. It was time.

At the edge of the river Quaid handed the flashlight to Carlos. "It's going to be up to you to pull me out if this goes bad."

"I should go first—"

"No offense, I'm younger. I have a better chance."

Carlos took the flashlight and shone it at the water. "No offense, but how many times did you go under at the boathouse?"

"I don't have a body dragging at me this

time," Quaid said as he tied one end of the rope around his waist. As he said it, his gaze followed the beam of the flashlight. The waters were brown with silt, and deceptively calm. He could almost convince himself they weren't moving at all—then they would carry another large branch past, surprisingly quickly.

Quaid secured the other end of the rope to the root system of a massive tree that was now buried crown-first in several hundred tons of mud.

Quaid made sure the anchor was tight, looked back at the waters, and made sure again.

Quaid handed the slack to Carlos. "Let it out easy, a little at a time."

"You be careful."

"Now you tell me." Quaid edged down to the river.

The water seemed to be racing by him now, the illusion of stillness evaporating. He had chosen this spot because it seemed to be where the water was shallowest. About midway, a log was wedged giving possible purchase for a crossing.

Quaid sucked in a breath and stepped in.

The water was frigid, sucking the heat from his body as it battered his legs. He stepped carefully. The footing was treacherous, a combination of soft mud that sucked at his ankles and twisted branches that clawed at his legs. The river here was only about fifteen yards wide, but by six feet in, he was already having trouble. He was chest-deep in the water now, and the current was causing his feet to skip across the bottom. He tried to push against the current, but it only shoved him into deeper waters where his feet couldn't find purchase at all.

Quaid's head went underwater, for a moment it seemed, but he'd been whisked fifteen or twenty feet down from where he wanted to be. Then the rope on his waist went taut, and his head was submerged again.

Quaid struggled for air and broke the surface. In the darkness, he could barely see Carlos straining against the rope, pulling him back. He saw chain lightning flash across the sky and the first real sheets of rain began falling down on them.

They didn't have the time.

Quaid waved at Carlos that he was all right, and he started to swim toward the opposite shore. The cold water sent daggers of ice through his kidney with every other stroke.

Quaid felt as if he'd inhaled two lungsful of water before he reached a downed tree he could hold on to. Once he grabbed it, he hung on for dear life as the current swept past him. The bark was slippery and bit into his hands, but he managed to hold on and pull himself slowly to the opposite shore.

It seemed endless, pulling himself hand over hand, stopping twice to untangle the rope from a stray branch. But near the roots of the half-submerged tree, his feet found purchase again and he could slog his way up to shore.

Once his feet were out of the river, he pulled the rope taut and secured it to another solidly downed tree. Rain was coming down in hard sheets now. He could barely see Carlos at the other side of the river. "Come on," he yelled over the storm.

Several lightning flashes streaked across the sky, followed almost immediately by thunderous cracks, as if the spine of the sky were breaking.

Quaid looked up to where the flares still glowed by the helicopter.

Please hold, he prayed.

Carlos coming across was almost an anticlimax. With the rope to hold on to, he managed it much better than Quaid had. Thankfully, he didn't say anything about it when he reached the shore.

"Let's go see about them," Carlos said.

They started the tedious climb through the rain and the deadfalls.

Twenty-seventh Move

It took them nearly fifteen minutes to make their way to the edge of the woods, where the ground hadn't yet turned to sliding mud. To Quaid, it felt like hours.

Rain veiled the world around them, making the darkness even more impenetrable. The ground beneath them snaked with hundreds of tiny rivulets, undermining the fallen trees and making the deadfalls more unstable every minute.

Intermittently, the wind would pick up in a gale, blowing the rain sideways. Every time, the roar of the storm would be accompanied by the groaning of shifting lumber. Quaid had the sick feeling that every step he took, every handhold he grabbed, could all slide out from under him at any moment. In several places, when his feet stepped into running water, he felt as if the ground was already moving downslope.

When they reached the woods, they faced a sheer mud cliff. The ground level here, where the earth had moved, was six to ten feet lower than where the trees still stood upright. At the edge of the wound, the earth gaped open, facing them with its strata of mulch and topsoil, roots holding it all in as if the earth was ashamed of its nakedness.

What worried Quaid was that the rain had already undercut many of the roots, washing the earth and clay away, leaving a number of roots hanging in empty air. That gave them plenty of handholds to pull themselves up the cliff, but it made it increasingly likely that the trees on the edge of the great wound might collapse.

When they reached the top of the cliff, several trees down the slope did just that. One was already leaning when it started making an ominous straining sound and collapsed outward, into the mudslide, as if pushed by its still upright fellows. Four or five trees, all at the edge, followed it like a row of dominoes. Their impact raised a crash that he felt in the soles of his feet.

Quaid looked up to where the helicopter was. All that was visible from here were the flares he had set up to mark the site. It seemed tantalizingly close. . . .

As he watched, he thought he saw one of the flares move.

No time.

"Hello?" he shouted into the darkness.

"A. J.? Gordon?" Carlos joined him, shouting into the roaring rainstorm.

"Eve? Bobbie?"

They were answered by a strobing lightning

flash above their heads. This time close enough that the shuddering impact of the thunder followed before the flash had faded. Quaid's eyes were still dazzled when he saw the dim yellow eye of the flashlight again.

They both ran toward it, as fast as they could, through the soggy underbrush.

Team D was camped out in a clearing facing a small hill shrugged up by the ground. They had a small canvas sheet up as a shelter, tied between the trees. It wasn't doing much to shelter them from the sideways-driving rain.

A. J. faced them, holding the dim flashlight in his left hand. *Thank God he's alive and still ambulatory*, was Quaid's first thought.

Quaid's second, when he shone his flashlight on him, was: *What the hell happened to him?*

His right arm was in an improvised sling. He wasn't wearing a shirt—that was what his sling seemed to be made of—and his torso was striped with vivid bruises that wrapped around his body, turning black when they reached his right side.

His pants were torn, spattered with blood and mud. He walked with a limp, favoring his left foot.

"You don't believe how good it is to see you guys," he greeted them. "We'd almost given up."

Quaid nodded and walked into their little camp. He saw Eve lying on the ground. She was tied down to a construction made of a pair of saplings, and what looked to be the remains of several backpacks.

"We had to rig something so that Bobbie and I could move her." He pointed his flashlight down at her legs.

Most of her legs.

They had wrapped them in some sort of fabric. A. J.'s shirt maybe, or maybe they had packed a sheet. The cloth used to be white, it was now stained black and red, and the outlines it covered were crooked and incomplete. She was strapped to the makeshift device with rope and the straps from the cannibalized backpacks.

"A log fell on me when the mudslide happened. She was crushed between two trees," A. J. explained. "She needs a hospital. She's been continually delirious since we dug her out."

Quaid shone his light up where Bobbie was. She looked pale and shaken, but otherwise unhurt. She was holding the sides of Eve's head. "Someone found help?" she asked him.

"Long story," Quaid said. "We don't have time right now." He looked up and saw no sign of the storm letting up. If anything, the wind was becoming fiercer, more constant, the lightning more frequent. "We have to get you to the helicopter before this storm starts another mudslide."

"Where's Gordon?" Carlos asked.

The way Bobbie and A. J. looked at them gave

the answer before A. J. said, "He was in front of Eve. He was buried completely. . . ."

"Let's get moving," Quaid said. "Bobbie, help A. J. Me and Carlos will take Eve."

"Where are the others?" A. J. asked. There was the trace of fear in his voice, as if he was just beginning to realize where they were going.

"It's just us and the helicopter," Quaid said. "And there isn't going to be a second one."

"We have to move through that?" Bobbie stood and turned toward the slide area. You couldn't see it from where they were, not in the darkness of the storm, but he knew what she was thinking. Ten more minutes of this storm and the footing was that much worse, more dangerous than what they had scrambled over when they had come here.

Now they were going to cross it, one man with a single arm and two of them carrying a stretcher.

Quaid looked around the clearing and saw the hill overlooking them was snaking with its own storm-generated rivulets. He shone his flashlight around and saw where sheets of water were sliding down the slope, covering the ground an inch deep.

The water was all brown with silt and mud. The whole hillside was saturated. It wouldn't be long before the earth started flowing like the water. "We have to move you now, before there's another slide."

*   *   *

Quaid didn't like the way Eve was shaking her head. Her mouth moved, but whatever she was saying was lost in the roar of the storm. Her eyes were closed, and she didn't seem to be responding to anything. Moving her couldn't be good, but what choice did they have? They couldn't stay put, this whole hillside was liable to go.

That's what he kept telling himself as he and Carlos carried her to the edge of the woods.

They had to hunt down the lowest portion of the mud cliffs so they could lower Eve down. They came upon a crater that had been left by a recently collapsing tree. It gave them a semi-stable place to stand that was about halfway down to the slide area.

Among the four of them, they managed to first lower the stretcher to the crater, the giant root ball of the fallen tree hovering above like a tentacled monster about to devour them. From there they managed to get her the rest of the way down.

Then they were on the shattered hillside. The rivulets had turned into actual rivers by now. Streams the same color as the mud they cut grooves through. The trees were illuminated in the lightning and distorted in the rain—as if the hillside was rotting away, exposing its twisted skeleton.

"You, A. J." Quaid yelled at Bobbie. "Take the lead. That way." He tilted his head toward the bluff where one flare was still dimly visible through the rain. The bluff it perched on, from this angle, seemed ominously tall and narrow now. Quaid might have seen a sheet of earth slide off of it as he watched, piling into the river that cut at its base.

"We left a rope to help you cross the river."

In a flash of lightning, he caught A. J. looking at him. His expression told him that he knew exactly how bad this situation was. He grabbed Bobbie's arm and started dragging her toward the river.

Quaid's march to the river was the longest distance he had ever walked in his life. They didn't have the luxury of a free hand to steady themselves. Every step was a potential disaster as every branch, rock, or patch of ground they stepped on tried to slide downhill, taking them with it. Most of the way, Quaid's feet were ankle-deep in rushing mud and water, keeping him from even seeing what he had to put his weight upon.

They didn't even have the help of the flashlight. They had no way to carry it. Their way was illuminated by the now nearly constant flashes of lightning.

Several times he saw Carlos slip ahead of him, causing Eve's mangled legs to dip toward the shifting ground and causing his own heart to try and slam through his chest. He could feel every move in his side where the pilot had kicked him.

Three quarters of the way there, he slipped

and fell to his knees. Quaid's right knee slammed into a submerged branch so hard that he blacked out for a moment. He managed to keep hold of his end of the stretcher without pulling Carlos down after him.

Quaid got slowly to his feet, and as he did, he saw a new flare up on top of the bluff. Bobbie and A. J. had made it up to the helicopter.

"Get in," Quaid whispered. "You don't have the time to wait for us."

If anything, their progress seemed to slow as they closed onto the bluff. The mud pulled at their ankles, and dead roots and branches grabbed for them at every step.

When they reached the banks of the now-swollen river, they had to set Eve down so they could find where they had crossed before. The land was mutating as they watched, the river changing its shape, shifting its banks. The rope he had strung over the river was much closer to being submerged now, and the edges of the river had overtaken the tree he had tied it to. The rope now *started* ten feet from the bank. As he watched, every few moments, a new slide of mud fell into the river from the edges, widening it even more. . . .

"We take her to the rope," he called to Carlos. "We're going to have to carry her one-handed."

"This is fucked up, Quaid." Carlos called back to him. "You think we can make it across there?"

"Yes," he lied.

They carried the stretcher normally, until they reached the rope. By that point, the water was coursing past them at waist level, faster than he remembered. Carlos reached the rope first. He let go of the left side of the stretcher so he could grab the rope. Quaid winced as muddy water coursed over Eve's battered legs, but there wasn't much he could do. At least the stretcher floated, mostly.

They kept moving, until it was his turn to grab the rope. He moved the stretcher so that the left pole rested its end on the rope. Carlos must have realized what he was doing, because he let go of the rope—a dangerous thing, as he was already in the water up to his armpits. Somehow he managed to turn around to face him, across the stretcher.

"What are you doing!" he called to him.

"We can do this!" Quaid shouted back.

Carlos got his end of the stretcher on to the rope. It was easier on his end, because the rope was almost submerged at that point. Now they had the left side of the stretcher up on the rope. They only had to support the other side.

In theory, it should work.

In practice it was like pushing a car uphill with four flats. The stretcher caught the rope every two or three feet. And after they had moved a few yards into the river, the water was rushing over all three of them so badly that the only way he knew that they weren't tumbling downstream was the fact that the rope was still taut.

Both his hands were raw and bleeding, his right hand clamped on to the stretcher so tightly he thought he would tear the fingers from his hand.

For an eternity it seemed like that, waves crashing over his head, only able to break the surface long enough to gasp for air and make sure that Eve's head was above water.

Then they reached the other end of the guide rope, and the real nightmare began. The river had widened here as well, and the area on this bank was a swamp of sliding mud. They walked toward the bluff, and he could feel the mud suck halfway up his calves. Occasionally past his knees.

Every step was a struggle, the water still rushing past their waists . . .

Around them, sides small and large collapsed from the edges of the eroding bluff. Quaid lost count of the times he fell, plunging himself underwater. Half the time, he managed to hold on to the stretcher. He didn't know if Carlos fell or not, his focus had narrowed to a small universe of himself, and the few feet of his end of the stretcher.

Then, when he fell a final time, he lost the part of his world that was Eve and the stretcher.

He panicked, trying to push himself up, his hands plunging into the semi-liquid mud that was trying to suck his legs under. He sucked a mouthful of liquid clay into his lungs and started coughing.

Quaid was convinced that he was going to die at that moment.

Then someone grabbed his shoulder and pulled his head out of the mud where he had fallen. Quaid's immediate thanks to A. J. was to vomit a stream of black mud, blood, and bile onto his chest. He gasped a few times. His breathing was raw, and it hurt, but he was alive. In a flash of lightning, he could see Bobbie and Carlos ahead of them, carrying Eve up the slope to the helicopter.

"Come on," A. J. said, pulling at him with his good arm. He'd hooked it under his armpit. The effort caused him visible pain, but Quaid needed the help to free his legs.

In a few moments, he was moving again. With A. J.'s help, he made it up the crumbling hillside.

Twenty-eighth Move

Time was even more critical than Quaid had thought. In the glow from the flares he could see that the edge of the bluff, once comfortably twenty feet away from the skids of the helicopter, was now within a foot, or less. The helicopter had also developed a perceptible list, the rotors angled toward the bottom of the hillside some three hundred yards down.

Once this hillside started moving in earnest, it wouldn't stop down there, when the ground turned level. When the momentum took this earth, it wouldn't stop for a mile, maybe more.

The ground was moaning, rumbling, as if it was on the verge of waking.

"How's the pilot?" he yelled as Carlos piled in with A. J. The words tore the skin from his throat.

"Still out," Bobbie said.

Fuck.

"Tell me that you can fly this thing." He turned to A. J.

A. J. was shaking his head, staring at the pilot

who was still trussed up where they had left him. The blood had all clotted now, and the pilot was drooling a little.

"I don't know—" A. J. said.

"Damn it, you're a pilot."

"I've only had about a dozen hours in two-man helicopters—without a busted arm."

Quaid pulled him into the cockpit. "Well, you're going to tell me how to fly this thing. We don't have the time to wait for him to wake up."

In a few minutes they were both strapped in up front, and the storm was overwhelmed by the sound of the engines starting. Quaid's hands were sweating on the stick between his knees.

"Wait for the RPMs," A. J. was telling him. "Wait."

The engine whined. He wanted this thing to take off *now*, but A. J. had warned him that the engine had to get up to speed before he pulled the stick back and tried to take off. The wait seemed endless. With every moment, the helicopter seemed to nose farther and farther down. He couldn't even see the bluff out the windscreen anymore. It had eroded away to some point almost under his feet.

The cockpit tilted again and A. J. said, "Now."

Quaid pulled and felt the rotors bite the air, trying to lever them airborne. The movement of the helicopter was too much for the bluff. Beneath them, he could see much of the hill slide

down, smashing logs together in its race to reach
the bottom. Fortunately, they didn't go with it.

Quaid didn't have much time to congratulate
himself. The helicopter was shaking, fighting the
wind as he battled weather a veteran pilot
shouldn't have been flying in.

With A. J. stepping him through the points of
steering, and changing the pitch of the rotor
blades, he managed to fly the thing, after a
fashion.

He found the switch for the spotlight, and
suddenly he had a circle of reality below him,
cut out of the darkness. Right now it shone
down on the mudslide zone, and it had the appearance of a giant mile-wide river—the earth
moving everywhere, flowing like water.

Quaid turned them north.

In a few minutes the spotlight found the one
landmark he had. The road. The helicopter was
moving erratically in the storm, and several
times they were blown aside and he had to fight
his way back to within sight of it.

They reached the Alphomeg compound, only
taking about twice as long as it had to get out
there.

"What is this place?" A. J. asked.

"Old Japanese base from World War II, taken
over by Alphomeg Entertainment."

"Alphomeg—that sounds familiar. . . ."

"They couldn't make you forget everything,"
Quaid said. "This is their game."

Then they were too busy to talk. A. J. giving

him orders on how to land this thing. It was a nightmare, the wind trying to smash the helicopter into the trees. He slammed the thing into the ground, half off the pad.

Quaid didn't shut off the engine.

"What are you doing?" A. J. asked him.

Quaid told him.

"Are you insane? You need to shut down the rotor."

Quaid shook his head. "No, I don't have the time to start it up again." He pointed out the windscreen. Half a dozen khaki-clad guards and a pair of Hummers were heading toward them through the driving rain.

"Start it up again? You can't fly this thing—"

"You told me enough to get where I'm going."

A. J. shook his head. "I don't understand—"

"I can't let Tage win."

"It's a *game*," A. J. said. "It really is just a game."

"Not anymore," Quaid said. "Are you going to go back there and get what I need?"

A. J. stared at him.

"We don't have time. Get it for me, or just get the wounded off. I can't spend time debating."

A. J. shook his head and slipped into the back. In a few moments he was back with a sheet of paper and Oyler's gun. "This might not even work anymore. It's been submerged a couple of times."

Quaid nodded and took the paper. It had been

torn off a clipboard that sat next to the pilot's
seat. Quaid didn't look at what was written on
the back; he knew what it said.

A. J. shook his head and told him, "You can't
seriously think this game—"

"Get back there and help move the injured
off—"

A. J. left the gun on the copilot's seat.

Quaid didn't know if he was acting sane or
not. All he did know was that this wasn't over,
not with Tage Garnell still lording it over the
Game.

Quaid's greatest fear right now was that some
of the Alphomeg people might try to board the
helicopter before he lifted off. He reached over
and picked up the gun, in case.

After an endless period of time, he heard the
door slide shut, muffling the sounds of the
storm outside.

Quaid looked back out the windscreen and
saw the Alphomeg people taking Eve and the
pilot. Quaid hoped he had done the right thing.
He hoped they had the facilities to at least stabi-
lize Eve.

He looked for the others, and saw two men
apiece on Carlos and Bobbie.

A. J.?

"Wait for them to get clear," A. J. told him as
he took the seat next to him.

"You don't—" Quaid started.

"Quaid, you are nuts if you're thinking of flying in this weather alone." He pulled the re-

straints across himself one-handed. "You barely
made the landing."

"This isn't your fight—"

"The hell it isn't." A. J. glanced out the windscreen. "Pull up, *now*."

Quaid started levering the helicopter into the
air. And suddenly A. J. was shouting orders at
him again. As they rose, he tossed the gun back
to A. J., because he needed two hands to control
this thing. The wind was making the helicopter
skip sideways on its skids, toward the trees. If
the rotors cut into that, it would be a very
short trip.

A. J. yelled at him to turn the machine. Quaid
struggled for control and they stopped skipping
toward the jungle. Now the tail was swinging
in that direction.

A. J. was screaming at him now.

Quaid yanked the stick and began a shaky
corkscrew ascent. The tail cleared the trees before cutting into them. Once they were airborne
and fairly steady, A. J. gave him a look that said,
I told you so.

At least they had a tailwind on the way back
to the hotel. The helicopter dipped and rose, it
seemed, with no rhyme or reason, whatever
Quaid did with the controls. He was grateful
that there weren't any power lines, or other air-
craft, to worry about.

From the occasional glance at A. J.'s pale expression, his passenger was even more grateful.

A. J. had him overshoot the hotel. The front of the building, the long sloping lawn, was the clearest place to try and set the thing down. The single flagpole, and the cannon below it, were the only obstacles.

The spotlight passed over the top of the sprawling Victorian as they headed toward the chosen landing area. The hotel was a great W-shaped building, its two wings enclosing the garden and the ballroom. Above it, like some obscure foreign accent mark, Quaid could even see the ruin of the greenhouse.

Then A. J. was yelling commands, and Quaid had to fight the machine and the wind to keep from landing in the lagoon. Even with A. J. telling him every move, he still barely made it. As Quaid tried to land, the skids slid across the ground again. The whole machine tipped as the skids left the lawn and dug into the sand of the beach.

They bounced twice on the left skid, then the wind shifted direction and slammed the other side down into the sand.

"Shut her down," A. J. yelled at him, and Quaid shut down everything he could think of to shut down. The rotors whined to a stop, but the wind continued to batter them, shaking the helicopter as if they were still in danger of tipping over.

A. J. looked pale and ghostly in the glow from the instrument lights. "I am never going to do that again."

"We made it—"

A. J. nodded and said, "Don't let that inspire you to get a pilot's license." He unbuckled himself and looked up at the hotel. "Before we go up there—"

"A. J., you're injured. There's no reason for you to—"

"Before *we* go in there, you should give me the full story."

"Okay. I'll give you the details on the way."

Quaid slid open the door to the helicopter and they stepped out.

The rain was a driving, almost solid force. But even in this weather, Quaid would have expected someone to come out. Could anyone have missed the fact that a helicopter had almost crash-landed in their front yard?

But no one came. In the blue flashes of lightning, he could see the lawn between here and the hotel entrance was completely empty.

He shouted the story of Alphomeg to A. J. as they made their way toward the hotel.

The ground here was as saturated as the hillside had been. The lawn was drowning under a sheet of water that was flowing downhill to the lagoon. They walked up the center of the lawn, slowly, because the wind and the slick grass were conspiring to topple them. He had to hold the gun because A. J. needed his good arm to hang on to him.

Quaid told him about Steven Combs as they passed the flagpole.

Above them, on top of the bluff, light blazed in the hotel's windows. It stared down, an alien creature from another dimension. Not only was it from a different era than the one it lived in, it was something that never belonged in this place to begin with.

It might have been his state of mind, but just looking at the building gave him the sense that something corrupt was living inside it.

They reached the lobby doors without seeing anyone.

Quaid pushed the doors in, letting in the wind and driving rain as he stepped into the room. "Hello!" he called out. "Is anyone here?"

A. J. stared around the lobby as if he was seeing it for the first time. "So Tage stole the one thing that would explain what we were doing here?"

"Yeah, that's what Diomedes said."

"And you believe him?" A. J. said.

Quaid shook his head. "Not by himself, but the evidence was pointing at Tage even before Carlos pulled my jailbreak."

"I don't know, Quaid. From what you've said, it's Alphomeg that would have the motive to kill Coombs, not Tage. He's supposed to be just another random player like the rest of us."

"I've been thinking about that. If Tage stole those briefing books, his strategy for this game was to keep the rest of us—except maybe his allies—from knowing what the game was. If Coombs was a reporter infiltrating Alphomeg's 'game' he would have known what this was long before he ever took Oyler's place. If Oyler ever existed. Alphomeg's amnesia treatment wouldn't have erased that prior knowledge, and any gaps were probably filled by that notebook."

"You think Oyler was killed because he knew what the game was?"

"That would fit."

A. J. shook his head. "Then why didn't the bastard tell all of us when he had the chance?"

"I don't—"

A groan came from the direction of the ballroom.

Quaid slammed through the double doors ahead of A. J., afraid of exactly what he would find—

Quaid stopped dead in the doorway. He held up the gun, but it shook because he didn't know where to aim.

A. J. ran into him, came to a stop, and said, "Good lord."

The moan had come from Olivia Grossmann. The woman who had thought so much about God and the Devil was bound at the wrists and hung up on the stage so her feet barely brushed the ground. Dr. Yanowitz was strung up next to her, unconscious but breathing. Frank Pisarski was on the stage, neck twisted unnaturally far away from them and colored a vicious purple. Otherwise his skin was almost bluish-white.

Frank wasn't moving at all.

"Oh, fuck, don't shoot me, man!"

Quaid swung the gun down to cover Duce, who was busy falling out of a folding chair and trying to hold his hands up at the same time. *"What are you doing?"* Quaid yelled at him.

"Guarding the prisoners," Duce said. "That's all."

"Get them down!"

"I can't—"

Quaid's practice with the pilot must have had some effect, because he had pretty much convinced himself that he *would* shoot Duce if he didn't do as he said. Duce must have seen it in his eyes, because he half stumbled, half ran, to the stage and started lowering Olivia.

"Where's Tage?" A. J. asked him. From the tone of his voice, Quaid could tell he'd lost any reservations about Tage being the man behind all this.

"And the others?" Quaid added.

"I don't know," Duce said as he scrambled to free the doctor.

"What the hell do you mean, 'you don't know?'" Quaid kept Duce covered with the gun while A. J. walked up on the stage to check out the victims. He checked Frank first. Quaid winced as A. J.'s fingers sank into the flesh of Frank's neck. A. J. shook his head and went to free Olivia and Yanowitz.

Quaid had to bite down his anger enough for his words to be coherent. "Sit down, Duce."

Duce backed away from him and A. J.

"No," Quaid said. "Right there."

Duce looked at him, looked at the ground, looked at the gun.

"Now!"

Duce dropped to the floor of the stage.

Quaid climbed carefully up to the stage. Keeping his attention on Duce, he called aside to A. J. "How're the other two?"

"They've both been roughed up. Yanowitz has a nasty knock to the head, Mrs. Grossmann has some bruising to the neck. But they're both breathing all right, and they don't seem to be in shock." He lifted their eyelids, one at a time. "Reacting okay to light."

Quaid felt some small relief at that. He edged sideways and picked up the rope that had bound Olivia's hands and tossed it to Duce. Duce stared at him. Quaid glared back, and Duce started tying his wrists together.

He obviously couldn't do a good job all by himself, but once he seemed somewhat entangled, Quaid handed the gun to A. J. and drew the rope tight and wrapped it around Duce's wrists and forearms a few more times for good measure. The last two loops he wrapped around Duce's ankles as well, immobilizing him.

Quaid stepped back. "How long have you been here?"

"Six, eight hours," Duce said. "What the hell

could I do? He would have killed me." He looked at A. J., as if seeing him for the first time. In the light, A. J. looked even worse. Shirtless, and the bruises wrapping his torso were a rainbow of colors from yellow, to crimson, to blue-green to a livid black. Even after the downpour, his hair was spiked with mud, and several day's worth of beard gave him a crazed look.

"What are you going to do?" Duce asked.

"What matters is what *you're* going to do," Quaid said.

"W–what's that?" Duce asked him. He still looked at the gun. His wise-ass bravado was gone. He looked a lot younger now

"You're going to talk to us, Duce."

Twenty-ninth Move

Duce was grateful for the excuse to unload on someone. Even Quaid Loman, the guy most likely to jeopardize his share of the take. Tage had been getting weirder and weirder, colder and colder, since all this shit began. The only reason Duce had been following his lead was out of fear. Even the money wasn't that much of an incentive anymore, not after that chick slit her wrists.

Duce had always imagined himself able to survive some hard-core scenes, but this was a little beyond what he wanted to deal with. He told Quaid that. He told Quaid that this shit really wasn't his fault, after all, what could he do when that shit Tage waved a share of twenty-five million dollars in his face, huh?

You'd have to be a fucking saint to resist that, huh? And Duce knew he wasn't no fucking saint. And damn straight he wasn't no martyr.

So, Duce laid it out from the beginning—

The last thing he remembered—the last thing Alphomeg let him remember—was his eighteenth birthday.

Duce had celebrated it on a Greyhound bus that he'd slipped aboard without a ticket. He had no clue where he was going, or even what state he had been in. All he had were the clothes on his back and fifteen dollars in his pocket, on the sixth month of running away from his mother and the trailer park they'd lived in.

Duce didn't like the righteous look Quaid gave him and told him that he'd rather sleep on the sidewalk than go back to that place. The night he'd left, his mom's boyfriend had dropped a crack pipe on the sofa bed and set the thing on fire. Duce had asked himself the question, *Where am I going to sleep tonight?*

The obvious answer was: *Not here.*

The story he put together later, was that during the blank spot in his memory, one of Alphomeg's recruiters caught sight of him. Something caused them to glom on to him as a potential candidate for their game. Who knows if it was his charm or good looks, or the fact that no one would give a shit if he disappeared for a few months.

Who the fuck gave a damn. Duce knew that once someone mentioned the quarter mil he would be in, and God help anyone who'd try and pull him out.

Of course, Duce didn't *remember* Alphomeg, or anything else. At the time, it seemed as if he'd fallen asleep on the bus and had woken up in this hotel room God-knows-where. Still dark outside when he left his room to look around.

All Duce knew was that he was seriously fucked up.

He'd never done any really hard drugs before, some pot, some acid, but nothing that had done up his memory like this. He had gone through most of the hotel before dawn.

Duce ended up in the lobby, and by then he was pretty sure that there wasn't any staff around. No maids, no one in the kitchen, no guys manning the desk. However, there were lots of thick manila envelopes, one with his name on it.

What Duce found was a bit different than what everyone else found. There was the sheet of rules, which Duce found bizarre. But there was also a small pamphlet with Alphomeg's logo on it.

You have been selected to play a very special game . . .

Duce read the details, wondering if it was some bizarre joke. They were paying him two hundred fifty thousand to play a fucking game at some empty resort hotel? It was nuts. Then he read the part about the grand prize . . .

God, was that a beauty deal if you were one of the winners.

Duce had started rifling through everyone else's envelopes when he felt a cold pressure on the back of his neck. Nothing was touching him, but there was a presence behind him, a weight. He turned around slowly, feeling as if a cop was about to bust him.

Duce turned, faced Tage, and slowly put a pile of envelopes on the desk.

The guy must have been watching him for a while. He was just standing there in the doorway. Duce knew at once the guy wasn't a cop, even though he was giving him a cop look—arrogance with obvious distaste . . .

Duce didn't like the way the guy was looking at him. "Who the hell are you?"

Tage smiled at him. Duce didn't like the guy's smile. He didn't like the guy's whole attitude. He was stressed out just by finding himself here.

Duce vaulted over the desk. The guy was still smiling. Still hadn't said a word to him. Still had that damn shit-eating grin on his face. Duce wanted to wipe it off.

"I asked you a question," Duce said. He walked up to the guy.

Tage never moved. He simply cocked his head and asked, "Is there some sort of problem?"

The guy was looking at him as if he were some interesting species of fungus. It infuriated Duce, who grabbed for the guy's arm—

Suddenly, and without any warning, Duce was facing the desk, his own arm levered up between his shoulder blades. Pain was shooting through his arm and all that went through Duce's mind was wonder at how quickly the guy had moved.

"*Fuck*," Duce muttered.

"I'm sorry you didn't choose to be more polite," Tage chastised him. "Now are you going to tell me nicely, what's happening here?"

Duce spilled his guts, his words breathless from the pain. He had to stand on tiptoe to keep from feeling the arm rip out of its socket. His free hand scattered envelopes in front of Tage.

"Interesting," Tage muttered. He managed to keep Duce pinned while he pulled out his own envelope from the pile. It seemed he perused the pamphlet forever.

Then he heard Tage say, "This is rich. *Tage Garnell!* The poor fuckers don't even know—"

"Christ, let me go, man!"

Tage increased the pressure on Duce's arm, and he gasped. "Now, son, didn't I tell you to be polite? If you respect your elders, we might both benefit from this grand prize, don't you think?"

"Okay, okay," Duce nodded maniacally, just to get the guy off of him. "What do you want?"

"An ally."

It happened like that, too quickly for Duce to understand exactly how. Within moments, Tage had freed him and was liberating the orientation packets from the envelopes.

Quaid asked Duce why.

So simple, man. Everyone suffered from the same fucking memory block, right? The orientation said so. If we don't let them know what kind of cash is riding on this game, they ain't going to fight for it. Chances were, everyone would panic, forfeit left and right, and leave him and Tage to split the twenty-five mil.

The pilot, who looked like he'd just come from a train wreck, asked why Tage had laughed at his name. *What* exactly did the fuckers not know?

He was getting to that.

First, they could see how he was conned, right? Tage waved, what was it, twelve and a half million in his face. How could you not go for that kind of money?

And he had believed it, too. Stepped right into Tage's conspiracy as if the guy had been his best bud for life—not someone who'd just about amputated his arm within thirty seconds of their first meeting. Tage convinced him that they were going to win the game together, and he made it sound so sensible, so reasonable, that Duce could almost taste the money.

Of course, by the time Duce realized that things weren't going to work that way, he had other reasons to keep his mouth shut.

"You got to understand, man. Who the fuck was this Oyler guy? Somehow he knew, right? You saw that, didn't you? He'd known and he *hadn't* seen one of those booklets."

Duce had watched the guy flipping through his notebook all through that first meeting. After the meeting broke up, Duce had run off on his own to find this Oyler character.

Duce found him back in his room, still flipping through his notebook. Asked him point-blank what he thought was going on. Oyler was cagey, said they had to go someplace private, someplace that wasn't monitored.

Okay, Duce told him. They'd ended up in the darkness of the root cellar. That was where Oyler showed Duce his notes. Alphomeg this, Alphomeg that. He knew exactly what was going on. He was a fucking reporter or something, investigating rumors of this damn game. He knew all about it. The notes he'd smuggled in told him all about it.

Including the fact that someone had swiped the orientation pamphlets.

Okay, fine. Duce was starting to panic, this guy had just screwed the deal with Tage. But, Duce was thinking, maybe they could still deal. Trade some sort of exclusive, or bribe this guy with a share—

After all, he hadn't come out and told everyone what was going on.

Then Oyler dropped a nuke on Duce's carefully constructed fantasy world. He told Duce *why* he hadn't spelled things out at the meeting.

"I never expected this," he said to Duce. "I had figured that the absence of the pamphlets was either someone's creative gameplay, or Alphomeg introducing a new wrinkle on their game. So, at first, I was playing along to keep my cover. Now I have a better reason."

What?

"Someone else lied to Alphomeg about his identity. The man's name is Damien Cristovos.

I only recognized him here because I've investigated the Mob and the gaming industry. I got to know some of the high rollers by sight."

"Who the hell is he?" Duce asked.

"The eighties. Colombia, Honduras, Panama. The guy was ruthless. He had a free ride because his profits funded the Contras—supposedly, though I think we're talking about three cents on the dollar. His rivals—do you know what a Colombian necktie is?"

Duce shook his head, and Oyler—who was calling himself Coombs now—explained. Cristovos was one bad dude. Someone you didn't want to cross.

In the nineties, he retired. The U.S. Government—which did not want to have an embarrassing scandal—cut him a beauty deal. He gave information on a few minor Colombians, and he disappeared into the witness protection program. He got to keep a pile of money, and the CIA didn't have to admit to a Grand Jury that they had him on the payroll.

Now, Oyler/Coombs explained, if he'd let on he knew how the game was set up, he would have to let on *how* it was that he knew. That would lead to the chance that Cristovos would figure out exactly who Coombs was, and that Coombs knew who *he* was. Prosecution might not be a threat to Cristovos, but if all this came out, it might jeopardize his share of the twenty-five million.

Cristovos' history did not lead Coombs to expect him to take that prospect peacefully. Coombs thought discretion was to keep his mouth shut and bow out of the game, so he didn't threaten Cristovos' victory. If he wasn't a direct threat to that, he was probably safe.

But, how would he know about the money—

"I'm pretty sure now, he was the one to swipe the orientation books. He fixed card games. It's something he would do."

Duce's palms were sweating when he asked, "Who is he?"

He already knew the answer when Oyler told him it was Tage. All Duce kept thinking about was that Coombs, Oyler, whoever he was, had just signed his death warrant. This guy talks to a few more people, and that twenty-five mil goes bye-bye, and he was sure that Tage would take it out on him.

Duce didn't know exactly how it happened, but one moment he was in a blind panic, the next he was standing over Oyler/Coombs' body with a rock in his hand. Duce never even remembered hitting the bastard.

"God, that fucker was a bitch to move."

"You took him to the boathouse and tied him up," Quaid said.

Duce nodded. He was staring at the scalloped plaster ceiling, wondering exactly how he was going to die.

"What about his notebook?"

"I ditched it in the underbrush on my way to the boathouse. I knew Tage—Cristovos—was going to . . ." Duce shook his head. "I didn't know what the fuck else to do. And I couldn't let him find the notebook—"

"Henry found it, didn't he?"

Duce nodded. "Poor bastard didn't even get a chance to read it." He lowered his head and looked at Quaid. "You want to know the irony? I don't think Cristovos even cared about the notebook. He never asked me how Henry found it."

"What did you tell him about Coombs?"

Duce swallowed. "Everything, except that he knew about Cristovos. That didn't matter either. Cristovos—Tage—never said what he would do, but I knew, damn it. I couldn't stop it."

Grossmann and the doctor slowly regained consciousness, shaking their heads, and looking at Quaid as if he was some alien creature. Duce looked at Quaid himself. What the hell was he doing here? Why did he come back after escaping this insanity?

"You're pathetic," Quaid told him.

For once in his life, Duce wasn't going to argue. Instead, he asked, "What do you want, Quaid?"

Quaid slipped a hand into his pocket and withdrew a ragged, water-stained piece of paper. "The same thing he wanted," Quaid said, "allies."

Thirtieth Move

Quaid did a quick mental head count as he mounted the stairs to the second floor of the hotel.

They had started with a total of twenty people. They had lost Mr. Oyler-Coombs, Louis LeMonde, Henry, Susan Polk, Gordon Hernandez, and, down on the stage, Frank Pisarski. Quaid hoped that Carlos' blow didn't contribute to Frank's death. That was six people. Carlos, A. J., Bobbie, and Eve were back at the Alphomeg compound. That accounted for half the population. A. J. was escorting Olivia, Dr. Yanowitz— both conscious now and ambulatory—and Duce out of the hotel and away to the boathouse. Out of range of whatever was going to happen here.

That left six people here, aside from Quaid himself. Jarl Theodore, Erica, Connie, Iris, and Beatrice Greenhart.

And Tage, of course.

Quaid accounted for most of them when he topped the stairs.

The door to Erica Urquort's room was shut,

and Quaid could hear a woman's voice coming from behind it. It sounded like Connie. Quaid walked up and tried the door, but it wouldn't budge.

"Who's that?" came the sharp voice of Beatrice Greenhart. She sounded frightened.

"Quaid," he called out.

"Quaid?" It was Erica's voice, distant, not as authoritative as it had been. "But they took Quaid, didn't they?"

"Quaid, you have to get out of here," Connie's voice was rushed and breathless. "Tage's crazy. He's one of them—"

"I know," Quaid said.

"He thinks he's won the game. He said the keepers—Alphomeg—are going to come and pay him for what he's done. That's crazy, isn't it? He killed Frank just so a vote would go his way—"

"Abe," Iris interrupted Connie. "Have you seen Abe?"

"Yes, Dr. Yanowitz is fine, so's Olivia." Quaid tried the door. It wouldn't budge. "Can you open this door?"

"No one enters," Erica said, "no one leaves. Those are the rules now. Have to mind the rules. Can't forfeit."

"Tage nailed the door shut," said Mrs. Greenhart.

Quaid ran his hand along the edge of the doorjamb, and sure enough his fingers rested on one of two dozen roofing nails that'd been driven diagonally into the doorjamb. It would take ten or fifteen minutes to open this door with a prybar . . .

"I'll be back," Quaid said.

"Oh, I wouldn't bet on it," came a voice from behind him.

Quaid turned just in time to see Jarl Theodore swing something at his head.

Smooth, Quaid, you even had the goddamn gun.
Quaid blinked his eyes a few times and saw that gun. It was in Jarl Theodore's hand, pointing at him.

Okay, Quaid thought, *this is bad . . .*
He was sitting in an overstuffed armchair in the library. He wasn't restrained, and he felt a little dizzy. His vision was blurred, and he panicked a few moments until he realized that he had lost his glasses. That pissed him off royally, and it took a moment to realize how incongruous that was.

Someone holding a gun to his head, and he was worried about his glasses. That was rich. He even laughed a little—and at the same time wondered if his sanity had completely gone. He felt drunk.

"He's awake, boss." Jarl gestured with the gun. Quaid stared at his blurred form. Was the guy actually wearing those mirror shades inside, at night?

"Welcome back, Mr. Loman." Tage Garnell walked in front of Quaid. Jarl edged to the side to keep a clean shot at Quaid's head. "You're just in time for my victory party."

Quaid squinted to make out his adversary. It was amazing really, still the same immaculate goatee. No trace of a shadow on his cheeks. His black shirt unwrinkled as if it had just come fresh from the laundry. It was as if the guy couldn't perspire.

It might have been the accumulated stress, it might have been the blow to the head, but Quaid wanted to see this guy sweat. Confrontation wasn't the sanest thing at this point, not with a gun to his head, but it wasn't a sane situation.

"So you've won, Mr. Cristovos?"

Without his glasses, Quaid couldn't really read Tage's expression. However, he could have sworn that the man backed away slightly. Tage's voice didn't change. It was still the level reasonable tone that it had always been, and the aura of superiority that backed it was as powerful as ever. "That isn't a name that I've used in a long time."

"How many people have you killed?" Quaid asked. If he got Tage talking, he hoped that he could rattle Jarl. If the trucker had some idea what Tage was all about, maybe he'd reconsider pointing the gun.

"Are you talking about since we came here, or total?" Tage laughed as Quaid kept staring at Jarl. "Oh, Quaid, after making it all the way back here, I expected a little more. I don't have

any secrets from Jarl." He walked up and patted
Jarl on the back.

"You knew?" Quaid asked.

Jarl shrugged. "Looking out for number one,
Quaid. Twelve million is a lot of money."

"Who do you think cleaned up Susan Polk's
little mess?" Tage asked. "Do you think Duce
could show that kind of creativity and
initiative?"

"God, you're a cold bastard."

"Please, Mr. Loman," Tage shook his head.
"Let's not descend to personal insults. I simply
chose an effective strategy to win the Game."

"You murdered three people," Quaid said,
"in the name of a *game*?"

"In the name of twelve million dollars, Quaid.
People have been killed for much less. I don't
lose, Quaid. I don't allow it."

"And Duce?" Quaid said. "Does he share in
this victory of yours?"

Tage chuckled. "Duce is a weak sister, an unstable loose cannon. He doesn't deserve the
quarter million that Alphomeg will pay him. If
I didn't need his votes, I would have finished
him off just to dispose of the irritation." Tage
walked up and knelt so he looked Quaid in the
eyes. "If it wasn't for Duce, no one would have
died. Save your anger for him."

"Who slit Coombs' throat?"

"Who?" Jarl asked.

"Mr. Oyler," Tage said, "had already shown
a healthy respect for me by bowing out of the

Game. If that brainless teenager hadn't chosen
to panic, I am sure I could have convinced him
to hold his tongue for the duration of the
Game." Tage shrugged. "He might have gotten
a Pulitzer, and an exclusive interview with the
winner."

"Christ," Quaid said. "Why kill him?"

"Someone had to cover Duce's tracks," Tage
told him. "I could not have Duce lose a vote
because of his stupidity."

Quaid made the mistake of standing up. "You
bast—"

The pistol connected with Quaid's cheekbone
with an impact that snapped his head sideways.
His vision went black, shot with color, and his
next conscious moment found him draped over
the arm of the chair trying unsuccessfully to
retch.

Quaid saw Tage's feet walk in front of him.
"Ill-advised, Mr. Loman."

"What about Susan?" Quaid sucked in a
breath and rolled back into the chair. "You kill
her, too?"

"The unfortunate woman slit her own wrists."

"I know," Quaid looked at Tage. "But you
killed her. Didn't you? She trusted you . . . Was
she sleeping with you when she told you
about Henry?"

"Shut up—" Jarl pressed the gun into the side
of Quaid's head.

Quaid swallowed and slowly turned to look
at Jarl. "No. *You*."

"Look, you don't know nothing about it," Jarl said.

Tage shook his head. "My advice would be not to force the issue with Mr. Theodore. Miss Polk had become too close to him, and her decision to take her own life upset him greatly."

Quaid gritted his teeth. "I see. Not quite enough to keep you from staging it as a murder—"

Jarl swung the gun at him again, but this time Quaid was expecting it. He ducked enough that it just cut a gash in his scalp.

"Mr. Theodore is a practical man," Tage said. "He knew that what Susan did could not be undone."

"Yeah, might as well fix things so you could win the game, right?" He looked at Jarl again, the blood was further blurring his vision. "Right?"

"She killed *herself*, man."

Yeah, Quaid thought, *but you know who's responsible.* "I know, Jarl. No reason that should cost you your share of that twenty-five million."

Jarl nodded. The gun was still perilously close to Quaid's face, shaking. He didn't know how he could manage to talk while someone had a gun on him, much less intentionally upset the man. Somehow, Quaid managed to say, "And you're sure Tage is going to share."

The gun shifted a fraction, and Quaid saw that he'd hit another nerve. Tage, however, remained as calm as ever. "Again, a clumsy at-

tempt, Mr. Loman. The Game is already over.
Once I had achieved total control of the rules, I
declared Jarl as my cowinner. Alphomeg is
monitoring our progress. They will retrieve us,
I presume, when the storm is over. I cannot
renege."

*Yeah, I figured, or else this guy wouldn't be
your toady.*

"And," Quaid continued, "you're convinced
that you'll get away with complicity in these
murders?"

"Do you understand the nature of this Game
at all?" Tage said. "They've purposely set it outside any national jurisdiction. Alphomeg has too
much at stake to try and legally penalize anything that occurs in one of their Games—"

"You gathered all that from the brochures
you swiped?"

" 'The rules we choose are the only law,' a
direct quote," Tage said. "If they were concerned with such matters, wouldn't they have
abandoned the Game as soon as I dispatched
Mr. Coombs? Miss Urquort was right about one
thing. They have so much obvious investment
in their Game, that they wouldn't do anything
to disrupt it."

Quaid nodded and looked at Jarl. He couldn't
tell if he was looking in his eyes, but he talked
as if he was. "I see, Tage. You pretty much have
Alphomeg pegged, don't you? You might be interested, during my little field trip, I met with a

Mr. Diomedes, the owner of Alphomeg Entertainment."

"I'm sure you did," Tage's voice had a hint of sarcasm to it. "I suppose he told you how wrong I am. How they'll abandon the Game to international publicity just to bring us to justice."

"No, he didn't." Quaid said. He kept staring at Jarl. Jarl lowered the gun a fraction. It pointed at Quaid's chin now, not his nose. *He wants to see my face. Figure out if I'm lying.*

It was Jarl who asked, "What did this Mr. Diomedes say?"

"That Tage's right, more or less. There's too much riding on this game for them to abandon it. He's here specifically because of Tage's 'unorthodox' gameplay. Right now their adjudication committee is coming to a decision on Tage's declaration of victory."

"Well, there. You see, Jarl?" There was a note of reassurance that crept into Tage's voice. "I really don't see your purpose in coming here, Mr. Loman. You should have stayed at whatever staging area you found, taken the quarter million—"

"Wait a minute," Jarl said. "What the hell is there to come to a decision about? It's clear-cut. We've followed the rules—"

"And no one voted to outlaw killing people," Quaid couldn't help getting that dig in.

"We won, Mr. Theodore," Tage said. His voice was hard, but was there, perhaps, a hint of nervousness in it at last? "Nothing he can say can change that."

Jarl backed up. The gun was now pointed at a spot on Quaid's abdomen. "Then why aren't they here, Tage "

"Look at the weather," Tage said. "You can't fly in that."

"He did," Jarl said.

"I think I've had enough of you, Mr. Loman." Tage stepped toward Quaid.

"But you haven't heard the punchline."

"Enough," Tage repeated.

"No," Jarl said, moving the gun to cover Tage. "Let him finish."

"You aren't going to let this drunken lowlife manipulate you—"

"Let him finish," Jarl said. He swung the gun back to Quaid. "And you better make it good."

Quaid swallowed and felt the paper in his pocket. His trump card. "I had an interesting talk with Mr. Diomedes. They're very possessive about their game. He's so obsessed about 'outside influences' that he was going to take me off the island to keep me from returning to the game and contaminating it—"

"You're too late for that," Tage said. Now he sounded a little nervous.

"—despite the fact that I was still officially a player. However, you and Oyler—excuse me— Coombs and Cristovos—had already demonstrated that Alphomeg wouldn't void a game because of that kind of influence. You could say that you set a precedent—Alphomeg's policies outside the game have no bearing on the game itself."

"Jarl, this is pointless. The man's talking in circles."

Jarl shook his head and said, "And I should care, why?"

"It's in their orientation booklet, isn't it? That they disqualify players if they know any of the other players, even by reputation? They didn't know that Oyler knew Tage because both had assumed identities. By the time Alphomeg knew the mistake, the game was underway. They didn't end the game at that point, so the precedent was set. The rules of the game are supreme—"

"You're starting to bore me," Jarl said.

"I'm sorry. That speech was for the adjudication committee who's going to rule on this."

"Rule on what? The Game is over," Tage said.

"You asked the question yourself, Jarl. I had to wonder myself. In terms of the game, Tage's win does seem cut and dried. I haven't seen what you've done to the rules since I left, but I could count. It puzzled me that there was a debate on Tage's win. I mean, if murder didn't disqualify him—"

"Get to the fucking point before I put a bullet in you."

"The only reason Mr. Diomedes would be worried about me contaminating the game, is if it wasn't over yet." Quaid pulled the sheet of paper out of his pocket. He did it slowly as Jarl tensed. It was drenched and bloodstained, but fortunately, even to Quaid's blurred vision, it was still legible.

Tage grabbed it. "What's this?"

"Proxies," Quaid said. "From Carlos, Bobbie, A. J. . . ."

Tage crumpled up the paper. "This is meaningless, the Game's over."

". . . Dr. Yanowitz, Olivia, Duce. Gordon's dead, and Eve was in no condition to sign."

"What the fuck are you talking about?" Jarl's gun hand was shaking.

Quaid smiled. "When's a vote over?"

The room was silent. Tage dropped the crumpled proxies on the carpet. He was smart, Quaid knew that he got the punchline the moment Quaid posed the question.

"What're you playing at, Quaid? It's over, we won." Jarl didn't get it. "Twelve million. *Right?*" Jarl turned toward Tage.

Tage was shaking his head. "Stupid mistake." His voice was barely a whisper.

"What fucking mistake? They voted you in, a lock." Jarl looked at Quaid. "You can't change an election after the vote's over—"

"It's not over," Quaid said, "until *every* Player votes. Rule three, 'majority vote of *all* the Players.' " He let that sink in for a few moments. Then he clarified things for Jarl. "We've all had our share of memory lapses, but I don't remember voting or granting my proxy since you guys locked me up."

"What the fuck?"

"The Rules haven't changed since you locked me up," Quaid said. "The vote's still ongoing on Tage's supremacy. And, unfortunately, you both have since forfeited."

"The hell I have," Jarl said.

Tage stayed silent.

"You wrote my guard rotation into the rules, last vote I was in on. I believe I voted against. Have either of you kept up with the six-hour shifts since Carlos liberated me? Or did you think you voted them away?"

"No, he's fucked up." Jarl shook his head and whipped around to face Tage. "Tell him he's fucked up!"

Tage straightened up and said, "It's a technicality. They are going to Rule in my favor."

"*Technicality?* You're telling me he's right?"

While Jarl was distracted, Quaid pushed himself up from the chair. Standing brought a wave of dizziness that almost made him topple over.

"Goddamn it! You fucking weasel. Mr. Big Time We-Can't-Lose."

"I don't lose, I don't allow it."

Quaid put a hand on a table to steady himself. One of the ubiquitous Tiffany lamps rattled as his weight tilted the top. Jarl and Tage didn't seem to notice. Tage was saying something low that Quaid couldn't quite make out. He wasn't really paying attention. There were too many flashes of pain from too many places for him to pay attention to more than one thing at a time.

He looked at the lamp and remembered Connie.

"You dragged me off to watch you finish Henry, just so we wouldn't break your fucking rules."

"Alphomeg keeps score," Tage said. "They're watching us now."

"You typed the goddamn rules yourself," Jarl yelled at him. "You fucked me out of twelve million dollars."

"Let's not become unreasonable," Tage said, a plaintive note breaking the calm, reasonable veneer of his voice. "We have Mr. Loman at a disadvantage. If *he's* actually in control of the rule set, I'm sure he can be convinced—"

Tage's voice was cut off by the sound of a gunshot.

Quaid's thought was: *Well, damn, the thing survived.*

Another shot broke the silence and Tage was on his knees, blood staining the Oriental carpet beneath him.

Quaid grabbed the neck of the lamp. It was cold bronze, very heavy. Heavier than he remembered.

"Great fucking leader," Jarl shouted at him. "But you're right. I'm sure Quaid can be convinced to share the win—"

Jarl turned to bring the gun to bear on the chair. Quaid could see surprise in his posture when he saw that the chair was empty. He kept turning, toward where Quaid stood.

The lamp's base came down on Jarl's skull with a satisfying thud. Tage watched the trucker drop like a wet sack of manure. Quaid moved to grab the gun. The movement made him dizzy again, and he almost threw up all over Jarl.

"Help me," Tage whispered. He had fallen on his side, clutching a wound in his chest. Blood poured through his fingers, bright red. His skin was already waxy and pale. The guy was already gone, he just didn't know it yet.

By the time Quaid reached him, he was already dead. He rolled the corpse over and saw that Tage's other hand grasped the note with the proxies on it.

"I don't lose, I don't allow it."

"It's just a game," Quaid told him, "and you lost."

Vampiric Thrillers from
S. A. SWINIARSKI

THE FLESH, THE BLOOD AND THE FIRE
During the Kingsbury Run murders over a dozen bodies—
mutilated, decapitated, and drained of blood—were found along
the railroad tracks and waterways of Cleveland, Ohio. With the
whole city gripped by terror, safety director Eliot Ness instituted
the largest manhunt in Cleveland's history, one that would eventually involve the entire police force. Despite these efforts, only two
of the bodies were ever identified and the killer was never found—
or was he? For one member of Cleveland's finest, Detective Ste-
fan Ryzard, refused to give up the case. And his search for the
truth would send him down a bloody trail that led from the depths
of the city's shantytowns to the inner citadels of industrial power
to the darkest parts of the human soul.

☐UE2879—$5.99

RAVEN
He awoke in a culvert, with no memory and no knowledge of how
he had gotten there. The only thing he knew for sure was that
he had become a vampire. . . .

☐UE2725—$5.99

Prices slightly higher in Canada.   **DAW 213X**

S. Andrew Swann

Elizabeth Forrest

□ **DEATH WATCH**   UE2648—$5.99
McKenzie Smith has been targeted by a mastermind of evil who can
make virtual reality into the ultimate tool of destructive power. Stalked
in both the real and virtual worlds, can McKenzie defeat an assassin
who can strike out anywhere, at any time?

□ **KILLJOY**   UE2695—$5.99
Given experimental VR treatments, Brand must fight a constant battle
against the persona of a serial killer now implanted in his brain. But
Brand would soon learn that there were even worse things in the
world—like the unstoppable force of evil and destruction called KillJoy.

□ **BRIGHT SHADOW**   UE2695—$5.99
When a clandestie FBI invasion of a cult ranch blows up, Vernon
Spense manages to rescue one little girl, Jennifer. Though Spense
finds what he thinks is a safe haven for her, to one man she's far too
important to let go. Either he will get her back or he'll make sure she's
beyond everyone's reach. And to that end, he will eliminate Spense
or anyone who gets in his way. . . .

□ **RETRIBUTION**   UE779—$6.99
A former child art prodigy, Charlie has begun to paint again. But now
her vibrant paintings bring to life a shocking revelation of undiscovered
murders and the killer whose identity would soon become clear—unless Charlie herself becomes the stalker's next victim. . . .

Prices slightly higher in Canada.   **DAW 134X**